Woman of Valor

In a world of tradition, she forged her own destiny.

By

Kurell Vidal

i

DEDICATION

This book is dedicated to my grandchildren, proud descendants of the Philogene Clan. It reflects my journey, my strength, and my unwavering spirit. May I always embrace challenges, celebrate victories, and shine brightly in everything I undertake.

I thank my incredible support system: my mother and sister Dee, my children, and grandchildren, along with all the strong women who have shaped my life and inspired me to embrace my own path. To my wonderful colleagues, your love and encouragement have been a driving force in my journey.

Table of Contents

In a world where silence is expected, I choose to raise my voice and embrace the power within me

Lorde, Audre.

ACKNOWLEDGMENTS

I would like to express my deepest gratitude to those who have supported me on this journey. Thank you to my mother and sister Dee for your unwavering love and encouragement. To my children and grandchildren, your joy inspires me every day.

Special thanks to my childhood friend Christine Jno Baptiste, my prayer warriors Celia Bertrand, and Gloria Tavernier, my friends Mr. D.C Cameron, McPherson Barber, Claudette Barber-Josephs, for your friendship and support. Lastly, I am grateful to my colleagues for your camaraderie and collaboration. Each of you has played a significant role in shaping my path as a woman of valor.

PROLOGUE

WOMAN OF VALOR

In the heart of the Caribbean, the island of Dominica blossomed in vibrant hues of green and blue, a hidden jewel blessed with stunning rivers and cascading waterfalls. In the 1960s, its lush landscapes bustled with life, but beneath the serene façade lay a current of change—a tide of socio-political movements sweeping across the island as the people yearned for independence and a voice of their own.

This was a time of both opportunity and tension, where the rich cultural heritage of Dominica, woven from the threads of African, European, French, and indigenous influences, began to stir with the restless spirit of empowerment. The air hummed with the fervor of those who dreamed of a brighter future, and the warm sun painted the fields with golden light, illuminating every corner of the island's beauty and strife.

In the modest village of Colihaut, framed by the embrace of the mountains, Isabella Philogene stood on the threshold of her family's land, her heart mirroring the vibrant pulse of the community around her. In her late twenties, she possessed a fierce determination borne from her lineage as the daughter of a farmer and a seamstress. The sweat of labor was etched into her skin, yet her spirit soared with dreams that transcended the fields she had grown up to know.

As a child, Isabella roamed the verdant expanse of her father's farm, where the smell of earth, fresh from the rain, intermingled with the fragrant blooms of hibiscus and ginger lily. Each plant and every river told stories of resilience and toil, echoing the voices of generations past. But Isabella's dreams were not confined to the simple life of

2

cultivation; they extended into the realm of empowerment for the women of her community.

The heart of her vision? To transform her family's modest land into a thriving agricultural cooperative—one that would serve as a beacon of strength for local women, offering them livelihoods, education, and a platform to harness their talents. She envisioned workshops where individuals could learn sustainable farming practices, spaces where skills could blossom, and a community united in purpose.

But the road to her dream was fraught with obstacles. Skepticism clouded the eyes of some, rooted in the traditions that had long defined their roles. The winds of change roared with possibility, yet uncertainty rippled through the air, mingling with the fragrance of blooming vanilla and the sounds of laughter that echoed from nearby homes.

Standing at the edge of her family's land, Isabella felt the weight of her dreams pressing against the backdrop of impending change. She was a woman of valor, ready to embrace the struggles ahead with unwavering resolve. The land beneath her feet thrummed with promise, and the vibrant community that surrounded her held the key to transformation. It was more than just soil and crops; it was the potential for a future where women could rise together, defined not by their circumstances but by their aspirations.

As the sun dipped toward the horizon, casting a warm, golden glow across the land, Isabella whispered her aspirations to the wind. The shadows of the past danced around her, and she could feel the spirits of resilient women who had come before her urging her forward.

This was just the beginning—a prologue to a journey that would unveil the strength of a woman determined to carve a legacy for herself, her community, and her island. In a time of change, Isabella Philogene stood poised to transform not only her own destiny but the very fabric of her beloved Dominica. The world awaited her, and she was ready to rise.

ONE

ROOTS OF AMBITION

Isabella Philogene took a deep breath as she stepped outside her family's modest home in Colihaut. The salty tang of the sea mingled with the earthy scent of the lush mountains, grounding her as the sun peeked over the horizon, bathing the world in a soft, golden light. Colihaut, a quiet village poised between the vibrant sapphire waters and the emerald, green hills, was a tapestry of simplicity and strength, where fishing boats bobbed in the bay and farmers tended to their fields beneath the watchful gaze of the peaks.

Born and raised in this humble village, Isabella was deeply woven into the fabric of its community. As the daughter of Wizen Philogene, a hardworking farmer, and Theresa Philogene, a seamstress renowned for her intricate patterns and vibrant dresses, her childhood was marked by both love and the challenges of economic struggle. Their modest home was filled with laughter—her father's hearty chuckles rolling like thunder, and her mother's gentle hums of lullabies weaving through the air alongside the delightful aromas of Theresa's cooking.

Each day began with the crowing of roosters, and the rhythm of life pulsed through their household as they prepared for the day ahead. Wizen would rise before dawn to tend to the crops, while Theresa spent her mornings crafting clothing that would eventually adorn the village's children, brides, and celebrations. Isabella often helped her mother, fascinated by the way she transformed plain fabric into vibrant garments that spun stories through colors and stitches. It was in those moments that Isabella first understood the power of creation, not just in art but in nurturing dreams amidst the harshness of reality.

5

With her parents as her role models, Isabella learned the value of hard work early on. Wizen instilled in her the principles of resilience, often reminding her that the best crops come from the most stubborn seeds. "It's the struggle that makes us strong," he would say as they labored in the fields under the sweltering sun. Meanwhile, Theresa taught her the significance of community—how a single stitch could mend more than just fabric, but also the bonds that held people together.

As she wandered the paths of Colihaut, Isabella observed the intricate dance of life around her: women gathering at the market, their laughter mingling with spirited conversations; men hauling in their catches of the day; children racing along the shores, their shouts echoing against the waves. Yet beyond the laughter and camaraderie, Isabella was acutely aware of the challenges that loomed over her village. Economic struggles cast long shadows over their lives, limiting opportunities for growth and prosperity. It was this reality that ignited a determination within her, a fierce flame kindled by her parents' sacrifices and the dreams they had for a better future.

With aspirations stretching far beyond the fields, Isabella imagined transforming their land into a flourishing agricultural cooperative—one that would empower the women of Colihaut to cultivate not only crops but also the strength to define their destinies. The seeds of her ambition were planted in the nurturing soil of her upbringing, watered by the love and hard work of her parents, and bathed in the light of possibilities.

As Isabella looked out over the fields that had been tended for generations, she felt a rush of gratitude for her roots, anchoring her amidst the vision of what could be. Every sunrise created new opportunities, and the whispers of the past encouraged her to dream boldly. She was ready to weave her own story into the rich tapestry of her community, driven by the love of her family and the resilience she had inherited.

The morning light illuminated the path before her, and Isabella took her first step into the day, where the promise of her dreams awaited like the blooming bougainvillea that graced the village—their colors as vibrant as the spirit of the woman who dared to dream.

Isabella often found solace in the warmth of her grandmother Isabelle's presence. On afternoons filled with golden sunlight, she would nestle in the old wooden rocking chair on the porch, listening intently as her grandmother spun tales of a time long past—stories rich with the essence of their family's history. Isabelle, with her silver-streaked hair and weathered hands, held an undeniable air of strength and wisdom, the remnants of a legacy that had shaped their very existence.

A former plantation owner before the land had been divided and kindred spirits scattered, Isabelle was a living embodiment of resilience. The colonial disruptions had stripped her of wealth and power, but it had never diminished her dignity. Instead, she cultivated a rich garden of memories, sharing the past with Isabella like a precious heirloom. Each story was infused with lessons of courage, tenacity, and the importance of standing firm against the currents of change.

"You must remember, my dear," Isabelle said one afternoon, her voice steady yet soft, "the strength of our lineage courses through your veins. Our ancestors worked the land not just with their hands, but with their hearts. They knew the value of hard work and the dignity it brings, even when faced with adversity."

Isabella watched her grandmother's eyes sparkle with fervor as she recounted tales of formidable women in their family—women who had defied the societal norms of their time, refusing to be confined by the expectations that sought to limit them. There was Aunt Cecile, who had opened the first school for girls in the village, fighting against the belief that education was unnecessary for women. Then there was Grandmother Clara, who had forged a thriving marketplace from nothing, a testament to the spirit of entrepreneurship that flowed through their blood.

Isabelle's voice would rise with passion as she spoke of these women's dreams, ambitions, and the legacies they had carved for future generations. "Education is our strongest weapon," she would insist, her gaze fierce, "and independence, my child, is a treasure that no one can take from you. It is not merely a right; it is a responsibility—to yourself and those who follow."

Isabella absorbed each word, feeling the weight of her grandmother's narratives settle around her like a warm embrace. They were not just tales; they were callings that stirred something deep within her soul. Inspired by the courage of her female ancestors, she began to forge her own vision. To reclaim the legacy that had been diminished, to uplift her community and empower the women around her through education and cooperative efforts—this became her goal.

Isabelle's spirit was a guiding force, a compass that directed Isabella toward her ambitions. Whenever doubt crept into those fleeting moments when the enormity of her dreams felt overwhelming—she would remember her grandmother's unwavering belief in her potential. It was in those moments she felt a kinship with the women of her lineage, a connection that fueled her hope that she, too, could be a catalyst for change.

One sunny afternoon, as they sat together on the porch, Isabella turned to her grandmother, curiosity brimming in her eyes. "Grandma, do you really believe I can do this? Transform our land? Inspire the women of Colihaut?"

Isabelle regarded her with a knowing smile, the kind that contained the wisdom of generations. "Oh, my dear Isabella, you are already on your way. You have the heart of a true Philogene. Remember, the journey of a thousand steps begins with one. Every seed you plant—whether in soil or in the minds of those around you—holds the promise of tomorrow."

As twilight enveloped the island, casting a warm glow over their faces, Isabella felt a renewed sense of purpose. The stories of her family danced in her mind, igniting her ambitions like a flickering flame that refused to be extinguished. She would honor the legacy of the women who had come before her. She could almost see it now—a flourishing agricultural cooperative, bustling with life and laughter, where the women of Colihaut worked side by side, empowered and equipped to transform their futures.

Standing, she embraced her grandmother, filled with gratitude for the roots that anchored her ambitions. "I promise, Grandma. I will make our dreams a reality."

Isabelle squeezed her tightly in response, her heart swelling with pride and hope. "Then let that promise guide you, my dear. The spirit of our ancestors walks with you—never forget that.

As the stars began to twinkle above, Isabella knew she stood on the brink of something extraordinary. With her family's rich history coursing through her veins and the light of her grandmother's wisdom illuminating her path, she was ready to reclaim her legacy and forge her destiny. The journey had begun, and the roots of her ambition were stronger than ever.

From an early age, Isabella's insatiable curiosity knew no bounds. While other children played among the wildflowers and climbed the mango trees that dotted Colihaut, she often found herself engulfed in thick textbooks or lost in the pages of novels that transported her to distant lands and different lives. The small schoolhouse, built of weathered wood and crowned with a thatched roof, became her sanctuary, a place where knowledge blossomed like the bright hibiscus flowers that adorned their village.

In the classroom, Isabella excelled, particularly in history and literature, subjects that resonated with her deep-seated desire for understanding the world around her. History lessons often came alive for her, especially when the narratives turned to stories of strong women who had shaped nations. Figures like Emmeline Pankhurst and Rosa Parks ignited a fire within her spirit, and she would return home from school, fueled by the knowledge that women, just like her, could challenge the status quo and inspire change.

Her teachers quickly recognized Isabella's passion and potential, encouraging her to embrace her talents. Miss Lorne, her history teacher, was particularly instrumental in nurturing her ambitions. With her fiery red hair and a knack for storytelling, Miss Lorne would often linger after class, engaging Isabella in conversations that sparked her imagination. "You have a voice, Isabella—a powerful one," she would say, her green eyes sparkling with encouragement. "You must use it to inspire others."

The annual Fishermen's Feast was the highlight of the social calendar in Colihaut. Every year, the village erupted into a vibrant celebration marked by a traditional church service, lively music with a procession to the bayside, and an abundance of local food and cheer. This year, the festival took on a deeper significance for Isabella, serving as both a backdrop for her ambitions and a stage for the community's spirit.

On the morning of the festival, Isabella joined the congregation at the small, weathered church that had withstood storms and sunlight alike, much like the village itself. The familiar scent of incense mingled with the salty sea air as the congregation gathered, filling the wooden pews with laughter and chatter. The church bells rang out, guiding the villagers from their homes, each heart pulsing with anticipation.

As the service unfolded, Isabella listened intently to the sermon, the priest's words a reminder of resilience and gratitude. "Today, we come together to honor the sea that provides for us and the strength of our community," he proclaimed. "Let us proceed to the bayside for the blessing of the boats, our fishermen, and the families that depend on them."

Isabella sat quietly, the warmth of the crowd enveloping her. She glanced around at her neighbors, feeling the pulse of unity that flowed through the village—a strength that she longed to tap into in her own endeavors. The importance of community was more palpable than ever, and she felt the weight of her ambitions resting heavily on her shoulders.

The service concluded with spirited singing, voices rising in harmony, echoing hope and tradition. As the congregation filed out of the church, Isabella felt a surge of energy. She was ready to take her place in the procession, a symbolic bridge between the past and the future she envisioned for her community.

The festive spirit engulfed her as they began the rhythmic journey down to the bayside. Villagers of all ages clapping their hands, moving together in a vibrant procession, singing songs that celebrated not only the sea's bounty but their collective identity. Isabella joined in, her voice blending with the crowd as they danced and swayed, leaving behind the barriers of doubt and fear.

As they reached the bay, colorful boats bobbed gently on the water, their hulls painted bright blue, yellow, and green and decorated with flamboyant flowers. The sight of the boats—symbols of the village's livelihood—filled Isabella with renewed purpose. This was more than just a celebration; it was a testament to the strength and resilience of her community, a reminder that they had thrived through adversity, much like the sea itself.

The priest stepped forward, holding a ceremonial oar adorned with flowers, as he prepared to bless the boats. This was the moment when hopes and prayers were cast into the wind and sea, and Isabella felt a stirring within her. She knew this was her defining moment, a turning point for her ambitions.

"Join me in prayer for our fishermen, our families, and the abundance of the sea," the priest called out, hands raised high. "May our boats be safe and our nets be full."

As the words flowed from his mouth, Isabella felt the energy of the gathering surge around her, rippling like the waves of the bay. It became clear that her dreams for the cooperative were intrinsically tied to the spirit of this gathering. She envisioned her cooperative standing as a parallel to these blessed boats—vessels for her community to navigate toward a brighter future.

As the blessing concluded, Isabella stepped forward, her heart racing. The villagers turned to her, some uncertain, others curious. This was her chance—the moment she had been waiting for to tie her dreams to the collective hopes of her neighbors.

"Everyone," she called out, her voice stronger than she felt, "thank you for being here today. This festival is not just about celebrating our fishermen; it is about celebrating our community. It is about honoring our land, our traditions, and our dreams for the future. I stand here before you not just as a dreamer but as your neighbor, committed to ensuring that our family land remains in our hands. Together, we can create something beautiful—a cooperative that will allow us to work the land together, feed our families, and empower women in our community."

Murmurs of support bloomed amongst the crowd, the energy shifting from hesitant questions to enthusiastic encouragement. She could see the realization dawning on faces around her; they were beginning to understand the synergy between their fishing heritage and her vision for agricultural sustainability.

"Let us come together," Isabella continued, her confidence growing as she spoke, "to honor the land that feeds us. Just as our fishermen rely on the sea, we have the power to cultivate the earth that nourishes our community. With our combined strength, we can protect it from those who seek to take it away and transform it into a sanctuary for future generations."

Cheers erupted from the crowd, voices blending in support of a common cause. Isabella felt tears prick in her eyes as she saw the seeds of unity being sown right before her. This was the moment she had been waiting for—the affirmation that her dreams resonated with the aspirations of the people surrounding her.

The festive atmosphere swelled in a joyous crescendo as people began to gather around her, offering words of encouragement and sharing their own hopes for the cooperative. Friendships strengthened; they discussed strategies.

"Did you hear her? She speaks like a leader," one woman said, taking another's hands.

"What a bright future she has," another replied, and Isabella felt a swell of pride mixed with responsibility settle over her like a comfortable shawl.

That night, as she lay in bed, the weight of those words rested heavily on her shoulders. She realized that her ambitions were not just personal; they had the power to ignite change within her community. Inspired and empowered by the support of others, Isabella reaffirmed her resolve to challenge the limitations placed on women in Colihaut.

With each lesson learned and every opportunity grasped, Isabella's determination bloomed like the fragrant roses that bordered their home. She began to envision a broader mission: a world where the women around her did not just exist as caretakers and nurturers, but as leaders, educators, and pioneers of their own destinies.

Encouraged by her teachers and the wider community, mixed with the wisdom and tales of strength passed down from her grandmother, Isabella's small-village ambitions began to unfold into dreams of a larger crusade. The journey toward that vision had truly begun, and she felt as if the roots of her ambitions were reaching deep into the rich soil of her ancestry, drawing strength from the sacrifices and triumphs of those who came before her.

The path ahead would be challenging, but she felt ready. With her heart set on reclaiming their legacy, Isabella envisioned the empowerment of her community—and that vision shone brightly as she stepped confidently into her future.

As the years flowed into the late 1960s, the island of Dominica was on the brink of significant transformation. The air hummed with a palpable energy, charged with discussions of independence and social justice that rippled through every corner of the community. While the sun cast its golden glow over Colihaut, Isabella's heart was aflame with a growing awareness of the struggles faced by the women around her. The oppressive societal norms weighed heavily upon them, confining many to domestic roles and denying them the opportunities that could expand their horizons.

The stark realities of their lives filled Isabella with urgency. Women who worked tirelessly on the fields, returning home only to cook and clean, often looked to her with admiration for her ambition, yet seemed resigned to their fates. This juxtaposition fueled her desire to advocate for change. They were strong, smart, and capable women who deserved to be seen as more than caretakers and laborers—women like her mother, Theresa, who spent her days transforming fabric into beauty yet confined by the expectations of her role.

Driven by this realization, Isabella began seeking avenues to channel her passion into activism. She recalled the fervent discussions shared at family gatherings about the broader socio-political climate. Independence was not merely a political objective but a chance to reclaim identity and self-worth—especially for women whose voices had long been stifled. With every story shared by her grandmother about the sacrifices of their ancestors, Isabella felt a growing determination to honor that legacy and fight for the rights of those still bound by the chains of tradition.

Her first step into activism came on a crisp Friday evening when she attended a local meeting organized by a group advocating for women's rights. The community center, usually a hub of laughter and celebration, was alive with debate. People gathered, their passionate voices blending into a chorus of aspirations, fear, and hope. Many spoke of the impending independence from British colonial rule, but Isabella found her attention drawn to those discussing the need for equality and education for women.

As she sat in the back, listening intently, Isabella's heart raced. She absorbed the stories of women who had risen against the constraints of societal norms. One woman spoke of her struggles as a single mother striving to provide for her children while battling local prejudices that deemed her unworthy of respect. "We deserve better," she declared, her voice firm and unwavering. "We deserve opportunities to educate ourselves, to work without stigma, to forge our own paths!"

Encouraged by the resolve she witnessed; Isabella felt a fire ignite within her. These were not just distant issues; they were intricately tied to her own life and the lives of her friends and family. After the meeting, she approached a group of women who had been discussing the need for a local women's coalition. "I want to help," she said, her voice tremulous but resolute. "I believe we can create programs for education and skills training. We can make a difference in our community."

In the following weeks, Isabella became increasingly involved. She participated in rallies where women marched through the streets of Roseau, their voices ringing out for change. Sign in hand, she shouted, "Women's rights are human rights!" The messages proclaimed how education was the key to empowerment and independence. The energy of those gatherings captivated her, and the rush of adrenaline lit a fire in her soul.

Through conversations and connections at these events, Isabella met women from all occupations—students, teachers, market vendors, and healthcare workers—all united by a common goal. They shared their stories, their passions, and their frustrations. Each interaction chipped away at the insecurities she had felt in earlier years. No longer burdened by isolation, Isabella embraced her role as a leader among them, inspiring them to speak out for their rights and pursue their dreams, just as she had.

Moreover, Isabella's own education deepened through this engagement. She delved into books about social justice and women's rights, absorbing the revolutionary ideas of the works by authors who had paved the way for civil rights movements across the globe. She found herself drawn to voices that echoed the sentiments within her heart—the words of audacious women who dared to claim their space and demand respect.

In line with the urgency of the era, Isabella began organizing community discussions to address pressing issues affecting women.

From access to education and healthcare to mental health and domestic violence, she aimed to create safe spaces for women to voice their experiences and needs. At each meeting, Isabella felt the presence of her ancestors—the strength of her grandmother, the courage of her aunt, and the resilience of the countless women before her—bolstering her resolve.

One afternoon, as the sun hung low in the sky, casting a warm amber hue over the hills of Colihaut, Isabella stood before a gathering of women at the community center. "Together, we are stronger," she proclaimed, her voice resonating with conviction. "If we support each other, lift each other up, and share our stories, we can change the narrative. We can reclaim our dignity and pave the way for future generations."

The murmurs of agreement and snippets of encouragement filtered through the room, igniting a spark of hope among them. That sense of unity swept over Isabella like a warm bath. In those moments, she recognized that this was not just activism; it was a movement born from love, solidarity, and a shared vision for a brighter future.

As the socio-political climate continued to shift, she knew she was embarking on a journey that would test her limits and challenge the very fabric of the society she had known. Yet, every challenge further stoked her determination. Isabella felt a sense of purpose stronger than ever, ignited by the struggles of her community and the promise of an empowered tomorrow.

She was no longer just a girl with dreams; she was becoming a woman of action, a catalyst for change, driven by a mission to uplift the women of her village and reclaim the dignity that had long been denied to them. The flame of activism had sparked within her, and she was ready to fan it into a blazing fire.

With the breathtaking landscape of Colihaut as her backdrop, the lush greenery and vibrant flora became more than just a setting for Isabella's adventures; they evolved into a canvas upon which she painted her dreams for the future. Standing atop a gentle hill overlooking her family's abandoned sugar cane plantation, Isabella felt the whispers of the land beckoning her to reclaim its story, intertwining it with her vision for empowerment and progress.

The estate, once a symbol of wealth and prosperity, had fallen into disrepair after the colonial disruption. Overgrown with wild grasses and thick vines, it echoed the voices of the past—voices of toil and resilience—but also of lost potential. Isabella envisioned transforming this neglected land into an agricultural cooperative, a vibrant hub that would empower the women of Colihaut to rise economically and socially.

Her heart raced as she imagined this cooperative bustling with activity—a place not only for cultivating crops but also for nurturing ambition and fostering community. She envisioned workshops dedicated to sustainable farming practices, where women could learn modern techniques that paid homage to ancestral wisdom. It could become a space where they could plant not just seeds in the soil but also seeds of knowledge—lessons about sustainable practices, nutrition, and food security. The cooperative would be a sanctuary for growth—both agricultural and personal.

In her mind's eye, Isabella saw a classroom filled with laughter and learning. Women of all ages would gather to discuss financial independence, budgeting, and entrepreneurship. They would share stories of hardship and resilience, inspiring one another and igniting a collective determination to forge new paths. She envisioned mentorship programs linking young girls with experienced women, creating a ripple effect of knowledge and empowerment.

Isabella knew that the cooperative would be more than just a means of economic survival; it would be a place of support and connection. There would be community meetings under the shade of the mango trees, where women could gather to share their struggles, celebrate their achievements, and build each other up. She imagined discussions filled with laughter, encouragement, and a shared commitment to uplift one another. In a village where voices had often been muffled, this cooperative could become a chorus of empowerment.

As these ideas blossomed in her mind, Isabella began to develop a more concrete plan. She reached out to local agricultural experts, inviting them to a workshop where they could share sustainable farming techniques. She approached women leaders in the community to gauge their interest in partnering on this initiative. Each conversation fueled her enthusiasm and inspired new ideas, and before long, a small group of dedicated women began to form around her vision.

By forging connections with fellow activists and community leaders, Isabella discovered resources available in Dominica and beyond— grants intended to support women's cooperatives and initiatives focused on economic development. She was determined to apply for funding that would help her revitalize the plantation, transforming the very site of historical exploitation into a testament of resilience and empowerment.

Her dreams extended beyond the physical cultivation of crops. Isabella sought to create a model of social enterprise that could educate and uplift generations to come. She envisioned baking classes that utilized the produce harvested in the cooperative, transforming raw ingredients into income-generating products. Women could learn skills in marketing and sales, showcasing their baked goods at local markets, and gaining confidence in their abilities to generate their income.

As she walked the serpentine paths of the old plantation, surrounded by towering sugar cane stalks that whispered secrets of a past life, Isabella felt the weight of history settle around her shoulders—not as a burden but as a mantle. She was no longer just a young woman with a dream. She was an inheritor of a legacy, and a pioneer poised to reclaim it.

One evening, while sharing her plans with her grandmother, Isabelle's eyes sparkled with pride. "You're planting seeds of hope, my dear," she whispered, her voice laced with emotion. "You remind me of the women who built our family's history. Just as they worked the land, you are working toward the future."

With her grandmother's words resonating in her heart, Isabella felt an unwavering resolve. She delighted in hearing Isabelle's stories and wisdom during their evening talks, which not only fueled her ambition but also connected her to her roots. Every tale of strength and resilience she heard became a steppingstone towards her dream, grounding her as she ventured into uncharted territory.

As Isabella began to weave together her plans and dreams, she invited the women of Colihaut to a gathering at the community center. The air buzzed with anticipation as she spoke candidly about her vision. "This cooperative will be ours," she declared passionately, her voice rising above the chatter. "It will be built on our values, with our dreams for the future."

The faces of the women before her illuminated, and the sense of excitement was palpable. Many had been waiting for someone to spark this energy, to channel their collective desires into action. Some raised their hands as they shared their ideas—about handicrafts that could be sold, about the vegetables they each loved cultivating, about how they could reach out to others in the village and invite them to be part of this new chapter.

As the evening wore on, the room filled with the sound of laughter and camaraderie, the weight of shared aspirations lifting their spirits. Isabella felt a rush of joy wash over her; it was confirmation that her vision had struck a chord. Together, they were forging a bond stronger than the roots of the tall sugar cane that surrounded them.

Under the vast Caribbean sky, Isabella reflected on the journey that lay ahead. This was more than a project; it was the manifestation of her dreams for a better tomorrow—a place where women could reclaim their agency, cultivate their potential, and build a future that honored their resilience. She felt the energy of the island flowing through her, the spirit of her ancestors guiding each step she took toward this new endeavor.

With each passing day, Isabella's dream of the agricultural cooperative grew closer to fruition, nurtured by the hopes and aspirations of the women around her. They were not just participants; they were co-creators of a movement that would reshape their community. Together, they would transform the abandoned plantation into a thriving space of empowerment, cultivating not just crops but futures ripe with promise and possibility.

The vision was becoming a tangible reality, and Isabella stood ready to embrace the challenges ahead, her roots deeply entrenched in the rich soil of ambition and community. Her journey was just beginning, and she was determined to ensure it flourished into something extraordinary.

As the vision for the agricultural cooperative began to take shape, Isabella felt a surge of excitement coursing through her veins. Yet, along with that exhilaration came an undercurrent of self-doubt that threatened to undermine her resolve. The weight of societal expectations pressed heavily upon her shoulders, whispering insidious doubts in her ear.

In Colihaut, tradition held a firm grip on the hearts and minds of many. The notion that a woman should lead or aspire to heights beyond domestic roles was met with skepticism, and Isabella was not immune to the scrutiny of those who believed her ambitions were misguided. The whispers began as mere murmurs—concerned comments about her "overreaching" and "forgetting her place."

At community meetings, she noticed the subtle glances exchanged between some of the older women, their expressions a mix of disbelief and disapproval. "What does she know about farming?" one would mutter, while another would scoff, "Women should focus on their families, not try to run a plantation." Each comment, though seemingly small, landed like heavy stones in her heart, chipping away at her confidence.

One evening, after a particularly challenging meeting where her ideas had been met with resistance, Isabella returned home feeling defeated. She sat on the porch, staring into the distance as the sun dipped below the horizon, painting the sky in hues of orange and purple. The vibrant colors mocked her turmoil, a stark contrast to the shadows of doubt creeping into her mind.

"Maybe they're right," she whispered to herself, her voice barely audible. "Maybe I am not cut out for this. What do I know about leading a cooperative? What if I fail?"

Just then, her grandmother, Isabelle, stepped onto the porch, sensing Isabella's turmoil. She settled beside her, the warmth of her presence a comforting balm. "What troubles you, my dear?" she asked gently, her voice a soothing melody amidst Isabella's storm of thoughts.

Isabella sighed, the weight of her worries spilling forth. "I feel like I am fighting against the tide, Grandma. Some people think I should just accept my place and not aim so high. What if I am not good enough? What if I cannot make this happen?"

Isabelle listened intently, her wise eyes reflecting the fading light. "You are stronger than you believe, Isabella. Remember, the strongest trees grow in fierce winds. It is not the opinions of others that define your worth; it is your courage to pursue your dreams, despite the obstacles."

"But what if I fail?" Isabella pressed, her voice trembling. "What if I let everyone down?"

"Failure is simply a steppingstone on the path to success," her grandmother replied, placing a reassuring hand on Isabella's knee. "Every great leader face challenge and criticism. It is how you respond to them that shapes your journey. You must trust in your abilities and the vision you hold in your heart."

Isabella took a deep breath, her grandmother's words resonating with her. Yet, the doubt lingered like a stubborn fog. It was not just the traditionalists she had to contend with; it was the fear of disappointing her community, the women who looked to her for inspiration, and even herself.

In the days that followed, she found herself grappling with these conflicting emotions. Each time she envisioned the cooperative, the doubts would creep back in, casting shadows over her dreams. What if she was not equipped to lead? What if her ideas were too ambitious?

One afternoon, while meeting with her close friend Lydia, Isabella confided her fears. They sat beneath a sprawling almond tree, its branches offering a cool respite from the sun. "I'm starting to wonder if I'm just a girl with a dream," Isabella admitted, her voice heavy with uncertainty. "What if I can't make it happen?"

Lydia, with her fiery spirit and unwavering support, shook her head vigorously. "Isabella, you are so much more than just a dreamer. You have the passion, the vision, and the heart to make this work. Remember all the women who have stood by you? They believe in you, and so should you!"

"But what if I disappoint them?" Isabella replied, the weight of her worries pressing down on her. "What if I can't live up to their expectations?"

"Expectations can be suffocating, but you must remember that your journey is your own," Lydia urged, her eyes bright with conviction. "You're not just doing this for them; you're doing it for yourself and for all the women who've been silenced for too long. Embrace the challenges; they will only make you stronger."

Lydia's encouragement pierced through the fog of doubt, igniting a flicker of resolve within Isabella. She realized that she needed to confront her fears head-on, to embrace the challenges that accompanied her ambitions.

Determined to fortify her resolve, Isabella began seeking out women who had successfully navigated similar paths. She attended workshops and seminars, where she learned from female leaders who had faced criticism and adversity, yet had emerged victorious. Each story of resilience resonated deeply, reminding her that she was not alone in her struggles.

As she immersed herself in these experiences, Isabella began to shift her perspective. She understood that self-doubt was a natural part of any journey, especially one that challenged the status quo. Instead of allowing it to paralyze her, she would use it as fuel to propel her forward.

With renewed determination, Isabella returned to her plans for the cooperative. She organized a community gathering to share her vision, inviting women from all levels of society to join her. As she stood before them, she felt the weight of their expectations, but this time, instead of fear, she felt a surge of strength.

"I know there are those who doubt us," Isabella began, her voice steady and clear. "But we are here to change that narrative. Together, we can create a space where our voices are heard, where we can learn and grow, and where we can support one another. This cooperative is not just my dream; it is ours."

The room erupted in applause, and Isabella felt the warmth of their support enveloping her. The smiles and nods of encouragement from the women around her ignited a fire within her—a fire that dispelled the shadows of self-doubt and replaced them with a fierce determination to succeed.

As the meeting continued, Isabella found herself invigorated by the collective energy of the women. They shared their own dreams and aspirations, and together they forged a bond that transcended the limitations imposed by tradition. In that moment, she realized that her vision was not just about her own ambitions; it was about creating a legacy for future generations of women who would dare to dream.

With each passing day, Isabella grew more confident in her abilities. The lessons imparted by her grandmother and the unwavering support of friends like Lydia became her guiding light. She learned to embrace the challenges and criticisms as part of her journey, understanding that they would only serve to strengthen her resolve.

Isabella stood at the precipice of her dreams, ready to confront the obstacles ahead. With the support of her community and the wisdom of her ancestors, she felt empowered to carve her own path, one that would lead not only to her success but to the empowerment of all the women in Colihaut. The roots of her ambition had taken hold, and she was determined to nurture them into a flourishing reality.

As the days turned into weeks, Isabella's commitment to the agricultural cooperative deepened, yet she continued to face the challenges of self-doubt—until a pivotal moment threatened to derail everything for which she had worked.

It was a balmy Friday evening when the community hall buzzed with the familiar sounds of chatter and laughter as neighbors exchanged news and updates. Isabella was preparing to present her plans for the cooperative. Huddled in a corner, she was reviewing her notes when the conversation of two women drifted toward her.

"I hear they're thinking of selling the plantation to a foreign investor," one woman whispered, her voice laced with concern. "They think it'll bring in money, but we all know those companies don't care about our community."

The other woman nodded, her expression serious. "It is a shame. If they sell, what will become of our land? What will happen to the generations who have worked it?"

Isabella's heart raced as she listened, her breath catching in her throat. The thought of losing her family's land place steeped in history, memories, and hopes for the future—was devastating. This land had been her sanctuary since childhood, a place where she had imagined her dreams taking root and blossoming. The idea of it falling into the hands of a foreign investor felt like a gut punch.

The women continued their conversation, their voices escalating with emotion. "We need to do something! We cannot let them take it away from us."

Suddenly, a fire ignited within Isabella. This moment crystallized her ambition, propelling her into action. She understood that this was not just about her dreams; it was about saving a legacy that belonged to her family and, indeed, the entire community. The desire to preserve what had been built by her ancestors kicked into high gear, intertwining with her vision for the cooperative.

The weight of the moment surged through her, sharpening her focus. Over the weeks, Isabella had nurtured her dreams of creating a space that empowered women and transformed their lives. Now, that dream felt even more necessary, more urgent than ever. If the land was sold, not only would her aspirations be shattered, but a part of their shared cultural heritage would be lost forever.

As the meeting began, Isabella stood taller, a newfound clarity pulsing through her veins. When the time came for her to speak, she launched her presentation with fervor. "What we have here is not just land; it's our heritage, a living testament to our resilience and strength," she declared, her voice rising above the murmurs of the crowd. "We cannot allow it to be sold to outsiders who will only exploit it for their own gain!"

Immediate reactions surged through the hall. Some faces displayed skepticism, while others sparked intrigue and determination. Isabella sensed the urgency she felt mirrored in the eyes of those listening, and the energy of the room shifted. She painted a vivid picture of her cooperative plan, outlining sustainable farming practices that would not only honor the land but also provide jobs and learning opportunities for women in the community. Would they come together to reclaim their heritage, to build something meaningful from their collective ownership?

"Together, we can cultivate this land into a beacon of hope, not just for ourselves but for generations to come," Isabella continued, her words gaining momentum. "We will not only save our heritage; we will work together to uplift everyone in Colihaut. This cooperative will be a sanctuary for our community—a place where we can teach our daughters the value of the land and the strength of their voices."

As Isabella spoke, she caught sight of her grandmother in the audience, her eyes glistening with pride. Awareness of the significance of this moment surged through Isabella; she was embodying the spirit of all the women who had come before her—those whose dreams had been stifled by societal expectations and traditional norms. She felt their strength coursing through her, igniting a fire that was impossible to dim.

When Isabella finished, silence filled the room, followed by a wave of applause. It was as if she had given voice to the unspoken fears of her community. Women began to rise and share their own stories of connection to the land, expressing their hopes for the future and their determination to support Isabella's vision.

"I've lived here my whole life; I don't want to see our land go to someone who won't care for it," one older woman declared. "We need a cooperative, and we need it now!"

Another voice added, "If we come together, we can ensure that our traditions and values thrive."

As these voices intertwined, Isabella felt buoyed by the growing momentum. The fear of losing her family's land transformed into a unifying force, solidifying her commitment to this cause. The possibility of the land being sold was no longer a distant threat; it was a fight she was willing to lead, igniting a resolve she had never known.

The evening culminated in a passionate discussion about strategies to protect the land from sale. Ideas flew like sparks in the air—community petitions, regular meetings to address concerns, and outreach to local government officials to express their opposition.

As the meeting ended, Isabella stepped outside, her heart racing with adrenaline. The stars twinkled overhead, casting soft light on the moments that would define her future. She felt a profound connection to her ancestors and the land beneath her feet, anchoring her ambitions into a reality that required not only her voice but the voices of many.

After the meeting, her friends surrounded her, gratitude and excitement lighting their faces. Lydia beamed at Isabella. "You were incredible! I knew you had it in you. This is just the beginning."

Though exhaustion tugged at her, Isabella felt invigorated. She exited the community hall, a sense of purpose thrumming through her. There was still much work to be done—gathering signatures, building alliances, and mobilizing the community—but for the first time, she felt like an integral part of something greater than herself.

The defining moment had arrived; the spark of action ignited by fear and hope swept her into a whirlwind of determination. She understood now that her dreams for the cooperative were not only rooted in personal ambition but situated squarely within the heart of her community's fight for its heritage. Isabella was resolute, she would save the land, and in doing so, she would uplift not just herself but the entire village of Colihaut.

With the wind at her back, she stepped forward, ready to confront whatever challenges might arise. She had become not just the dreamer of a vision but a leader stepping boldly onto the path of change. This was her time to act, and she was prepared to seize it with both hands.

TWO
THE CALL TO ACTION

As the 1960s progressed, Dominica found itself at a crossroads. In the air hung a palpable sense of change, an awakening that rippled through its villages as communities fervently discussed independence from colonial rule. The push for self-determination intensified, and with it came waves of unrest and blossoming activism. Isabella, now in her late twenties, felt the surge of this changing tide in every corner of her life.

She observed the world around her shifting—the creaking of long-held traditions under the weight of new ideas. The streets of Colihaut were alive with conversations that had not been voiced before: discussions about rights, representation, and the importance of empowerment. Community gatherings and rallies became more frequent, resonating like a drumbeat of urgent resolve. More than ever, Isabella felt the urgency of her own ambitions intertwined with the aspirations of her fellow villagers.

Isabella had dedicated herself to the cooperative, tirelessly organizing meetings and mobilizing support among the women in her community. She recognized that many were still marginalized, their potential stifled by societal expectations and a lack of opportunity. The stories of her own grandmothers, who had fought against cultural constraints to carve out paths for themselves, resonated deeply within her. They had faced hardships and discrimination but had forged legacies of resilience and strength that she longed to amplify.

One humid evening, as the sun dipped low over the bay, casting golden hues across the gathering clouds, Isabella hosted an informational meeting at the community center. The air buzzed with anticipation as women of all ages filed in, their faces lit by the soft glow of oil lamps. They whispered among themselves, uncertain at first but curious about what Isabella had to say.

"Thank you all for coming," she began, her voice steady in the flickering light. "Tonight, we gather not just to discuss our cooperative but to recognize that our dreams cannot be achieved in isolation. The winds of change are upon us, and now is the time to harness that energy. It is a call for action, especially for us women who have so much strength and potential."

Nods of agreement rippled through the room, and Isabella felt a swell of hope as she looked around at the diverse faces: mothers, daughters, grandmothers, and a few men who had come to support. The recent political climate was undeniably dire, but the spirit of the women gathered there was unyielding.

"I know many of you face challenges every day—balancing work, family, and all the responsibilities placed upon us. But our voices matter, and we must find ways to be heard. This cooperative can be a powerful tool for our community, a beacon of hope for all women to break free from the limitations imposed upon us," she continued, her enthusiasm infectious.

As she spoke, Isabella painted a vision of what a united front could look like. "Imagine a place where women share resources, develop skills, and uplift one another. Imagine standing together, not just for ourselves but for every woman in Dominica who has felt unheard, invisible, or trapped in a cycle of limitation. We need each other now more than ever."

The room was electric with energy, and Isabella's words hung in the air like an unlit fuse, waiting for something to ignite it. She could see that her neighbors were beginning to awaken to their own voices, emboldened by the collective spirit filling the room. They shared their stories of struggle—Margot, who had been denied a position at the local school simply because she was a woman, and Gwendolyn, whose dreams of becoming a seamstress were thwarted by her family's traditional expectations.

"It's time for us to claim what is ours," Isabella declared, her heart racing as the adrenaline surged through her veins. "We are capable, and together we can not only change our own circumstances but inspire the next generation."

As the meeting progressed, the tensions outside mirrored the resolve building within the center. News of protests and rallies in the capital reached Colihaut frequently, and the village buzzed with discussions of politics and rights. The government responded to the growing unrest with increased police presence and occasional raids on known activists, stifling voices to maintain control.

One evening, as Isabella walked home from a particularly spirited meeting, she could not shake the feeling of urgency settling over her. The winds were shifting, and she could sense that her life was on the verge of transformation. Growing political tensions pushed her toward a pivotal decision: she needed to take a stand for the voices of the women who had been silenced for far too long.

As she neared her home, she paused for a moment, looking out over the bay. The water shimmered under the moonlight, reflecting her hopes and dreams back at her. An idea began to form—a rally, a gathering that would not only urge women to unite but would also attract attention from the political leaders who needed to hear their voices.

"Tomorrow," she whispered to herself, "I will begin planning a rally—a call to action for every woman in Colihaut." Her determination solidified with each heartbeat, and as she stepped into her home, she felt buoyed by the sense that she was no longer just responding to the changes around her, she was becoming a part of them.

The next few weeks unfolded like a fever dream. Isabella worked tirelessly, rallying support, and crafting a message that resonated with the women of the village. Posters were handmade plastered up around the town, calling all women to come together in a united stand. The buzz grew, and soon the date of the rally became the topic of discussion at every food stall and front porch.

Then, as anticipation swelled, tensions in the village began to rise. Voices of dissent emerged: a small fraction of men questioned the necessity of a women's rally, arguing that it would distract from the greater political struggle for independence. Rumors spread, painting Isabella's intentions as misguided or overly ambitious.

But Isabella's resolve only deepened. She refused to let fear or opposition deter her. "We have every right to be heard," she declared to her supporters, fueled by the power of their shared experiences. "Our fight is not separate from the fight for independence; it enhances it. An empowered woman is an empowered nation."

As the rally day approached, it became clear that this was not just a moment for Isabella; it was a moment for all women in Dominica to rise and reclaim agency over their lives. They were no longer mere bystanders in the tides of change; they were architects of their destinies.

The stage was set for a historic gathering, one that would challenge not only the social dynamics of Colihaut but also send ripples through the broader movement for independence sweeping the nation. With her heart and spirit ignited, Isabella stood at the precipice of a new chapter marked by courage, solidarity, and the unwavering belief in the power of collective action. She was ready to answer the call to action, knowing that as a woman of valor, she would leave a legacy that would inspire generations to come.

The bustling la Place dame market was alive with the sounds of laughter, haggling, and the aroma of fresh produce and spices wafting through the air. Isabella wandered through the stalls, absorbing the vibrant atmosphere and marveling at the creativity on display. From colorful fabrics to intricate beadwork, the market highlighted the artistic talents of the villagers. Yet amidst this celebration of local craftsmanship, Isabella's gaze was drawn to a frail older woman struggling to attract attention.

Aunt Miriam sat at her modest stall, surrounded by handmade crafts—colorful baskets, woven mats, and delicate ornaments. Despite the beauty of her work, few people paused to engage with her. Instead, the crowd flocked to the more commercial vendors, their stalls overflowing with imported goods and flashy advertisements promising the latest trends. Isabella watched as potential buyers brushed past

Aunt Miriam, their indifference a stark reminder of the broader societal dynamics that marginalized the women of her community.

Isabella's heart sank as she observed the older woman's weary expression, a poignant reflection of countless hours spent perfecting her craft, only to be overlooked for flashy alternatives. Aunt Miriam's hands trembled slightly as she rearranged her wares, but her spirit remained unbroken. Isabella could see the pride in the woman's eyes flicker of hope that someone might recognize the value in her hard work.

Unable to look away, Isabella approached Aunt Miriam's stall, feeling a surge of empathy and shamefulness. "Good morning, Aunt Miriam. Your crafts are beautiful," she said softly, her voice laced with sincerity. The older woman looked up, gratitude shining through her sadness.

"Thank you, dear," Aunt Miriam replied, a weak smile breaking through the lines of weariness etched on her face. "I have worked all year on these. Just hoping someone will see their worth."

Isabella's heart ached for her. Here was a woman who dedicated her life to her art and family, yet the world around her seemed to render that dedication invisible. In that moment, Isabella was confronted with the stark reality of her own privileges—her education, her community support, her stable life compared to the struggles faced by women like Aunt Miriam.

As she stood by the stall, a wave of realization washed over her. This was not just about her dreams for the cooperative; it was about something larger, a responsibility to uplift those who had been silenced and sidelined. Aunt Miriam was a symbol of the many women in

Colihaut, each one with stories of struggle and resilience, each one worthy of respect and opportunity.

"Would you let me help you?" Isabella asked, her resolve firming. "I could share your story at my upcoming rally. We need to ensure that our community values the work of women like you."

Aunt Miriam's eyes widened, a glimmer of hope igniting within her. "Oh, girl, that would be wonderful. But what if they do not listen?"

"They *must* listen," Isabella asserted, her determination solidified. "We have to show them that the strength of our community lies in our women—their skills, their dedication, their voices."

The frail woman nodded slowly, and as Isabella helped her rearrange the crafts, they drew the attention of passersby. For the first time that day, people began to stop, curious about Aunt Miriam's beautiful creations. With each piece she presented, Isabella shared snippets of Aunt Miriam's story, the sacrifices she had made, the love woven into every item she crafted.

As the crowd gathered, Isabella felt a profound shift inside her. This was the catalyst she had been searching for. Aunt Miriam's experiences were emblematic of greater societal issues, and they resonated deeply with the themes of her rally. She realized that her work could be a platform for other women, a way to amplify their voices and ensure their stories were heard and valued.

The realization ignited a fire within her, stronger and more urgent than ever. Her vision was not just about creating a cooperative; it was about catalyzing change, about acknowledging the dedication of women like Aunt Miriam who poured their lives into their crafts only to have them dismissed. This rally had the potential to elevate every woman in

Colihaut and beyond, launching a collective call for respect, opportunity, and empowerment.

Returning home that day, Isabella reflected on the profound impact of this encounter. She could no longer think of her ambitions solely in terms of personal achievement. Her dreams had to extend beyond herself and envelop the community she loved. As she sat in her small room, ideas began forming in her mind—a program that could highlight the crafts of local women, a series of workshops where they could share their skills, and initiatives that could redefine the parameters of craftsmanship and entrepreneurship in Colihaut.

Isabella knew that with every word spoken at her rally, she would channel Aunt Miriam's strength and spirit—her trials and perseverance would resonate with the collective voices of women in Dominica who had long yearned for recognition. The way forward was clear; she must center this work around stories, making the personal political.

In the subsequent days leading up to the rally, Isabella poured her energy into organizing. She reached out to the women in her community, inviting them to share their experiences and dreams, encouraging them to speak out and stand together. Each story she gathered deepened her understanding of the struggles faced by women across Dominica and solidified her resolve to ensure that their voices were not just heard but celebrated.

The closer she got to the date of the rally, the more nervous energy flowed through her veins. But now, it was nervous excitement—an anticipation that bubbled up from the very core of her being. This was more than an event; it was a movement in the making. It was a call not just for women but for the entire community to recognize the worth and potential of every individual, especially those who often went unseen.

As the day approached, the village hummed with potential and possibility. Isabella felt the energy shifting, the undercurrents of change deepening as Colihaut prepared to rise together. She was no longer just a dreamer; she was a woman of valor, ready to ignite a spark of empowerment that would transcend her own ambitions and galvanize an entire generation of women—and men—ready to stand for the dignity and respect their community deserved.

The rally would not only be a space for sharing, but a platform for action, a declaration that the fight for independence must include the fight for equality and opportunity for all. And at its heart, Isabella understood that her mission was to ensure that women like Aunt Miriam—and countless others—would finally be seen, heard, and celebrated.

Isabella stood at the front of the dimly lit community hall, her heart racing as she surveyed the gathering crowd. The room buzzed with whispered conversations and the rustle of fabric as women from different backgrounds settled into their seats—fisherwomen with salt-kissed skin, farmers with dirt-streaked hands, teachers with weary eyes, and homemakers with hopeful hearts. Each had come with their own stories, their own burdens, yet there was a shared determination in the air, a spark of possibility that Isabella could sense pulsing through the gathering.

"Thank you all for coming," Isabella began, her voice steady but passionate. "I know that life has not been easy for any of us. We face challenges that often feel insurmountable. But I believe we can change that. Together."

Some faces showed skepticism, brows furrowed with doubt. A fisherwoman spoke up, her voice edged with concern. "And what can we do? Who would listen to us?" The room fell silent, eyes shifting to Isabella, waiting for an answer.

She remembered the stories woven into her childhood, tales her grandmother told of communities banding together, of women rising in times of need. Drawing from that well of inspiration, Isabella replied, "Our voices are stronger than we realize. Remember the days when the tides were rough, and we still cast our nets, pulling in what we could? Or how can the land yield a bountiful harvest if we sow together? By sharing our struggles and aspirations, we can create a support system that empowers us all."

The atmosphere shifted slightly; curiosity mixed with skepticism. Isabella continued, sharing her grandmother's stories of resilience—how women had rallied in their village to fight for access to education and healthcare, how they had banded together to secure fair wages for their work. "If we harness that same spirit, we can create change," she urged, her eyes shining with conviction. "We all want better lives for our children, for ourselves. Let us not just talk about our hardships; let us turn them into a cause for action."

One by one, women began to share their stories—some about the struggles of caring for aging parents while working multiple jobs, others about the frustrations of being overlooked in decision-making processes that affected their lives. As they listened to one another, a bond began to form among them, igniting a sense of solidarity.

A farmer's voice broke through the conversations. "We need more than just support—we need resources, training, and representation. How do we even begin to tackle that?"

Isabella nodded, recognizing the complexity of their challenges. "We can organize workshops, share skills, and create networks that help us amplify our voices. Together, we can approach local leaders, advocating for our rights and needs. Power lies in our unity."

As the discussion progressed, the women brainstormed ideas, jotting down notes fueled by newfound energy. They spoke of creating a cooperative for their goods, a platform for advocacy, and mentorship programs for the younger generation, ensuring that their knowledge and stories of resilience were passed down.

The meeting concluded with a renewed sense of purpose. As the women filed out of the hall, Isabella felt a swell of hope. They were no longer just individuals facing their struggles alone; they were a collective force ready to challenge the status quo. If they could just hold onto this momentum, harness their voices, and support one another, they could truly shape their destinies.

As she cleaned up the empty chairs and tables, Isabella's heart soared. She had seen the spark ignite amongst her community, and she knew this was just the beginning. The journey ahead would be filled with challenges, but they would face them together, drawing strength from one another, ready to enshrine their place in history.

As the cicadas chirped outside, filling the air with their rhythmic song, Isabella stood in front of the assembly, a sense of purpose enveloping her like a warm embrace. The energy in the room was electrifying; their shared stories were now the groundwork for something greater. It was time to channel that energy into action. She took a deep breath and began to share her vision collective dream that could transform their futures.

"Imagine with me," she started, her eyes glimmering with excitement, "what we can achieve if we reclaim the abandoned sugar cane plantation on the outskirts of town. We could cultivate not just crops but also the very spirit of our community—a place where we can nurture our skills and harvest the fruits of our labor together."

Murmurs of interest rippled through the audience. Isabella paced slowly, ensuring her words resonated with every person present. "This cooperative would be a haven for women of all backgrounds. It will provide jobs that pay fair wages and create an environment where we can learn from one another. We would not just be workers; we would be entrepreneurs, growers, teachers, and leaders."

A seasoned farmer raised a hand, curiosity gleaming in her eyes. "How would we go about starting something like this? Isn't that a monumental task?"

Isabella welcomed the question, eager to dive into specifics. "It will take hard work and dedication, yes, but we have a remarkable chance to develop sustainable farming practices that respect our land. Imagine working with local agricultural experts who can teach us about organic farming, soil health, and eco-friendly techniques. We can grow our crops responsibly, ensuring we protect the environment while feeding our families and the community."

Isabella paused, allowing her vision to settle in. "Moreover, we would incorporate business management training. It is essential that we do not just cultivate plants but also cultivate the knowledge to run this cooperative successfully. Learning how to manage finances, market our products, and create a brand can empower us to take control of our economic futures."

A soft voice spoke from the back of the room, a homemaker with a wise, weathered face. "But what about our daughters? How can we ensure this knowledge continues?"

Isabella smiled, recognizing the importance of legacy in her vision. "That is a critical point. I want the cooperative to be a place where the next generation can thrive. We can develop mentorship programs that teach our daughters about leadership and entrepreneurship. They should know they can carry this torch forward, and with each passing generation, our community grows stronger."

As Isabella spoke, she could see the skepticism ebb away, replaced by hope and determination. Women nodded in agreement, their faces reflecting a burgeoning belief in the possibility of change. "And let us not forget—we will also join forces with local health initiatives to foster discussions about nutrition and wellness within our community. This cooperative can promote health and well-being as much as it promotes economic stability."

The fisherwoman who had spoken earlier raised her hand again, now animated. "And what about selling our goods? How will we reach customers?"

"Great point!" Isabella replied enthusiastically. "We can leverage local markets, establish a community-supported agriculture (CSA) program, and even explore partnerships with local restaurants and retailers who prioritize sourcing from women-owned businesses. Together, we can create a brand that not only represents quality but also embodies our shared stories of resilience and empowerment."

As the meeting progressed, conversations flourished like the crops they were envisioning. Women began to break down tasks: forming committees for each aspect of the cooperative—agriculture, marketing, education—and brainstorming ways to raise initial funds. Ideas flew around the room like sparks, igniting creativity and inspiration.

Eventually, Isabella brought the gathering to a close. "This is just the beginning, but together, we have the power to create something transformative. This cooperative can be more than just a source of income; it can become the heartbeat of our community, an incubator for knowledge, skills, and sisterhood."

As the women stood to leave, a palpable sense of excitement and commitment tinged the air. They were ready to take on the challenge of building this cooperative, to cultivate not just the land but their own potential. Isabella felt a warmth glow within her, knowing that they were embarking on a journey that would redefine their lives and secure a legacy for future generations.

With newfound determination, the women dispersed into the evening, weaving through the pathways of their neighborhood, each step echoing the promise of what was to come—a cooperative born from the ashes of their shared struggles, ready to rise and thrive.

As the women trickled out of the community hall, a palpable tension hung in the air. The initial excitement that had sparked during Isabella's presentation began to face the realities of skepticism and fear. Some women were fueled by the possibility of change; others, however, carried the weight of doubt like heavy stones in their pockets.

Isabella gathered a handful of women who appeared particularly animated. Among them, Maya, an energetic teacher, spoke first. "I love this idea, Isabella! We can really make something of ourselves, especially with our knowledge of farming. It is time we eliminated the stigma that we are just caregivers. We could transform the community!"

But before Isabella could respond, a voice cut through the building tension—a woman with a face hardened by years of toil, Clara, a seasoned farmer from the next town over. "You are dreaming, Isabella! Women around here do not get to decide their fates. We have families to care for and men to answer to. Why would we risk everything chasing a fantasy? This sounds like a lot of work for nothing!"

Gasps could be heard from those nearby. Isabella felt a wave of emotions wash over her—disappointment, but more importantly, a resolve to address the self-doubt gripping her community. "Clara, I understand your concerns. Change is daunting, especially in a world that expects so little from us. But think about our potential. What if we did not just conform to those expectations? We have the talent, the knowledge—if we combine our strengths, we can create something real.

Another voice joined in, this time from Eliza, an older homemaker known for her unwavering practicality. "And who will support us? We cannot be naive; the men will surely resist the idea of women controlling land and profits. We must also be willing to confront those who will stand in our way."

Isabella's heart raced, but she knew she had to stand her ground. "You are right, Eliza. We may face resistance, but that is why we need each other now more than ever. Together, we can be a formidable force. And let us not forget, women have always faced adversity and proven their strength when they unite. Look at the stories of women in history—those who fought for their rights and changed the world around them."

Clara shook her head, her skepticism palpable. "That sounds noble, but what about our families? The demands of work and home will not magically disappear because we have a dream. What if we fail? What then?"

"Failure is possible, but so is success," Isabella replied, keeping her tone calm yet firm. "The hard work will be there, no matter what we choose to do. But we can invest in ourselves and our community. If we fail, we learn and adapt, we do not give up. And we will support each other through thick and thin."

In the audience, a few women began to nod, swayed by Isabella's entreaties. Maya stepped forward; her voice filled with encouragement. "Clara, think about what we have already accomplished as individuals. Isn't there glory in banding together? We could redefine what it means to be women in this community. Besides, we could start small—initiate workshops to build skills and collaborate before we jump into major projects."

Another woman, Lena, a recently retired teacher, added, "We can organize a trial run—set up a small garden on the land to see what we can grow together. It does not have to be all or nothing right away. We can test the waters and prove to ourselves that we are capable."

Isabella seized this moment, her heart swelling with hope. "That is an excellent idea! A trial garden could showcase our potential—and we can invite the community to participate in its growth, fostering interest. Imagine the impact we could make by not only producing food but also demonstrating our capability to lead and innovate!"

Clara's brow still furrowed, but she seemed to waver, conflicted between tradition and aspiration. "I suppose starting small could be manageable. But what if our families do not support this? We face generations of expectations."

"I fully understand," Isabella replied softly, her tone soothing. "Change does not come easy, especially when it challenges long-held beliefs. But if we demonstrate our commitment to this vision, others may start to believe in it too. Let us not forget, we are not doing this solely for ourselves. We are doing it for future generations of women who will not have to fight as hard as we have."

The discussions continued late into the evening, as women debated and deliberated, visions of their cooperative forming clearer through the haze of doubt. While not every woman left the hall convinced, many were intrigued by the potential for collaboration, ready to take that first tentative step into uncharted territory.

As Isabella watched them leave, she felt a mix of pride and trepidation. Change was rarely greeted with open arms, but she recognized that each small victory, each budding belief, was a seed planted in fertile ground. They faced considerable challenges ahead, but armed with conviction and community, they had a real chance—to rewrite their own narratives.

The days following the initial meeting were filled with a whirlwind of ideas and conversations. Isabella understood that to turn the tide of skepticism into enthusiasm, she needed to demonstrate the potential of their collective talents. Fueled by a resolute spirit, she began to formulate a plan—a public demonstration to showcase the skills of the women in her community, a celebration of their hard work, resilience, and creativity.

She called a gathering at her home, inviting those who showed interest during the last meeting. As the warmth of the afternoon sun filtered through the open windows, Isabella laid out her vision. "We need to show our community what we are capable of," she declared, her tone passionate. "Let us organize a demonstration where we can spotlight the skills of women artisans, farmers, and cooks. This event could not only celebrate our abilities but also highlight our contributions to society.

Maya leaned forward, her eyes brightening at the prospect. "That sounds wonderful, Isabella! We can invite everyone—families, friends, and local leaders. It will be an opportunity to show what we can do, to gain their respect and support.

Clara, still cautious but intrigued, crossed her arms. "And how exactly do you plan to pull this off? It sounds great and all, but we need a concrete plan."

Isabella smiled, grateful for Clara's practicality. "We will organize it around the town square. With the help of a few volunteers, we can set up booths where artisans can display their crafts—pottery, textiles, and handmade jewelry. We will have a section for farmers to bring fresh produce and one for cooks to prepare tastings of local dishes.

Lena added, "We could incorporate a storytelling segment where women share their personal stories and experiences. It would highlight our journeys, the obstacles we have faced, and the strength we have developed. That would resonate deeply with the audience."

"Yes!" Isabella exclaimed, enthusiasm bubbling within her. "By sharing our stories, we create connections. We show them we are not just women but visionaries, caretakers, and innovators. And we can include an open forum for discussion afterwards—an opportunity for community input on our cooperative idea."

With a plan forming, the women dove into the details, brainstorming logistics and assigning tasks. They took on roles that best matched their skills: some would gather supplies, others would reach out to potential participants, and a few would handle logistics for the day of the event. Clara even volunteered to rally the farmers, while Maya enlisted her students to help with promotion, creating flyers and banners to hang around town.

As the days passed, the word of their demonstration spread, and the excitement in the community grew. Shops began to display the flyers, and passersby started to inquire about the event. Many women who had previously remained skeptical now found themselves curious, even eager to take part.

The day of the demonstration dawned bright and warm, the sun casting a golden hue over the town square. Banners depicting images of resilience and community spirit fluttered in the gentle breeze. The air was filled with the rich aromas of home-cooked dishes, mingling enticingly with the scent of fresh produce.

Isabella stood at the center, taking in the vibrant scene with a mixture of pride and nervousness. Women set up their booths with care, arranging handmade crafts and fresh vegetables, all while chatting and laughing. A small crowd began to gather, intrigued by the buzz of activity.

When it was time for the storytelling segment, Isabella took a deep breath and stepped forward to welcome everyone. "Thank you all for being here today! We have come together not only to showcase our talents but to share our experiences and dreams for the future. We are women of this community, and we have strength in our unity."

The stories flowed like a river, each narrative rich with emotion and wisdom. A fisherwoman spoke of the dangers she faced on the water, while a farmer shared the struggles of dealing with erratic weather patterns. Women mentioned their hopes for their daughters and how they wished to pave a better path for future generations. The crowd listened intently, clapping, and showing their support, and Isabella could see the shift in energy as empathy and admiration filled the square.

As the event continued, laughter erupted from the cooking station where local chefs prepared dishes using seasonal ingredients. Tantalizing flavors drew people to sample each dish, sparking conversations about nutrition and sustainability. Clara beamed as she watched the farmers' booth, where fresh produce was traded and sold, and women exchanged tips on growing techniques.

The culmination of the day came when Isabella invited local leaders to the center stage. "We are here asking you to recognize the contributions of women in our community. We believe that by uniting our voices and talents, we can be a force for change, not just for ourselves, but for the entire community."

Encouraged by the audience's energy and the support from behind, several leaders stepped forward to speak. They expressed their respect for women's talents and offered to support the cooperative initiative, suggesting ways they could help facilitate grants and resources.

As the demonstration wrapped up, Isabella felt a deep sense of fulfillment. What had started as a call to action had transformed into a vibrant celebration of strength and solidarity. The walls of doubt that had once surrounded her community began to fracture, replaced by a newfound hope and collective ambition.

As people began to disperse, many lingered to help clean up, demonstrating a unity that went beyond the event. Women began making plans to meet again, to further solidify their ideas and to embark on the journey of the cooperative together.

Stepping back, Isabella watched the scene unfold, her heart swelling with pride. She knew there would be challenges ahead, but they had ignited a flame of determination that could not be extinguished. Together, they were no longer just a group of women with dreams—they were a movement, ready to reclaim their narrative and shape their destiny.

With the memory of the successful demonstration still fresh in her mind, Isabella felt invigorated. The energy and enthusiasm that had surfaced during the event were too powerful to let fade. She understood that to truly establish the cooperative and encourage participation from every corner of their community, she needed to sustain that momentum.

Isabella reached out to her close friend Lydia, a fellow activist known for her passion for women's rights and her ability to rally support. Over coffee at their favorite café, Isabella laid out her vision. "Lydia, we need to build on the energy from the demonstration. Let us mobilize more women and make sure that everyone knows about the cooperative and what it can offer."

Lydia's eyes sparkled with excitement. "Absolutely! We can start by creating flyers that highlight our mission, our needs, and how this cooperative can empower women. We could also use social media to spread the word."

Isabella nodded, invigorated by Lydia's enthusiasm. "Yes! And I want to emphasize the importance of community support as we reach out to local leaders and businesses. We need them to understand what we are trying to achieve. Their backing could really elevate our efforts."

The two friends strategized, setting goals for the upcoming weeks. They mapped out different neighborhoods, targeting areas where support could be enlisted. They began drafting flyers that stated the purpose of the cooperative, outlining the skills and resources women could contribute and how it would benefit the community. Their message was direct and hopeful: "Together, We Can Create Change!"

The first step was a grassroots effort, using word-of-mouth within their existing networks. Lydia organized small gatherings, where they could informally discuss the cooperative's vision and importance. They encouraged attendees to invite friends and family, creating a ripple effect that would expand their reach. With each meeting, the energy grew, and the number of voices amplifying the message increased.

As the flyers were printed and distributed, Isabella and Lydia crafted messages for their community's social media pages. They created posts that celebrated the talents showcased in the earlier demonstration, along with photos of women actively participating in the local economy. They shared stories of resilience and empowerment, highlighting the individual artisans, farmers, and cooks who would be involved in the upcoming initiatives.

Lydia also suggested they contact local farmers' markets and craft fairs, where they could set up information booths. "We can engage the community directly, inviting them to join our movement," she said. "Plus, it'll give us a chance to show what we're already accomplishing."

Excitedly, Isabella agreed. They reached out to the organizers of the local farmers' market, who were receptive to the idea of featuring their initiative. The market was always buzzing with activity, and it would provide a great platform for building community awareness.

As days turned into weeks, they intentionally reached out to local leaders—community officials, educators, and influential figures in the area. Isabella drafted personalized invitation letters that thanked them for their support of local initiatives and explained the cooperative's potential impact on the community. Each letter emphasized the importance of their

presence at the next demonstration, giving them a chance to see firsthand how the cooperative could flourish.

One morning, while preparing her letters, Isabella received an unexpected call from the mayor's office, expressing interest in learning more about the cooperative. Thrilled, Isabella scheduled a meeting, knowing this could be a pivotal moment for their initiative. She wanted to ensure the mayor understood the collective's mission and the resonance of its potential impact on both the community and the local economy.

During the meeting, Isabella was both nervous and excited. She arrived with her notes and an open heart, eager to share not just the statistics but the stories of the women behind the initiative. "Our aim is to empower women by providing a platform for skills development, economic independence, and community building," she explained, her voice steady.

The mayor listened intently, nodding at the appropriate times. Isabella described how the cooperative would create a ripple effect, improving the local economy and fostering pride among community members. "We're seeking your support not only to legitimize our efforts but also to inspire others to join our cause."

The mayor expressed interest in attending the next demonstration and promised to share their initiative within her networks. "It sounds like a promising direction for our community," she concluded. "As a woman in leadership myself, I understand the importance of initiatives like this."

Energized by the meeting, Isabella returned to Lydia, sharing the good news. "We are gaining momentum, Lydia! The mayor is on board, and she is committed to supporting our next event. Imagine the number of people we can reach with her backing!"

Overwhelm and exhilaration settled in as they planned further outreach, crafting messages and organizing mini events leading up to the main demonstration. They decided to host a series of pre-event brainstorming sessions to engage more women in the planning process, emphasizing collaboration and inclusivity.

On the day of those sessions, they welcomed women from diverse backgrounds—some were eager to contribute their skills, while others initially remained hesitant. Isabella and Lydia encouraged everyone to think broadly about what talents they could bring to the cooperative.

"Whether you've grown up farming, crafting, or cooking, every skill is important," Isabella said, her passion pulsating with each word.

"This cooperative has the power to change our lives, but only if we all stand together and contribute our gifts."

Gradually, women began to share their ideas and talents, and the sessions buzzed with creativity and collaboration. Artisans crafted decorations for the upcoming event, farmers brought produce to share, and cooks collaborated on recipes that would delight attendees. Each woman's contribution became a building block for their shared vision, transforming skepticism into shared purpose.

As the next demonstration approached, a palpable excitement filled the air. Women began to rally, their spirits lifting with each passing day. They shared stories of their ancestors' struggles and triumphs, lending meaning to their fight for their own identities and futures.

Isabella watched as her network expanded, feeling a sense of pride in the way they were coming together. This was more than just a cooperative; this was a movement, a collective spirit determined to carve out a rightful place in their community, standing strong against resistance and bound by the promise of unity. By gathering resources and support from diverse allies, Isabella was confident that the cooperative would soon take its rightful place as a beacon of empowerment within the community.

The sun rose over the mountains, casting its first golden rays across the island, and Isabella felt a wave of anticipation and purpose wash over her. She stood at the edge of the valley, flanked by Lydia and their guide, Samuel, who was well-versed in the natural wonders and hidden gems of the land. Today, they were embarking on a journey to the Boiling Lake, a destination that not only held breathtaking beauty but also represented the raw power and transformation that resonated with Isabella's current mission.

As they began their trek, the air was crisp, filled with the scent of damp earth and blooming flora. The path wound through lush vegetation, steep gorges, and rocky ridges, each step a reminder of the obstacles she faced both personally and for the cooperative. The beauty surrounding her was breathtaking; the vibrant greens of the trees and the sounds of chirping birds whispered of life and resilience. Yet, it was the thought of the Boiling Lake, with its fuming sulfuric waters, that loomed in her mind as a metaphor for her journey—a constant reminder of the potential for transformation amid challenges.

"Isabella, do you know the story of the Boiling Lake?" Lydia asked, as they navigated a rocky section of the trail.

"I've heard pieces of it," Isabella replied, her voice steady but contemplative. "They say it formed from an explosion caused by a volcanic eruption ages ago. The water is heated by geothermal activity beneath it. It is beautiful but dangerous."

Lydia nodded, clearly intrigued. "Exactly! It reminds us that beauty and danger can exist side by side. Just like our cooperative. We are stepping into uncharted territory, facing both challenges and possibilities. If we can harness our collective strength, we can create something truly transformative."

The three of them paused at a viewpoint, overlooking a vast gorge painted with hues of green and brown, the river winding like a silver ribbon below. Isabella felt a rush of exhilaration, the stunning view a testament to nature's power. "Every step we take is a step toward change," she said, her voice filled with conviction. "We're overcoming the fear of failure, just like the landscape we see here—always evolving, adapting."

As they continued onward, Samuel led them to the Valley of Desolation, a unique subregion where steam rose from the ground, and the air filled with the scent of sulfur. "This is where we can take a Sulphur bath," he explained, gesturing toward a series of natural pools bubbling with mineral-rich boiling waters. "They're supposed to have healing properties."

After a brief discussion, they decided to indulge in the experience, realizing the soaking in these natural thermal waters would not only refresh them but symbolize their willingness to embrace the challenges ahead. Stripping down to their swimsuits, they waded into the warm, milky water, its heat enveloping them like a comforting hug.

"This is incredible," Lydia said, submerging herself up to her shoulders. "It feels like nature's way of rejuvenating us before we face the boiling lake."

Isabella closed her eyes, allowing the warmth to seep into her bones. "I needed this. It is a reminder that, like the geothermal waters transforming the landscape, we too can change our community for the better. This cooperative will be a source of healing and empowerment for so many."

Once they finished their Sulphur bath, they felt invigorated, the energy renewed, and spirits lifted as they continued their journey toward the Boiling Lake. As they trekked further, the foliage began to thin, giving way to rocky terrain and volcanic soil. The landscape changed dramatically, showcasing the raw power of nature, a stark contrast to the lush valley from earlier.

Finally, they reached the rim of the Boiling Lake, and Isabella gasped at the sight. The vibrant blue water bubbled violently, steam rising in thick clouds that obscured the view momentarily before drifting away. The sight was both mesmerizing and intimidating, a perfect representation of the tumultuous journey she was navigating.

"Look at that!" Lydia exclaimed, stepping closer to the edge. "It's stunning and terrifying all at once."

Isabella nodded, her heart racing. "It is a perfect metaphor for our struggle. The lake looks serene from a distance, but up close, it is a powerful force that commands respect. We must approach our challenges with that same respect and understanding."

As they stood there, taking in the beauty and fury of the lake, Isabella contemplated the trials that lay ahead. Leading the cooperative required navigating the doubts and fears of others while also confronting her insecurities. It was about embracing the discomfort and acknowledging the power they held together, just like the bubbling water—an expression of both chaos and creation.

"Do you think we can really harness this energy?" Lydia asked, a hint of uncertainty in her voice.

Isabella turned to her, resolve flooding her being. "Absolutely. Just as this lake is a product of natural forces at work, our cooperative is born from our collective strength. It will not be easy, but if we can channel our passions, confront the hardships, and work together, we can create a groundswell of change. The power lies within us."

With renewed purpose, they stood at the edge of the lake, committing to the journey ahead and the challenges they must face. The boiling waters mirrored their turbulent emotions, always changing yet so full of potential.

After spending some time in quiet reflection at the lake, allowing its energy to infuse their spirits, Samuel ushered them back down the mountain trail. The descent was filled with animated conversations about the future, the women sharing dreams of what their cooperative could become a thriving hub of creativity and empowerment, bridging gaps between generations and enriching their community.

Isabella felt lighter with each step, buoyed by the unwavering support from Lydia and the inspiration drawn from nature's raw power. They were not just three women on a hike; they were a part of a movement, pushing back against traditional norms, determined to forge a path ahead that would benefit countless others.

Little by little, they transformed their fears into fuel for action, with the Flows of the Boiling Lake guiding their mission—ever-changing, fervent, and alive with possibilities.

As the day of the demonstration drew closer, Isabella could feel the weight of anticipation pressing down on her. The excitement that had sparked in the community felt overshadowed by a creeping anxiety, taking root in her mind—a nagging whisper that echoed the doubts some community members had expressed.

"Is this really going to work?" She found herself wondering time and again. Conversations with those who were skeptical reverberated in her thoughts. "Women can't run a cooperative." "What makes you think you can do this?" The doubts seeped into her consciousness, mingling with the insecurities of her past. She recalled moments of hesitation in her own journey—times when she felt overshadowed or deemed less capable because of gender or circumstance.

One evening, under the twilight sky, Isabella sat alone in her small living room, the soft glow of a single lamp illuminating her workspace strewn with flyers and planning documents. Each sheet depicted the vibrant vision of the cooperative, but instead of excitement, they filled her with unease. The pressure to make this demonstration a success felt insurmountable. What if it failed? What if the community turned against her again, dismissing her vision as naive?

Her mind drifted back to her grandmother, a woman who had faced countless struggles with unwavering bravery. Isabella could hear her voice clearly as if she were sitting beside her. "Courage is not the absence of fear, my child. It is standing firm in your convictions, even when your heart races with doubt. Remember that true strength often comes from the connections we create with one another."

A wave of nostalgia washed over her, and Isabella remembered the stories her grandmother had told her about overcoming adversity warrior spirit woven into the fabric of their family history. Her grandmother had faced societal pressures, discrimination, and heartache, yet through it all, she never wavered in her beliefs about justice and equality. Isabella felt the warmth of those memories slowly wrapping around her like a familiar blanket, reigniting her resolve.

A sudden wave of clarity washed over Isabella, and she realized that this cooperative was not just about her—it was about all of them, the women who had supported her, who stood shoulder to shoulder with her, striving for a common goal. The faces of the women she aimed to uplift filled her mind: Clara's fierce determination, Maya's creativity, Lydia's unwavering support, and the countless other women who had shared their stories and aspirations. Each of their journeys mattered, and together, they were stronger than any whisper of doubt.

Isabella rose from her chair, a renewed sense of purpose coursing through her veins. She moved to a nearby window and gazed out into the night, the stars shining brightly against the dark canvas of the sky. It was a clear reminder that beauty and light existed even in the darkest hours. "I can't let fear dictate my actions," she murmured to herself. "This is bigger than me, and it's time to show them what we can accomplish when we believe in one another."

The following morning, Isabella gathered her thoughts, and a deep breath filled her lungs as she made her way to the community center. She had called an impromptu meeting with all the women involved in the cooperative, urging them to join her. The chatter of voices filled the room as women arrived, surprised yet intrigued by the sudden call to gather.

"Thank you all for coming on such short notice," Isabella began, her voice steady now, infused with a newfound energy. "I know we've been building up to the demonstration day, and I want to take a moment to remind us all why we're here together."

She could see the curiosity in their eyes, the quiet nods of encouragement from Lydia and other friends in the crowd. Isabella spoke from her heart, sharing her recent struggles with doubt and fear. "I have been grappling with my own insecurities, hearing the whispers of disbelief from those who doubt us. But I realized something essential: THIS is our moment. We must remind ourselves of the strength we have when we unite."

The room stirred with energy, and she felt the increasing spirit of solidarity wrapped around them. Isabella looked into their eyes, drawing strength from the reflections of hopes and dreams she saw within them. "Each one of you carries the weight of your story, and together, those stories transform into a powerful narrative."

"Let's make sure everyone understands that this cooperative isn't just about running a business—it's about lifting each other up," Clara added, standing up to support Isabella. "We're showing women they have a voice and a place in our community."

Lydia chimed in, "This is our opportunity to reshape how others see us. Let us remind them of our capabilities—not just as individuals, but as a collective force!"

With each woman sharing her own motivation for being there, the room pulsed with renewed purpose. Bella felt as though they were weaving a quilt of strength and determination, and the energy spilled over, igniting their passion. Ideas flowed freely—ways to empower each other and ensure the event showcased their collective spirit.

They discussed plans for informational booths, storytelling sessions, and demonstrations of their crafts—everything that could encapsulate the essence of their initiative. Every voice mattered, and every contribution amplified their cause.

As the discussions flowed and organizational roles were assigned, Isabella felt gratitude for the connections she had forged over the past few weeks. It had taken all their voices, combined with her grandmother's wisdom, for her to find her footing again. She embraced that beauty lay not just in individual achievements but in shared journeys toward transformation.

As the meeting ended, they all stood together, hands raised, forming a circle of support that radiated unshakeable determination. "Together," Isabella declared, "we will rise above the doubt and fear, and on demonstration day, we will show the community who we are and of what we are capable. We are not just women—we are a force of nature!"

The laughter and cheers that erupted after her declaration filled the room, banishing any lingering doubts. Together, they sealed their commitment to one another and the cooperative, ready now to embrace the turning point in their journey.

Leaving the center, Isabella felt a profound sense of relief. She had reconnected with her purpose and found strength in the community of women beside her.

In the coming days, they will create something beautiful, transformative, and lasting.

As she lay in bed that night, her heart swelled with hope and a familiar rhythm emerged—one that promised courage in the face of adversity and the unwavering belief that together, they could indeed change the narrative of their lives.

THREE
THE SUGAR CANE DREAM

The early morning light bathed the sandy path in gold as Isabella made her way to the expansive fields of her family's abandoned sugarcane plantation. She could feel the warmth of the sun on her skin, the soft breeze brushing against her face—a gentle reminder that change was possible. This land, once a thriving epicenter of her family's livelihood, now lay fallow, the remnants of its past barely visible beneath an unruly carpet of wild grass and scattered debris. To the untrained eye, it might have appeared desolate, but to Isabella, it represented dreams, both realized and unfulfilled.

With each step, her heart raced, invigorated by the prospect of transforming this neglected land into something beautiful and powerful—an emblem of resilience and opportunity for the women in her community. Memories flooded back as she walked, images of her grandmother dancing among the tall Sugarcane stalks, the laughter of children echoing through the fields, and evenings spent gathering with family to celebrate the harvest. Those were moments of joy and pride, which now seemed distant echoes in the rustling grass.

It was time to reclaim that legacy.

Isabella paused at the edge of the property, looking out over the browning remnants of the plantation. The skeletal remains of old sugar mill machinery jutted out like silent sentinels of a bygone era, their rusty exteriors telling stories of sweat and toil, of dreams birthed and dreams dashed. "If only they could see this now," she whispered, feeling the spirits of her ancestor's hover nearby, urging her to act. "We can do more than just remember; we can create a future."

Armed with a renewed sense of purpose, Isabella sought a clearer vision for the land. She wanted to turn it into an empowerment hub— a place where women could gather, learn, and thrive through skill development and entrepreneurship. Imagining vibrant markets, workshops brimming with creativity, and community gatherings filled her with excitement. "This could be our stronghold," she mused, her imagination unraveling scenarios where women could share their crafts, sell their goods, and share their stories.

Driven by inspiration, Isabella recalled how her grandmother had spoken of the importance of land and community. "Our land is our legacy, Isabella," she used to say. "We cultivate not just crops but hope and dreams. To let it go to waste is to let our heritage slip away." That sentiment had lodged itself in Isabella's heart, a mantra that now resonated deeply as she stood before the remnants.

She decided to bring her vision to life by reaching out to the women in the cooperative. They had shared stories of their struggles, their dreams, and their aspirations during their meetings, and Isabella felt it was vital to involve them in the planning stages of what would soon become their shared venture. The sugarcane fields could become a canvas upon which they painted a lively tapestry of empowerment and opportunity.

Later that week, Isabella organized a site visit, inviting the women of the cooperative to step onto the land and envision its potential together. As they arrived, a sense of excitement filled the air. Some women walked gingerly through the overgrown grass, others marveled at the rusty machinery, while a few paused to listen to Isabella's vision.

"This land has been resting for too long," Isabella began, her voice rising above the whispers of the breeze. "What if we transform this abandoned plantation into a place of renewal? A hub where we can nurture our skills, support one another, and build something beautiful?

The women exchanged glances, pondering the prospect. Lydia stepped forward, her eyes brightening with enthusiasm. "We could establish a marketplace for our crafts and produce right here! Imagine women from all over bringing their goods to sell and share their stories!"

Clara added, "And we could create workshops where we can teach each other our skills! From gardening to crafting, cooking to sewing—there is so much we can learn together!"

Isabella could feel the energy building, her heart swelling with enthusiasm as the women began to dream aloud, voices mingling in an optimistic harmony of ideas. They envisioned community gardens, classrooms for skill-sharing, and spaces for local gatherings, where laughter and learning would intertwine.

As ideas flew around, Isabella saw the potential in the land beyond just a passive venture; it was a call to action, a revitalization of their shared history. She pointed toward the old sugar mill and its weathered walls. "What if we turn this building into a community center, a place where our stories and artistry can flourish?"

Nods of approval blossomed among the group, and soon, the air buzzed with possibilities. A sense of unity enveloped them, a bond forged in shared aspirations and a collective dream. Together, they could reclaim this land, not just for themselves, but for generations to come.

Days turned into weeks, filled with planning sessions and brainstorming meetings under the expansive sky. Isabella knew they needed a plan to revitalize the property, a vision that extended beyond mere appearances. They would need funds, resources, and community support. She reached out to local organizations, seeking partnerships to help in their efforts.

Gradually, the women of the cooperative began to cultivate the land, clearing away weeds and debris, while colorful banners were strung up to announce their presence. The transformation was not merely physical; it was a reclamation of identity, a re-establishment of roots that had long been lost to neglect.

The sugarcane fields began to feel alive again, resonating with the laughter of women and children who now played among the blooming flowers. Each day brought new opportunities for connection, collaboration, and growth as they sowed the seeds of hope into the very ground they sought to revive.

Isabella often lingered on the property after everyone else left, finding solace in the sound of the wind stirring the grass and the possibilities unfurling before her. In those quiet moments, she could almost hear her grandmother's laughter echoing through the fields, a melody interlaced with the dreams of generations past.

This was not just land—it was a garden of hope, brimming with promise and potential. The sugarcane dream would flourish, nurtured by their collective effort and fueled by their indomitable spirit. With every weed pulled and every seed planted, Isabella felt an unbreakable bond forming between the women of the cooperative and their heritage, a testament to the enduring legacy of empowerment and resilience.

Together, they would turn this neglected plantation into a sacred space, a beacon of opportunity where the dreams of their ancestors could intertwine with the aspirations of their future. And, just perhaps, the sounds of joy and laughter would return to the land, breathing life back into its soil, and transforming it into a thriving hub of possibility.

As the sun dipped low in the sky, casting a golden hue over the once-desolate sugarcane plantation, Isabella stood in the heart of the land, allowing her imagination to soar. In her mind's eye, she could envision the transformation of this sacred space. The rows of vibrant crops would stretch across the fields like a patchwork quilt, each plant thriving under the diligent care of skilled hands. She could see women—her friends, her allies—working side by side, laughter filling the air as they tended to the land, a tapestry of colors and life unfurling before them.

The hum of activity reverberated in her vision: workshops bustling with creativity, where the air was thick with the scent of herbs and spices, where hands crafted goods that reflected their heritage and ingenuity. They would share knowledge and skills, learning from one another to cultivate not only the crops but also the dreams that lay beneath the surface.

Isabella pictured a community gathering space—an inviting, open structure adorned with the vibrant colors of their culture, where chairs made from reclaimed wood invited conversations filled with passion and promise. This would be a hub for sharing ideas, a place where plans were forged, and new ventures took their first breath. Here, they would celebrate their unity, gathering for potlucks, storytelling sessions, and lively discussions about their future.

But alongside sugarcane, Isabella envisioned incorporating a diverse range of crops that would enrich their cooperative and reflect the needs of the local market. Rows of cocoa trees would line one side of the plantation, their broad leaves providing dappled shade while offering the tantalizing promise of dark, rich chocolate. Bananas would flourish on the other side, their bright yellow fruit brightening the landscape, providing sustenance and income. An herb garden bursting with medicinal and culinary herbs would serve as both a source of nourishment and a testament to their ancestral knowledge of healing.

"Imagine the markets we could attend!" Clara's voice echoed in her mind, brimming with excitement. "Everything from sweet treats to herbal remedies, and we could even host workshops to teach others what we know."

The more Isabella contemplated the land, the more she felt the stirring of purpose within her. She envisioned the women coming together not only to plant and harvest but to celebrate their victories, big and small. They would host harvest festivals, events that honored their hard work and gratitude for the land. Children would play among the rows of crops, learning from the rhythms of nature, while their mothers' shared stories of resilience and hope.

That afternoon, as dusk settled over the plantation, Isabella gathered the women around a fire pit constructed out of stones salvaged from the old sugar mill. The flickering flames cast playful shadows as they sat in a circle, animated discussions bubbling like the fire itself.

"Close your eyes for a moment," Isabella instructed with a soft smile. "Listen to the land and imagine the possibilities."

They complied, and the air grew quiet except for the crackling of the fire and the distant chirping of crickets. Isabella sensed a palpable energy among them, a collective heartbeat. "Picture what this place can become," she urged. "Visualize the crops, the laughter, the workshops. See the community center thriving, filled with people sharing their skills."

As they opened their eyes, excitement crackled in the air. "We can do this!" Lydia exclaimed; her face flushed with enthusiasm. "Think of all the women in our community who could benefit from this!"

"Yes!" Clara added, her voice steady with conviction. "We must draw in all the artisans, the farmers, and the healers. Let us diversify our activities. The more we offer, the more we will attract neighbors and friends who might join us."

Guided by their collective vision, the women began brainstorming ways to get the cooperative off the ground. They discussed applying for grants, seeking partnerships with local businesses, and organizing fundraising events to bolster their resources.

"We'll need to scale our production," Isabella suggested, excitement swirling within her. "We can set up a members-only market where we sell our goods directly to the community, ensuring they know who we are and what we stand for."

"I'd love to lead the kitchen workshops," Clara offered. "We can teach healthy cooking with fresh produce, encouraging everyone to connect to the land through their plates."

As the fire crackled and stars twinkled above, inspiration flowed freely, and dreams began to solidify into plans. They mapped out the layout of the plantation, indicated areas for crops, space for the hub, and spots for community gardens. It became evident that this venture was not just about growing food; it was about nurturing a community and reviving a legacy.

In the weeks that followed, their plans began to take tangible form. The women organized workdays to clear the land, uprooting weeds and restoring the soil. They gathered under the warm sun, laboring together, the air filled with conversation and camaraderie. Children played nearby, incorporating nature into their games as they watched the women transform their visions into reality.

The first designated area they tackled was the herb garden, which began to take shape. Isabella formed a close bond with Maya, who had extensive knowledge of traditional herbal remedies. Together, they mapped out the plots, debating which plants to include—lavender, rosemary, mint, and various medicinal herbs that had been passed down through generations.

During one such workday, Maya paused to reflect. "Isabella, this is more than just land we are working on. We are revitalizing memories, blending our histories into something new. It is healing."

Isabella nodded, feeling the weight of Maya's words. The cooperative could serve as a bridge between tradition and innovation, and she was determined to honor that connection.

As weeks turned into months, signs of life began to emerge amidst the overgrowth, and just like the crops they planted, women's relationships flourished. They cultivated not just plants but also a sense of unity and resilience, creating bonds that solidified their purpose and made their vision more powerful.

Isabella held regular meetings, involving everyone in the decision-making processes, ensuring each voice was heard. They embraced a democratic approach; ideas and aspirations shaped their journey. And as they worked, the stories of their ancestors whispered through the leaves, pushing them forward—a gentle reminder that they were rooted in something deeper, a legacy of strength and tenacity.

The cooperative began to attract attention within the community as word spread of their efforts. Neighbors came to see the changes and were drawn in by the spirit of empowerment that radiated from the plantation. People expressed interest in participating, contributing skills, and sharing resources.

One morning, as Isabella stood overlooking the herb garden, she caught sight of several familiar faces approaching. It was people from the neighboring farms, curious about the vibrant energy emanating from the once-abandoned land. Isabella felt a rush of excitement and apprehension all at once. Would they embrace this initiative, or would skepticism overshadow their vision?

The group approached cautiously, and Isabella took a deep breath. "Welcome! We are just starting to cultivate the land and ideas here. We would love for you to join us."

"Looks like you're doing something amazing!" one of the visitors replied, eyeing the colorful herb garden bustling with activity. "We heard about your plans and wanted to see for ourselves."

There, under the warm sun and surrounded by growing plants and enthusiastic women, Isabella felt the first stirrings of a broader community beginning to form. Her heart swelled as she envisioned these visitors' joining hands with the women of the cooperative, their collective efforts sowing seeds of opportunity that would stretch beyond the land.

As the day went on and laughter mingled with the sounds of nature, Isabella knew deep down that they were on the cusp of something remarkable. With each passing moment, as they worked the earth and turned dreams into reality, they were stitching together threads of hope, solidarity, and renewal. The sugarcane dream was no longer just an idea; it was a movement—a symphony of voices rising to reclaim their heritage and craft a future defined by unity, empowerment, and resilience.

As months passed, the plantation began to blossom under the dedicated care of Isabella and the cooperative's members. With every new sprout that pushed through the earth, Isabella became increasingly passionate about integrating sustainable farming practices that would respect the land and benefit the community. She envisioned a model of agriculture that honored the heritage of Caribbean women, who had cultivated the earth with wisdom and innovation for generations.

One evening, under the glow of a setting sun, she gathered the women around the fire pit once again. "We've made great strides," Isabella began, her voice filled with enthusiasm, "but we must think about how we are nurturing this land for the future. Sustainable farming is not just about what we grow—it is about how we grow it."

The women listened intently, intrigued by Isabella's vision of rejuvenating the soil and introducing methods they could all learn to apply. "For centuries, women in our communities have used techniques like crop rotation and organic pest control," Isabella continued. "These methods not only enhance soil health but also create a resilient ecosystem. Our ancestors lived in harmony with the land, and we can, too."

"Crop rotation sounds promising," Lydia said, her brow furrowed in concentration. "It helps prevent soil depletion and pests, right?"

"Exactly!" Isabella smiled, grateful for the woman's engagement. "By rotating different crops in each field, we can improve soil nutrients and reduce the need for chemical fertilizers. For instance, after sugarcane, we could plant

legumes, which naturally enrich the soil with nitrogen.

Maya, known for her expertise in herbal medicine, leaned forward. "And we could use organic pest control methods, like introducing beneficial insects that help with pest management. I have used ladybugs and certain types of wasps in my garden to keep things balanced."

"Yes! That is perfect," Isabella exclaimed. "We can cultivate a diverse environment that supports not just our crops but also encourages biodiversity. Imagine a landscape filled with different plants and creatures, birds, insects, and even small animals—that thrive because of our choices."

As ideas bounced around the group, excitement turned into a clear plan. Each woman began to contribute her knowledge about traditional farming practices, sharing stories from their families. It became evident that their collective wisdom was a powerful tool, one that could imbue their cooperative with the strength of their history.

"Let's create a schedule for our crop rotations," Clara suggested. "We can map it out based on the growing seasons. We should also document everything we do, sharing our successes and challenges. It will create a resource for others who want to replicate our success."

Amid the growing dialogue, Isabella felt a surge of hope. They were not just reviving the land; they were establishing a framework for future generations to thrive. She dreamed of launching workshops where they would teach others in the community about sustainable practices, empowering more women to join in this movement.

The women decided to dedicate one of the upcoming weekend workdays to planting their first rotation of crops. They would begin with sugarcane, legumes, and a selection of colorful vegetables like tomatoes, peppers, and greens, ensuring they cultivated both nourishment and economic opportunities.

Following their plans, the day of planting finally arrived, and the atmosphere was brimming with energy. Music wafted through the air as the women arrived, their laughter mingling with the sounds of rustling leaves and buzzing bees. Each woman took pride in the work ahead, eager to sow their dreams into the soil.

As they tilled the rich earth, Isabella moved from group to group, sharing insights and encouragement. "Remember, it is not just about efficiency but about creating a system that lasts. Every decision we make here reflects our commitment to our community."

Once the sugarcane was planted, they focused on the legumes. As they worked, Isabella and Maya discussed incorporating more native plants known for their resilience, like cassava and sweet potatoes, embracing techniques that these plants had perfected over centuries.

"Many of these crops thrive in local conditions and require minimal intervention," Maya explained. "They can nourish our families while also being commercially viable."

Isabella nodded, her heart swelling with pride for their collective endeavor, knowing this was just the beginning. They later gathered to set up the garden area, planting herbs that would not only attract beneficial insects but also provide healing remedies for their community.

As the sun began to set, they stood together in a circle, dirt on their hands and smiles on their faces. "Let's plant a tree together," Isabella proposed, selecting a shady moringa tree, known for its nutritional benefits. "This will symbolize our commitment to sustainability and cooperation."

They dug into the earth, feeling the soil give way and the roots nestle into their new home. As they placed the tree carefully in the ground, Isabella felt an overwhelming sense of connection and purpose. This moment embodied the life they were creating—rooted in the past, flourishing in the present, and reaching toward an abundant future.

To further their impact, the cooperative began organizing public workshops focused on sustainable farming. Word spread quickly, drawing neighbors from near and far to the plantation. Families showed up eager to learn about the techniques Isabella and her friends were adopting.

During one workshop, held beneath the shade of the newly planted moringa tree, Isabella spoke passionately to an attentive audience. "These practices are not just about our farm; they are about the collective good of our entire community. If we work together to share knowledge, we can uplift each other and create a sustainable future for everyone.

Participants asked questions, eager to delve deeper into the importance of sustainability as a shared responsibility. Isabella's heart swelled with pride as she saw the interest in their methods grow, envisioning a ripple effect of change spreading throughout the island.

With each workshop, a sense of unity blossomed beyond the cooperative's borders. Local farmers approached Isabella, inspired by her vision, eager to integrate similar practices into their own farms. The cooperative was no longer an isolated initiative; it was a burgeoning network of guides and innovators, each woman contributing to a movement that respected and nurtured both land and community.

By embracing sustainable methods, Isabella and the women were not merely farming; they were rewriting the narrative of agriculture on the island. They were proving that it was possible to cultivate abundance without exploiting the earth, creating a blueprint that could inspire future generations of farmers, especially women, who sought to reclaim their heritage and uplift their communities.

As she returned home one night after a long day of workshops, Isabella reflected on the transformation that was taking place, not only on the farm but within herself. She was learning, adapting, and growing alongside the women she admired. This journey was not just about the land; it was about healing, empowerment, and the interconnectedness of community.

In the quiet of her room, she felt a surge of determination coursing through her veins. "This is just the beginning," she whispered to herself, making plans in her mind. "We will show everyone the power of sustainability and community-driven action. Together, we are creating more than just a hub for crops; we are sparking a revolution."

With each step, they would redefine what it meant to farm on the island—honoring their ancestors while defiantly forging a new path forward. And as Isabella drifted off to sleep, she felt confident that their sugarcane dream was blossoming into a beacon of hope and resilience for all.

As the sun rose over the plantation, illuminating the vibrant greens and browns of the fields, Isabella's mind buzzed with ideas. It was clear to her that education and skill development were central to the cooperative's mission. She understood that empowering women through knowledge would lay a foundation for long-term success not only for themselves but for future generations.

After gathering the women one sunny afternoon, Isabella shared her vision. "We have come together to revitalize this land, but we need to build something greater than just a thriving farm. I believe we can create an educational hub right here—an inclusive space where women can learn, grow, and empower one another."

"What do you have in mind?" Clara asked, her interest piqued.

Isabella felt her excitement rise. "We can organize workshops on a variety of topics! We will start with sustainable farming techniques, but we can also offer classes on financial literacy and entrepreneurship. I want this to be a place where every woman, regardless of her background, can gain practical skills and knowledge."

"A great idea!" Lydia chimed in. "How can we ensure that everyone has access to these workshops?"

Isabella nodded, appreciating Lydia's foresight. "We will keep them free or low-cost. We can also invite local experts to lead sessions, and we can share resources with one another. It is vital that everyone feels welcome and encouraged to participate. If we learn together, we can forge bonds that extend beyond the fields."

With overwhelming support from the group, they began designing the first series of workshops. Isabella reached out to local agronomists, financial advisors, and entrepreneurs willing to share their knowledge and experiences. The cooperative was becoming a hub of innovation, not just in agricultural practices but in social empowerment.

Weeks later, the first workshop on sustainable farming techniques was scheduled, and excitement buzzed in the air. Isabella stood before a small ensemble of community members—women of various ages, from eager young adults to wise grandmothers. The atmosphere was charged with energy and determination.

"Welcome, everyone!" Isabella greeted me warmly. "Today marks the beginning of a journey towards sustainable farming and self-sufficiency. We will learn together how to cultivate our crops responsibly, ensuring our land remains fertile for future generations.

After spending the morning learning about crop rotation and organic pest control, the attendees gathered in small groups to brainstorm ways to apply their lessons to their own gardens and farms. The discussions were spirited and full of enthusiasm, with women sharing stories from their own experiences.

As the session concluded, Isabella felt a surge of gratitude. Participants expressed their appreciation for the knowledge and shared their eyes alight with the possibilities ahead. "Let's keep this momentum going,"

Isabella said, energized by their response. "We have more workshops lined up, and I encourage you all to spread the word. The more women we reach, the stronger we become."

The following workshop focused on financial literacy; a topic Isabella was particularly passionate about. She knew that understanding budgeting, savings, and investment was crucial for women who wanted to take charge of their livelihoods.

Local financial consultant Grace joined them, bringing a wealth of knowledge and practical advice. As Grace began explaining basic financial concepts, the room filled with questions and lively discussion. "It's not just about farming," Isabella reminded everyone. "It's about understanding how to manage your earnings so that every effort we put into our fields translates into security and independence."

The women shared their aspirations, discussing ideas ranging from launching small businesses to creating community-based products they could sell at the local market. The brainstorming session echoed with laughter and excitement as women mapped out their entrepreneurial dreams on a large piece of paper, creating a visual tapestry of hopes and aspirations.

Leah, a newcomer to the cooperative, stood up hesitantly, her voice barely above a whisper. "What if we start a small line of herbal products? I have made salves and tinctures for years. There is a market for it."

Her idea ignited a wave of inspiration. "We could combine various herbs and create educational workshops around them," Maya suggested. "Imagine selling herbal teas, balms, and remedies together at the market!"

"Yes! We can even host events to teach families about the benefits of these herbs," Isabella added, feeling the enthusiastic spirit grow among them. "It'll not only support our income but also bring the community together."

As the weeks turned into months, the educational initiatives expanded, drawing more women into their fold. Isabella envisioned the cooperative as a community of knowledge, where women felt empowered to share their experiences and learn from one another. They explored topics such as health and nutrition, cooking classes using their fresh produce, and even crafting sessions that encouraged creativity through sustainable practices.

One day, as the women crafted colorful baskets from local materials, Clara shared her experience working with artisans from neighboring islands. "They taught me how to create beautiful pieces while respecting our environment. We must carry these traditions forward," she said, her voice resolute.

"I love that! We could even start a market day showcasing our handmade goods," Lydia suggested, her enthusiasm infectious. "It would not only provide income but also strengthen connections within the community."

Isabella beamed at the unfolding ideas, realizing that they were not just cultivating crops but also sowing the seeds of a vibrant, interwoven community. With every workshop and every shared experience, they were building a legacy—a network of empowered women who could support one another and thrive in a changing world.

One evening, as twilight painted the sky in hues of pink and orange, Isabella sat beneath the shade of the mango tree outside their gathering place. The air was fragrant with the scents of herbs they had planted, and the sounds of laughter and voices surrounded her, creating a harmonious backdrop.

She watched as women shared stories, exchanged tips, and relished in the collective joy of learning and practicing together. It was a scene she had envisioned, and it felt like a beautiful reality unfolding before her.

In this moment, Isabella reflected on how far they had come. "This is just the beginning," she whispered to herself. "We are shaping a new narrative for our community. Our roots are deepening, entwining with knowledge, resilience, and the spirit of cooperation."

Little did she know the impact of their educational initiatives would extend far beyond the plantation. They would become a model for other communities seeking empowerment through shared knowledge and sustainable practices, transforming their cooperative into a beacon of hope across the island.

With a full heart and a determined spirit, Isabella knew they were on the right path. Together, they would continue to nurture not just crops, but a flourishing community rooted in education, support, and unwavering strength. The Sugarcane dream had blossomed into something far great vision that celebrated their past and inspired an enduring future.

As the weeks rolled on, Isabella found herself caught in a whirlwind of optimism and trepidation. The workshops were thriving, and the cooperative was steadily becoming a nurturing environment for learning and empowerment. Yet amidst the growth, a shadow loomed gnawing realization of the monumental challenges that lay ahead.

Reclaiming the land and transforming their collective vision into sustainable reality would demand enormous effort, resources, and resilience. The agricultural environment was fraught with uncertainties; weather patterns could be unpredictable, pests could threaten their crops, and the viability of their initiatives depended heavily on the fertility of the soil.

But most pressing of all, Isabella felt a growing anxiety about securing the funding necessary to support their initiatives. They needed tools, seeds, educational materials, and resources for their workshops, not to mention the ongoing maintenance of the once-neglected land. The financial burdens were daunting, and she knew they could not sustain everything with just the revenue from their initial crops and products.

One evening, as Isabella walked through the fields, she spotted a few of the older women sitting together, their concerns evident in their furrowed brows. She had noticed their skepticism during the meetings. While they admired the enthusiasm of the younger women, their hesitance to embrace the changes Isabella proposed cast a long shadow over her ambitions.

"Isabella," Clara said softly as she approached, recognizing the worry etched on her face. "We have heard whispers from some of the elders. Many of them are concerned about this new approach. They fear we are straying too far from our traditions."

Isabella sighed, a wave of frustration washing over her. "I understand their worries, Clara, but we cannot let fear hold us back. We can honor our traditions while also evolving to meet the challenges of the present and future. Our land has suffered for too long, and we need to adapt if we are to restore it."

Eager to prove that change could be harmonious with tradition, Isabella invited the elders to a special meeting, hoping to bridge the gap between fear and possibility. As the day approached, she felt a mix of hope and anxiety. She believes they could unite under a common purpose, yet she was very aware of the deeper-rooted beliefs that clung to many in the community.

When the day arrived, Isabella set up the gathering under the shade of the moringa tree. She arranged for some of the younger women to present their experiences and the knowledge they had gained from the workshops. The atmosphere was charged with anticipation, and the air was filled with the zest of fresh herbs and blooming plants, a stark reminder of the potential surrounding them.

As the elders arrived, Isabella greeted each of them warmly, hoping to ease their apprehensions. The older women took their seats, exchanging glances that spoke volumes about their skepticism.

"Thank you for coming today," Isabella began, heart pounding as she spoke. "We have gathered to discuss how we can respectfully blend our traditions with new practices that can rejuvenate our land and community. We believe that through education and adaptation, we can ensure a prosperous future for all of us."

She shared stories of the ways the cooperative had benefited from their workshops, highlighting the enthusiasm they had sparked among the women and the knowledge they had gained. As she spoke, a mix of attention and resistance came from the elders, their expressions revealing a tapestry of doubt and curiosity.

One elderly person, Aunt Rosa, finally spoke up, her voice steady but filled with concern. "Isabella, we respect your passion, but we are cautious. We have farmed this land for generations. You talk about change as if it was the solution, but our ancestors knew this land. They understood its rhythms. What if these new methods do not work?"

Isabella felt her heart race, recognizing the weight of Aunt Rosa's words. "I honor the wisdom of our ancestors, and I know that their practices are invaluable. But the climate is changing; the world is changing. If we cling too tightly to past methods, we risk losing everything they built for us. I believe we can learn from each other—combine your wisdom with our eagerness to innovate."

The conversation continued, the tension in the air palpable as the younger women shared their own stories of discovery and success. Maya stood up; her voice was strong. "I have seen how traditional practices can coexist with new ones. Using what our ancestors taught us about plants, while also incorporating science and new techniques, can create a powerful synergy. We are not abandoning our roots; we are strengthening them."

Gradually, the hardened expressions of the elders softened, but doubts still lingered. Aunt Rosa regarded the younger women, her gaze challenging. "We need to see results. Talk is not enough. If you want us to trust this path, you must show us it leads to something real."

Driven by Rosa's words, Isabella realized that she bore the weight of responsibility not just for her dreams but for the hopes of the community. They needed tangible proof that their efforts could yield progress. "You're right, Aunt Rosa," she replied, determination igniting her spirit. "We must prove that our collective dreams can be more than just dreams; they can manifest into reality."

As the meeting continued, strategies began to form in Isabella's mind. They would create a measurable plan to implement their ideas, focusing on pilot projects that could showcase the effectiveness of their sustainable practices.

Over the next few months, Isabella rallied the cooperative to focus on smaller, attainable goals. They decided to dedicate a section of the farm to showcasing a blend of traditional and contemporary farming techniques, making it a demonstration site where everyone in the community could see firsthand the benefits of their work.

"I'll organize the workshops to include hands-on demonstrations," Isabella said, her mind racing with possibilities. "We will document everything—the successes, the challenges, and the learning processes.

It will be a living resource, both for us and for the community."

The women rallied behind her, energized by the prospect of tangible outcomes. They brainstormed ideas for crops that could illustrate the effectiveness of crop rotation, pest management, and the cultivation of native plants. Each of these initiatives would not only demonstrate sustainable techniques but would also have the potential for economic benefit as they would eventually sell the produce.

As they laid out their plans, the challenges ahead still weighed heavily on Isabella's mind. She recognized that funding would be crucial for their pilot project to succeed. With limited resources, they needed to be creative and proactive. She realized they would need to seek grants, connect with local businesses for sponsorship, and even launch a crowdfunding campaign to engage a broader audience willing to support their vision.

The thought of these tasks was daunting, but Isabella was determined to confront them head-on. The stakes were high, and she felt the urgency to transform ideas into actions, navigating her way through the obstacles, fueled by the belief that their collective efforts could create lasting change.

Late one night, after a long day of planning, as she stared up at the stars from her porch, she reflected on the journey thus far. Doubts flickered in her mind, but they were met with a fierce resolve. Change was never easy, but it was the path they had chosen. She understood that sometimes the path to progress required patience and perseverance.

"I won't let fear dictate our future," Isabella whispered into the night, a sense of calm washing over her. "We have what it takes to honor our past while forging a new path—and I will fight for our dream."

With her heart set and a plan in place, Isabella felt ready to embrace the challenges ahead, trusting that, with each step they took, they were sowing seeds for a brighter future. The journey would not be without its trials, but she had faith in their resilience, hopeful that together, they could transform the land—and their community—into a thriving embodiment of their shared dreams.

Determined to turn her vision into tangible initiatives, Isabella understood the importance of unity and collaboration. To make their plans a reality, she needed allies within the community—supporters who shared her enthusiasm and commitment to sustainable practices and women's empowerment. Inspired by the energy from the last meeting with the elders, she began reaching out to the women who showed interest in her ideas.

With Lydia by her side, Isabella organized a series of community brainstorming workshops at the plantation, inviting anyone eager to contribute their ideas and skills. Lydia was an invaluable partner, known for her ability to rally people together with her infectious passion. As they spread the word, excitement sparked throughout the community, drawing an enthusiastic crowd to their first gathering.

As the attendees settled under the expansive branches of the moringa tree, Isabella felt a surge of hope. She surveyed the faces around her—women of various ages, each with stories and aspirations. "Welcome, everyone! Thank you for being here today," she began, her voice imbued with warmth. "As you know, we are embarking on a journey to revitalize our land and empower ourselves through education and sustainability. Today is about collaboration—together, we will brainstorm ideas and develop plans to make this dream a reality."

The atmosphere was charged with energy as the women began sharing their thoughts. Soon, ideas buzzed in the air like a lively rhythm. They discussed everything from crop selection to marketing strategies, and the conversation flowed freely, punctuated by laughter and occasional bursts of inspiration.

Lydia facilitated the first session, encouraging everyone to contribute. "Let's think about what we want to achieve with our cooperative," she said, jotting down suggestions on a large piece of butcher paper. "What are our priorities, and how can we make them happen?"

I think we should start with our identity," Clara suggested. "What sets us apart? We could focus on organic products and traditional knowledge, highlighting the connection between our heritage and what we offer to the community."

"Yes! We can create a brand that tells our story," Isabella chimed in, feeling the energy swell. "Our unique practices can attract attention, and we could even host events showcasing our produce and cultural heritage."

As they continued to brainstorm, the topic of financial sustainability arose. "We need a solid business plan to attract support," Lydia noted. "That includes analyzing costs, deciding on pricing, and planning for growth. We should also explore avenues for funding like grants, sponsorships, and partnerships."

Isabella nodded, her mind racing with possibilities. "We can outline all of this and present it as a comprehensive proposal to potential donors and local leaders. Our aim is to demonstrate how investing in our cooperative is not merely a financial contribution but a commitment to uplifting our community."

The group erupted in lively discussion; each woman eager to contribute ideas for practical logistics. They outlined specific roles, decided on strategies for marketing their products, and debated about the crops that would thrive in their environment.

Over the following weeks, the workshops continued, evolving into a focused series of meetings where they collectively crafted their proposal. They split into smaller groups, each tackling different aspects of the business plan: financial projections, product selection, marketing strategy, and operational logistics.

Isabella organized sessions where they could practice presenting their ideas, honing their public speaking skills, and ensuring everyone felt confident in their contributions. "We all have valuable insights,"

Isabella encouraged, "and together, we can weave our individual strengths into a cohesive vision."

One notable rainy afternoon, as the sound of gentle raindrops pattered on the roof, the women gathered indoors, sketching out graphs and charts detailing their projected sales and costs. Lydia stood before the group, passionately explaining their financial model. "If we focus on nurturing both traditional crops and innovative organic produce, we can capture various market segments," Lydia explained, her enthusiasm infectious. "Plus, we can highlight our workshops as an additional revenue stream, showing our commitment to education

alongside our products."

Under Isabella's leadership, they balanced their proposals, so their aims were clear: to cultivate not only healthy crops but also a skilled community of women dedicated to economic empowerment and sustainability.

With their proposal nearing completion, Isabella, Lydia, and several key women from the cooperative prepared for a critical moment— presenting their initiative to potential donors and local leaders. The selected venue was spacious, adorned with vibrant fabrics and decorations that showcased local crafts, creating a warm and welcoming atmosphere.

As the day approached, Isabella felt an exhilarating mix of nerves and determination. They meticulously rehearsed their presentation, ensuring each person had a chance to articulate their ideas, infusing the proposal with passion and authenticity.

On the day of the presentation, the room was filled with community leaders, local business owners, and influential figures who had shown interest in supporting sustainable initiatives. Isabella stood at the forefront, flanked by her allies, and took a deep breath before beginning.

"Thank you all for joining us today," she began, her voice steady and confident. "We are here to share our vision for a community-driven cooperative that blends sustainable farming practices with education and engagement. Our mission is to empower women, reclaim our land, and cultivate a future where our community thrives."

Isabella launched into their proposal, clearly outlining their goals, strategies, and anticipated impact. The women who had worked alongside her echoed their commitment, each adding their unique perspectives and experiences. They highlighted stories of growth from their workshops, challenges they overcame, and the motivation that radiated throughout their gatherings.

In the audience, Isabella noticed a few skeptical expressions, but as they unfolded their vision, the atmosphere shifted curiosity flickered in the eyes of onlookers. She ended the presentation with a call to action, inviting the audience to envision their role in supporting this transformative initiative.

"We believe together we can restore our land, empower our women, and create a sustainable model that can serve as an example for other communities. We ask for your support, guidance, and partnership in this journey toward fostering resilience and prosperity."

As the applause echoed through the room, Isabella felt a wave of relief wash over her. There was no denying that the journey to bring their dreams to life had its trials, but presenting their initiative stirred a sense of hope and possibility.

In the days that followed, responses began to trickle in. Some local leaders expressed their enthusiasm to their partner, while others offered technical support to refine their business model. Slowly, they secured small grants and promises of assistance—from resources for educational materials to help in building out their plans.

Yet Isabella knew this was just the beginning. Challenges remained, and the road ahead would still require perseverance and unwavering commitment.

As she reflected on the progress made during those weeks, the urgency of their mission grew more profound. They were no longer working in isolation; they were connected to a web of potential allies and advocates. The notion that their efforts could resonate with the broader community fueled her resolve.

Under the vast sky that night, as she stood at the edge of the plantation watching the last light of day fade, Isabella felt a deeper connection to the land and the women who stood beside her. Their dreams were woven together, each thread representing shared hopes and relentless spirits.

"Together, we'll make this happen," she whispered to the wind, determined to face the challenges ahead. They had created not just a proposal but a movement, a collective dream that would transform the heart of their community. The sugarcane dream was on the brink of blossoming into reality, and Isabella was filled with anticipation for the journeys yet to unfold.

In the sacred moments of quiet reflection, Isabella found solace by the river that wound beside the plantation. The water flowed rhythmically, a soothing melody that mirrored her thoughts—a blend of ambition, hope, and a deep sense of responsibility. Here, with the sun casting intricate patterns on the water's surface, Isabella dreamed of what the cooperative could truly represent, not just for her village, but for the entire island and beyond.

As she sat on a smooth stone, legs crossed and eyes gazing into the depths of the shimmering river, her imagination unfolded limitless possibilities. She envisioned the cooperative transcending its local roots, emerging as a beacon of inspiration across the Caribbean. "What if," she mused, "we become a model for women's empowerment in our region?"

Imagining it all vividly, she pictured groups of women from neighboring islands coming together at the cooperative. They would share stories steeped in resilience, passing down ancestral knowledge through workshops and discussions. Each meeting would be a gathering of diverse talents—women sharing their crafts, their agricultural practices, their voices in song.

In her mind's eye, the cooperative blossomed into a thriving hub of education and creativity, offering programs tailored not just to farming techniques but also to leadership, business practices, and arts. A place where women of all ages would feel empowered to express themselves, leading initiatives, influencing decisions, and forging new pathways for their futures.

Isabella envisioned collaborative programs that invited women to learn about environmental sustainability, food security, and health. The cooperative would host conferences, attracting speakers from various fields, all united by the mission of empowerment and shared knowledge. She imagined a network of women supporting one another across different islands—mentoring programs, online platforms for collaboration, and even exchange visits to learn from each other's experiences.

The thought ignited a fire within her. "We may be starting small," she whispered to herself, contemplating the challenges they still faced, "but our impact can echo throughout the Caribbean." She could almost hear the ripple effect of their work—a movement that would inspire women from distant shores to rise, to collaborate, and to take charge of their destinies.

Reflecting further, Isabella recognized that the role of the cooperative could extend beyond agriculture. They could advocate for policies that support women's rights, education, and sustainable practices at local and national levels. By sharing their successes, they could change perceptions about women in leadership and agriculture, sparking dialogues that would challenge societal norms.

Isabella felt invigorated, her heart racing with the enormity of it all. The river flowed gently, as if encouraging her dreams to take shape. "We will be the change-makers," she declared, her voice carried away by the wind. "We will show what's possible when women unite and support each other."

The vision of the cooperative as a model for empowerment became a cornerstone of Isabella's thoughts during those quiet hours at the water's edge. It was more than just a dream; it was a calling. She imagined mothers bringing their daughters to the workshops, instilling in them a sense of pride and ownership over their contributions to both the land and their community. Each generation would add to the legacy of resilience, nurturing a culture of empowerment that would reach far beyond what they could foresee.

Evenings by the river turned into ritualistic reflections where her heart and mind intertwined. She began to draft ideas for programs that could anchor their future endeavors, sketching them mentally as she envisioned women learning about financial literacy, marketing their products, and the science of sustainable farming.

The more Isabella dreamed, the clearer her path became. They would not simply cultivate crops; they would cultivate minds, spirits, and a resilient community. The cooperative could become a sanctuary for growth where women would reclaim their stories and their roles in the broader tapestry of their culture.

With each passing day, as they gathered to work on their plans, Isabella poured her dreams into the cooperative's framework. She invited feedback from the other members, encouraging them to share their visions and ideas, fostering an atmosphere of inclusivity and collaboration. As they crafted their mission statement, Isabella championed the concept that the cooperative was not solely about agriculture; it was about sisterhood, knowledge, and empowerment.

While the logistical aspects of building the cooperative were challenging, Isabella remained resolute. She organized community meetings where they discussed the many ways they could showcase their commitment to empowerment, creating scholarships for young girls, developing mentorship programs, and establishing connections with local businesses to foster partnerships and collaborations.

In one of those meetings, Clara spoke up, her voice steady and filled with conviction. "We're not just planting crops; we're planting dreams—dreams that can bloom into something magnificent if we nurture them together." The sentiment resonated deeply within the group and further strengthened their bond.

As the weeks turned into months, the vision of the cooperative as a model of empowerment transformed from a dream nestled in Isabella's heart into a vibrant tapestry woven from the aspirations of each woman involved. The energy and enthusiasm around their collective efforts were palpable, generating a palpable excitement that spurred them into action.

On one particularly radiant day, as Isabella walked along the riverbank, she felt a deep sense of gratitude wash over her. The water sparkled under the sun, mirroring the hope that coursed through her. The journey ahead would demand perseverance, but they were not alone in the endeavor. Each woman brought her own strength and resilience, weaving a strong community

fabric that could withstand the challenges they would face.

With renewed purpose, Isabella made her way back to the plantation, her heart swelling with determination. She envisioned the day when their cooperative would flourish, becoming a thriving model for women's empowerment throughout the Caribbean. Not just an economic enterprise, but a movement—one that would inspire generations to come, a legacy of empowerment rooted in the rich soil of their land.

As she stepped onto the familiar ground of the plantation, she looked out over the fields, imagining how they would transform into a vibrant hub of activity. Together, they could build something remarkable, a community anchored in strength, resilience, and shared dreams. The sugarcane dream was growing roots deep within them—now it was time to let it flourish.

As the trees shed their leaves and the vibrant hues of twilight filled the sky, the sugarcane plantation stood tall and resolute, embodying the spirit of resistance against the limitations imposed on women in their community. To Isabella, the plantation transformed from a simple agricultural space into a powerful symbol of resilience. It represented not only their agricultural ambitions but also the collective fight against the societal norms that sought to confine them.

The plantation became a sacred ground for women to reclaim their narratives and forge their identities. Each stalk of sugarcane swaying gently in the breeze echoed with the stories of the women who tended it, laced with their hopes, dreams, and struggles. The land, once marred by history, now thrummed with the energy of revitalization and purpose. Together, they were not just cultivating crops; they were cultivating a movement.

Isabella often gathered the women at the heart of the plantation, under the shade of the old baobab tree, where they could share their thoughts and ideas in an open forum. Here, the conversations ran deep. "This plantation isn't just about sugarcane," she declared one afternoon, her voice unwavering. "It is about breaking the barriers that have held us back for too long. Each of us has the power to transform our lives and our community."

The women nodded in agreement, their eyes brightening with understanding. They shared their own experiences, discussing the challenges they faced, whether it was the pressure to conform to traditional roles, limited access to resources, or the struggle for recognition in a male-dominated society. Yet with each story, a new layer of determination unfurled within them, reinforcing their shared commitment to not just endure but thrive.

Marta, a skilled agriculturalist, spoke up. "This land has seen our ancestors' hands and hard work. Now it is our turn to honor that legacy by making choices that reflect our strength. We need to show others that women can lead, innovate, and inspire change." Her words resonated deeply, serving as a rallying cry for the group reminder that their labor on the plantation was not just physical work, but a profound act of resistance.

Fueled by this renewed energy, they devised plans to integrate storytelling into their workshops, allowing women to share their personal journeys while teaching traditional agricultural methods. The women would gather to weave stories of struggle and triumph alongside their farming practices, sparking discussion around their roles as caretakers of the land. This approach not only enhanced their agricultural knowledge but built a powerful bond among them, fostering a sense of community and unity.

Isabella envisioned creating a monthly "Storytelling Sunday," where each woman would bring a dish made from the crops they cultivated, sharing not just their culinary skills but their family histories. They would transform the plantation into a vibrant space of learning and celebration, where each gathering served as a reminder of their resilience.

Through these shared narratives, they would highlight the rich cultural heritage inherent in their work, celebrating their identities as women in a community marked by labor and aspiration. The plantation would become an anchor for their stories, each harvest representing a chapter in their collective journey toward empowerment.

Isabella's heart swelled with pride when she reflected on how the plantation had become synonymous with hope and transformation.

News of their initiative spread beyond the village, attracting attention from neighboring communities and local organizations. They began to garner support from various groups interested in women's empowerment, sustainability, and traditional practices.

Their efforts led to a partnership with a nearby university, where students in agricultural studies sought to learn from the women's expertise. Isabella and her fellow farmers opened their doors for field trips, demonstrating their practices while emphasizing the importance of women-led initiatives. As students shared their own experiences in return, a dynamic exchange flourished, enriching both the cooperative and the education of future generations.

The sugarcane plantation had become a beacon not only of resilience but of aspiration—a place where women had stepped from the shadows of societal expectations and reclaimed their narrative. As the cooperative grew, it became clear that they were not alone on their journey; they were part of a movement echoing across the Caribbean.

As the sun dipped below the horizon, painting the sky in stunning shades of orange and pink, Isabella stood at the edge of the field, watching the last rays of sunlight glisten on the sugarcane. The sight stirred a deep sense of conviction within her. This land, once a breeding ground for limiting beliefs, was now synonymous with dignity and vibrancy.

"To reclaim our dignity is to reclaim our power," she whispered to the wind, her thoughts drifting toward the future. Their hard work was laying the foundation for future generations, teaching them the value of unity, determination, and perseverance.

Isabella pictured young girls learning about their heritage, empowered by the knowledge that they could forge their own paths. She imagined them standing proudly on this very land, discussing sustainable practices and leadership, knowing they had the strength of their mothers and ancestors behind them. The cycle of inspiration and empowerment would continue to flourish.

As she turned to leave, Isabella felt a quiet resolve settle within her. They were forging a path of resistance against limitations, reclaiming their stories and destinies. The sugarcane plantation, emblematic of their journey, was a testament to what could be achieved when women came together to pursue their dreams.

In that transformative space, every plant, every harvested stalk, every shared meal, and story echoed with the promise of resilience. Isabella vowed to continue nurturing this dream, fostering a cooperative that would shine brightly as a symbol of empowerment, not just for her village, but for all women seeking to rewrite their narratives under the expansive Caribbean sky.

As dawn broke over the lush hills of Dominica, an invigorating light spilled across the sugarcane plantation, illuminating the vibrant green stalks that stood tall and proud. To Isabella, this was not just land—this was the foundation of a dream, a vision that would shape the future for generations of women. The cooperative represented hope, resiliency, and the strength of women united in purpose.

Isabella's heart swelled with purpose as she looked out over the fields. Her dream was clear: she wanted the cooperative to be a beacon of empowerment for the next generation of women in their community. She envisioned young girls watching their mothers rise as leaders in agriculture and contributors to their household economies. With each success, these girls would come to understand that their potential was limitless and that the path to achieving their dreams began with believing in themselves.

To make her vision a reality, Isabella organized regular meetings with the women of the cooperative where they could share their experiences and celebrate their achievements. The atmosphere was electric with energy and hope as they exchanged stories of overcoming challenges, nurturing their crops, and supporting one another. "Every single one of us here is carving a path for our daughters," Isabella declared during one such meeting. "Let's lead by example and show them that they can achieve anything."

This focus on community cultivated an environment of encouragement that rippled through the plantation. Isabella encouraged the women to bring their daughters to the gatherings, letting them witness the camaraderie and determination of their mothers. Each meeting turned into a lesson, a chance for the girls to absorb the values of hard work, solidarity, and resilience that characterized their mothers' lives.

That spirit of empowerment manifested in tangible ways. Workshop sessions on leadership development, entrepreneurship, and sustainable practices became a staple of their gatherings. Girls watched as their mothers' shared insights, and in those moments, they absorbed the message that success was within reach, that their voices mattered, and that they too could lead.

Despite the promise of this vision, Isabella faced numerous obstacles. In a society steeped in traditional gender roles, skepticism often clouded their aspirations. Some community members doubted the viability of a woman-led cooperative, questioning the practicality of their efforts. Others warned them of stepping too far outside established social norms, insisting that agriculture was not a place for women seeking leadership.

But within Isabella burned a fierce determination. She drew strength from the bonds being formed among the women in the cooperative, recognizing that their unity was an indomitable force. "We are stronger together," she reminded her fellow members during challenging times. "Every barrier we break is a step toward a brighter future for our daughters. We cannot turn back now."

With resilience as her weapon, Isabella reached out to community leaders, sharing her vision, and building alliances. She organized open forums to discuss the benefits of women participating fully in agriculture and local commerce. By showcasing the successes of their cooperative, she aimed to shift the narrative. These efforts began to bear fruit as community members who once doubted started to see the positive changes in their neighborhoods, flourishing not just due to the agricultural yield but also through inspired women taking leadership roles.

As Isabella stood in the fields, her heart filled with hope, she imagined the future unfolding before her. She envisioned young girls, emboldened by their mothers' achievements, stepping confidently into roles they once thought unattainable. They would assume positions of leadership, create their own businesses, and participate actively in their communities.

To further nurture this emerging legacy, Isabella launched a mentorship program within the cooperative, pairing young girls with experienced women from diverse backgrounds. The program was designed to encourage skill development, instill confidence, and foster deep, meaningful connections across generations. Each mentorship relationship became an invaluable exchange of wisdom and encouragement. Isabella watched with pride as both mentors and mentees flourished in their roles, the young girls rising one step closer to their dreams as they observed and learned from those who had once walked the same path.

As the first harvest season approached, Isabella organized a grand community festival, celebrating their achievements and the bright future ahead. This event would serve as a culmination of their hard work—an opportunity to showcase the fruits of their labor and inspiring the next generation.

The festival buzzed with excitement. Colorful banners adorned the fields, and groups of women and children set up stalls filled with vibrant produce, handmade crafts, and traditional dishes. Young girls, adorned in bright clothing, danced, and laughed, embodying the essence of hope and possibility. It was a joyful celebration of not just agriculture but also the strength of women in shaping their destinies.

During the festivities, Isabella took the stage to address the crowd, her voice steady and filled with passion. "Today, we celebrate not just our harvest but the dreams we are nurturing together. To all the young girls here, look around you! Your mothers have worked hard, and they are proof that dreams can come true. Believe in yourselves, for you are capable of greatness—just as they are!"

As the cheers and applause reverberated around her, Isabella felt a profound sense of fulfillment wash over her. Her vision was beginning to take shape, and the cooperative was indeed becoming a foundation for the legacy she longed to forge.

As twilight descended over the plantation, painting the sky in hues of orange and purple, Isabella reflected on their journey. The struggles, the triumphs, the laughter was all part of the dream woven into the very fabric of the land.

Her commitment to the cooperative remained unwavering, anchored in her desire to see women empowered and future generations transformed. This was about more than just sugarcane; it was about cultivating a legacy of empowerment that would echo through time. She was determined to ensure that the stories of resilience, unity, and aspiration would continue to inspire, encouraging young girls to chase their dreams relentlessly.

The sugarcane fields, bathed in the warm light of a setting sun, represented more than crops. They symbolized a growing movement, a shift in the narrative of women in Dominica. Isabella stood firm in her resolve, ready to face the challenges ahead, inspired by the knowledge that with each step, they were turning dreams into reality— for themselves and for the future generations waiting to blossom just beyond the horizon.

FOUR

LOVE AND CONFLICT

Isabella stood at the edge of the vibrant rally, the warm Caribbean sun drenching her in light as colorful banners danced in the air. The excitement of the crowd pulsed like a heartbeat around her, the voices rising in a chorus of hope and determination. Today marked a pivotal moment not just for her, but for the future of Colihaut and Dominica by extension. She had come to understand that this community rally was a living testament to the collective yearning for change, and she could not help but feel a sense of belonging among those gathered.

As she scanned the crowd, Isabella's eyes fell upon a figure on the makeshift stage. Javier, the local journalist she had heard whispers about, was speaking passionately into the microphone. His dark hair fell slightly into his eyes, which sparkled with conviction, and as he gestured animatedly, the audience erupted in cheers. Isabella felt a rush of admiration. Here was a man who embodied the spirit of the movement, his words igniting a fire in the hearts of those listening.

Once the rally concluded, she found herself amongst a sea of enthusiastic supporters. Her pulse quickened as she maneuvered through the crowd, her heart set on meeting Javier. The energy in the air crackled as groups discussed strategies and dreams. However, all her focus was on the man who had captivated her attention.

Finally, she spotted him standing at the edge of the gathering, engaged in animated conversation with a few locals. Gathering her courage, Isabella approached, her cheeks flushing ever so slightly. As she reached him, he turned, and their eyes locked, an electric connection sparking instantly between them.

"That was an incredible speech," Isabella said, her voice steady despite the butterflies in her stomach. "You have a way of capturing people's hopes."

Javier's face broke into a warm smile. "Thank you! I believe in the strength of our people. If we do not advocate for ourselves, who will?"

The sincerity in his voice resonated with her deeply. In their small talk that followed, they discovered their shared passion for social reform and community empowerment. Each word exchanged drew them closer, the intensity of their conversation igniting an undeniable chemistry.

"Have you been involved with the cooperative efforts on the plantation?" Javier asked, curiosity glimmering in his eyes.

Isabella nodded, feeling a surge of confidence. "I want to revitalize the sugar cane plantation to benefit the entire community, not just a select few. Working together can empower us all."

"You have a vision," Javier remarked, his admiration palpable. "Change is often daunting, but with conviction and community, it's possible."

Exactly! And I feel that if we unite our efforts, we can truly transform this town." As she spoke, Isabella watched as his gaze shifted from her lips to her eyes, an unspoken understanding passing between them. Was it just her imagination, or was he equally mesmerized?

Javier took a step closer, lowering his voice conspiratorially. "The more I meet folks like you, the more I believe there's a chance for real reform here—something profound. Would you be willing to collaborate on some initiative? We could reach a wider audience together."

Her heart raced at the suggestion. "I'd love to! I've been hoping to find passionate allies in my mission."

As they exchanged ideas, the world around them faded into the background. Their excitement for shared dreams and aspirations wove an invisible thread between them, making everything else seem small in comparison. They discussed strategies for community workshops, potential grants for the cooperative, and plans for future gatherings aimed at rallying greater support.

Hours slipped away unnoticed, and as the sun began to set, painting the sky with hues of orange and pink, Javier stepped back, a hint of vulnerability in his voice. "Isabella, can I confess something?"

"Of course," she replied, her heart fluttering, sensing the weight of the moment.

He took a breath, his expression shifting to something more earnest. "I'm inspired by your spirit. I see greatness in you, and your bravery to lead is something I admire tremendously. I hope this isn't too forward, but I would like to get to know you better, beyond just the cause."

Isabella's cheeks flushed at the sincerity in his gaze. This was unexpected, but she felt a stirring deep within her, a warmth that spread to her fingertips. "I'd like that, too," she said softly.

Their conversation lingered for a moment longer before they exchanged contact information, promises of future collaboration thrumming like a heart. As they parted, there was an unspoken agreement hanging in the air, one that encompassed not just their mission but also the undeniable chemistry they had ignited.

The next few weeks were a whirlwind of community meetings, planning sessions, and collaboration on projects that sought to empower the local workers. Together, Isabella and Javier navigated the delicate dance of activism, their conversations growing deeper, often lingering after hours as they shared thoughts not just on their work, but on their lives, their dreams, and the intertwining paths they hoped to forge.

Isabella found herself captivated not just by Javier's passion for the cause but by the man himself. His laugh was infectious, filling her with warmth, and when he spoke about his vision for Dominica, she felt inspired and invigorated. They spent more day's side by side, laughing, planning, and dreaming of a future where they and their community thrived.

As the tension in the air thickened with each encounter, Isabella sensed that their burgeoning friendship was leading them into uncharted territory—territory she was both excited and apprehensive to explore. Would their shared values reinforce the bond between them, or would it complicate the passionate collaboration they had cultivated?

For now, though, she felt emboldened; she was a woman of valor, ready to embrace the changing tides, not just in her work but in her heart as well. And as she met Javier's gaze across a bustling meeting room, filled with hope and possibility, she knew they were on their own path toward something remarkable—together.

The weeks flowed like the gentle waves lapping against the shores of Dominica, each day weaving Isabella and Javier closer together. Their shared ideals became the foundation of a bond that transcended mere friendship; that blossomed into something deeper, something electric. They were two souls united by a common purpose, their hearts beating in rhythm with the dreams of their community.

Every project they undertook reinforced their connection. They organized workshops to educate local farmers on sustainable practices, hosted community meetings to discuss the cooperative's goals, and rallied support for social justice initiatives. Each event brought them closer, their laughter echoing through the air as they shared jokes and stories, their camaraderie evident to everyone around them.

One evening, as they prepared for a community rally, Isabella caught Javier's gaze lingering on her. She felt a flutter in her chest, the kind that made her acutely aware of how much he meant to her. "What is it?" she asked, brushing a strand of hair behind her ear.

Javier smiled, a hint of shyness coloring his cheeks. "I was just thinking about how incredible it is to work alongside someone

who shares the same passion. You inspire me, Isabella."

Her heart swelled at his words. "I feel the same way about you. Your courage to speak out against injustice is something I admire deeply. It gives me strength."

As the rally commenced, their hands brushed together, a fleeting touch that sent a jolt of electricity through Isabella. She noticed the way Javier's eyes sparkled when he spoke about their shared vision for a better future. It was in those moments, filled with passion and purpose, that she realized her admiration for him had blossomed into something more profound.

Late-night discussions became a ritual for them. After long days spent advocating for their community, they would often retreat to the quiet of Isabella's porch, the stars twinkling above like scattered diamonds. They shared their hopes and fears, their dreams intertwining like the vines that climbed the nearby trees.

"I worry sometimes," Isabella confessed one night, her voice barely above a whisper. "What if we fail? What if our efforts do not bring the change we hope for?"

Javier turned to her; his expression serious yet gentle. "Failure is a part of any journey. But what matters is that we try. We are planting seeds of change, and even if they take time to grow, we must believe in the future we are fighting for."

His words resonated deeply within her, filling her with a sense of purpose. "You are right. It is about the legacy we leave behind, not just for ourselves but for all the women and families in our community."

They sat in comfortable silence for a moment, the weight of their conversation hanging in the air. Then, Javier reached for her hand, intertwining their fingers. The warmth of his touch sent a rush of warmth through her, and she looked up to find him gazing at her with an intensity that made her heart race.

"Isabella," he said softly, "I have never felt this way about anyone before. Our connection is unlike anything I have experienced, and I want to explore it further with you."

Her breath caught in her throat, and she felt a blush creep up her cheeks. "I feel the same, Javier. You have become such an important part of my life."

As they leaned closer, the world around them faded away, leaving only the two of them enveloped in a cocoon of shared dreams and burgeoning affection. Their lips met softly, a tentative yet electric kiss that ignited a fire within them both. It was a kiss that spoke of promise, of a future intertwined with their shared ideals.

From that moment on, their relationship blossomed like the vibrant flowers that adorned the island. They began to navigate the delicate balance of love and activism, supporting each other in their endeavors while nurturing their growing affection. Whether they were planning community events or sharing quiet moments under the stars, their connection deepened.

Together, they envisioned a future where their efforts would empower women, uplift families, and foster a sense of community pride. Their late-night discussions evolved into dreams of a cooperative that not only provided economic stability but also served as a haven for those seeking support and guidance.

One evening, while sitting on the porch, Javier turned to Isabella, his expression earnestly. "What if we create a mentorship program for young women in our community? We could help them develop skills in leadership and advocacy."

Isabella's eyes lit up with excitement. "That is a brilliant idea! We could empower them to take charge of their futures, just like we are trying to do."

As they brainstormed ideas, their laughter filled the air, mingling with the sounds of the night. In those moments, they were not just partners in activism; they were partners in life, envisioning a world where their love could thrive alongside their shared mission.

Days turned into weeks, and their relationship flourished. They attended rallies hand in hand, their presence a powerful symbol of unity and hope. The community began to take notice, inspired by their commitment to each other and to the cause.

As they stood together at the forefront of a rally one sunny afternoon, Isabella could not help but feel a swell of pride. Javier's voice rang out, calling for justice and reform, and she felt a sense of purpose wash over her. She was not just fighting for change; she was fighting for a future filled with love, hope, and possibility—a future she envisioned with Javier by her side.

During their activism, they found solace in each other, their love acting as a guiding light through the challenges they faced. With every shared dream, every late-night conversation, and every rally they attended together, Isabella and Javier forged a bond that was not only rooted in their commitment to social justice but also in their unwavering affection for one another. Together, they were unstoppable, ready to face whatever challenges lay ahead, fueled by their shared ideals and the love that blossomed between them.

As the days turned into weeks, the initial thrill of their burgeoning romance began to intertwine with the heavy weight of their ambitions. For Isabella, the urgency of establishing the cooperative loomed larger each day. She poured herself into her work, often losing track of time as she strategized and organized, driven by a fierce desire to uplift her community. The vision she held for the cooperative was not just a dream; it felt like a lifeline for the families around her, and she was determined to see it through.

Javier, too, was consumed by his responsibilities. His journalistic endeavors demanded long hours and relentless dedication. He was determined to give a voice to the marginalized, to shine light on the injustices faced by the community. With each article he wrote, he felt the weight of expectation from his readers and peers, pushing him to dig deeper and speak louder. The political landscape was shifting, and he wanted to be at the forefront of that change.

As their individual commitments intensified, the time they spent together began to dwindle. What had once been late-night brainstorming sessions and shared laughter on the porch turned into hurried phone calls and stolen moments between meetings. The connection that had blossomed so beautifully now felt strained, overshadowed by their growing responsibilities.

One evening, as Isabella sat at her desk surrounded by papers and notes, she glanced at the clock and realized she had not heard from Javier all day. A wave of anxiety washed over her. She picked up her phone, scrolling through the messages that had gone unanswered. She missed his laughter, his insights, the way he made her feel understood.

Just as she was about to send a message, her phone buzzed, and Javier's name flashed on the screen. Relief surged through her, but as she read his text, her heart sank.

"Isabella, I am swamped with interviews and need to finish my article tonight. Can we talk later?"

She felt a pang of disappointment but understood the demands of his work. *"Of course. I am just busy with the cooperative too. Let us catch up tomorrow?"*

"Definitely. I am looking forward to it."

But as the night wore on, the anticipation of their conversation was overshadowed by the reality of their separate worlds. Isabella returned to her paperwork, but her thoughts kept drifting to Javier. She could not shake the feeling that they were both slipping away from each other, consumed by their individual pursuits.

The next day, they finally managed to meet at a local café, a small haven nestled between the bustling streets. As they settled into a corner table, the air was thick with unspoken tension. Javier looked weary, his eyes shadowed from lack of sleep, while Isabella felt the weight of her own exhaustion pressing down on her shoulders.

"Hey," she greeted him softly, trying to mask her concern. "How are things with the article?"

"It is a lot. There is so much happening politically, and I am trying to cover it all," he replied, running a hand through his hair. "But it is not just the work. I feel like I am losing touch with everything else—especially with you."

Isabella's heart dropped. "I feel the same way. I am so wrapped up in the cooperative that sometimes I wonder if I am neglecting us."

Javier leaned back; his expression hurt. "It is hard, isn't it? We are both fighting for something we believe in, but it feels like we are fighting against each other, too.

"I don't want that," Isabella said, her voice trembling slightly. "I care about you, Javier. I want to support you, but I also need to focus on this mission. It is just... it is so important."

"I understand," he replied, his tone softening. "But I worry that we are letting our ambitions come between us. I want to be there for you, but it feels like we are on different paths right now."

The weight of his words hung in the air, and Isabella felt a lump rise in her throat. "I don't want to lose what we have," she admitted, her voice barely above a whisper. "But I also cannot ignore the needs of the community. They are depending on us."

Javier nodded; his brow furrowed in thought. "We need to find a way to blend our efforts. We are both passionate about the same things; we just need to remember that we are on the same team, even if we are fighting different battles."

Isabella felt a flicker of hope in his words. "You are right. We can work together, even if it looks different than before. I do not want to sacrifice our relationship for our ambitions."

"Neither do I," he said, reaching across the table to take her hand. "Let us plan. We can schedule time for each other, even if it is just a few hours a week. We can support one another while still pursuing our goals."

Tears pricked at the corners of Isabella's eyes as she squeezed his hand. "I would like that. I need you in my life, Javier, not just as a partner in activism but as someone I deeply care for."

Javier smiled, the warmth returning to his eyes. "And I need you too. We can face this together, I promise."

As they talked through their ideas, the tension began to dissipate, replaced by a renewed sense of purpose. They discussed how they could intertwine their efforts—Javier could write articles highlighting the cooperative's initiatives, while Isabella could provide insights into the community's needs and the impact of their work. With each suggestion, they felt the distance between them shrink, their ambitions no longer a barrier but a shared journey.

However, as they left the café, the reality of their commitments loomed large. They both knew that the path ahead would not be easy. The demands of their respective roles would continue to challenge their relationship, but they were determined to navigate the complexities together.

Isabella walked away with a sense of hope, but also a lingering anxiety. Could they truly balance their ambitions without losing sight of each other? As she glanced back at Javier, who was already engrossed in his notes, she realized that while their love was strong, it would be tested time and again by the very passions that had brought them together.

But at that moment, she felt reassured. They had chosen to fight for their dreams side by side, and as long as they kept communicating and supporting one another, they could weather any storm. With the promise of shared efforts and understanding, Isabella felt a renewed determination to pursue her mission, not just for herself but for the love that had begun to blossom amidst the strain of ambition.

As Isabella delved deeper into establishing the cooperative, she found solace in the vision of women coming together, supporting each other, and creating a strong, united community. The more she engaged with local farmers and artisans, the clearer her goal became: to uplift the women who had been marginalized for too long. She believed that empowering individuals on a grassroots level would lead to a ripple effect of positive change for the entire community.

However, as proud as she was of the progress, Javier's voice echoed in the back of her mind. He had begun to challenge her approach, pushing her to see beyond their immediate surroundings and consider the larger political landscape. He often mentioned systemic issues that he felt were being overlooked, urging her to expand her vision.

"I appreciate what you're doing at the cooperative," Javier said one evening as they sat on the porch, enjoying the cool breeze. "But don't you think it is a bit insular? We need to be addressing the broader structural injustices that are affecting the community."

Isabella frowned, her fingers tightening around her coffee cup. "Javier, I am not dismissing the importance of systemic change. But local initiatives can create real change too, especially for the women who feel powerless. Isn't it valid to start where we are?"

"I understand that, but sometimes it feels like you are focusing too much on local issues without considering the bigger picture. There are political movements that require mobilization, and if we do not use our voices to address those, we risk being complacent while injustices continue," he replied, frustration creeping into his voice.

Isabella felt her heart race. "My focus on the cooperative does not mean I am ignoring broader issues! It is about building a foundation of support. If we empower women, they can then participate in those larger movements. Change starts small, Javier!"

"But what about the systemic barriers that keep women from being able to join these movements in the first place?" Javier countered, leaning forward in his chair. "We need to be fighting for accountability from those in power, advocating for policy changes. It is not enough to just uplift individuals; we need a revolution in the way systems operate."

His passionate words struck a nerve with Isabella. She interpreted his insistence as a dismissal of her hard work, the fruit of her labor for which she had sacrificed so much. "How can you not see the value in nurturing the very people who will eventually stand up to those systems? You are talking about politics while I am trying to empower individuals here and now!"

Javier sighed, rubbing the back of his neck in frustration. "I do see that value, but our efforts are limited by an overarching structure that cannot simply be ignored. You have a powerful voice, Isabella. Why not use it to bring attention to the wider issues we face?"

The tension thickened in the air between them as their differing perspectives brought them to an impasse. Isabella's gaze hardened. "Because I believe in the strength of grassroots movements. Change does not happen overnight. My focus is on these local initiatives because they matter to the women in our community. Maybe if you understood that better, you would not think I am being complacent."

"Complacent? That is not what I mean!" he shot back, his voice rising. "It feels like you are playing into the hands of the very systems we should be dismantling. What is going to happen if you succeed and nothing else changes? What about those who are still suffering because the larger dynamics remain the same?"

Anger bubbled within Isabella. "You are making it sound like I am not doing enough. I am out here building relationships and supporting my community while you are hidden behind your computer, chasing stories! It feels like you are looking down on me instead of supporting the work I am doing!"

Javier's expression shifted, a mix of pain and shock crossing his face. "I never intended to belittle your efforts. I just want to challenge you to think critically about the wider impact. We are both passionate—can't we see that our strengths can complement each other?"

Isabella felt a wave of frustration. "But it is hard to see it that way when it feels like you are criticizing me rather than collaborating. Our dreams for a better future cannot be at odds with each other, can they?"

A silence fell between them, heavy and taut. They both leaned back, trying to process the weight of their arguments. Isabella stared out at the darkening sky, her thoughts whirling.

Javier inhaled deeply, calming himself. "What if we set aside time to talk about our ideas more cohesively? Let us see how our missions can align instead of clashing.

Isabella nodded slowly, the anger beginning to drain from her. "That would help. I want to understand your perspective, and I just need you to see mine too."

"Absolutely," he replied, relief washing over his features. "Let us work together on this. We can explore how local initiatives can feed into broader systemic change. Can we agree on that?"

"Yes," she said, a small smile creeping onto her face. "I want to bridge that gap. Let us find ways to highlight the stories at the cooperative while also advocating for the changes needed in the larger political landscape."

As they talked late into the night, the tension began to recede, replaced by a sense of hope. They both acknowledged that they were passionate individuals working toward a common goal, albeit from different angles.

Whether it was through local action or larger political commentary, both paths were essential. Their love—once again—became a source of strength amidst the challenges they faced. And though they knew that their perspectives might clash again, Isabella felt reassured that together, they could navigate the complexities of their aspirations and continue to fight for the community and their relationship simultaneously.

As Isabella immersed herself in her work with the cooperative, a layer of pressure began to creep in—not just from her increasingly divergent visions with Javier, but from the very fabric of her community. The wind carried whispers that seemed to linger on the fringes of her efforts, and they were not all kind. Elders, once supportive, began to express their reservations about a woman stepping into a leadership role.

"Isabella," one elder, Aunt Liza, said sternly one afternoon as they gathered for a community meeting, "your heart is in the right place, but women should not be bringing attention to themselves like this. Leadership is for men, and your ambitions may disrupt the harmony of our society."

The words stung, and Isabella felt a mix of anger and disappointment. "But Aunt Liza, we cannot wait for change to come from the men in our lives. Women have voices too, and the community deserves to hear them."

"It's not about the voice," the elder countered, her tone firm. "It is about the position a woman should hold—supportive and nurturing, not leading. Remember, dear, it is the men who must guide our families and paths."

Isabella glanced around the room, noting the nods of agreement from some of the other elders. Her heart raced as she sensed the weight of their collective judgment pressing down on her. "Leadership is about making a difference, and change starts with us. We cannot allow tradition to dictate our future."

As she spoke, she met the gaze of Javier, who sat at the back of the room, his expression a mixture of admiration and concern. He had always been supportive of her endeavors, but

As much as he appreciated her spirit, he understood the cultural expectations that loomed large over them.

After the meeting, Javier walked alongside Isabella, sensing her frustration. "I'm sorry you faced that," he said softly. "It's frustrating to see how some people can't embrace the fact that women are capable leaders."

"It's infuriating!" she replied, her voice tight with emotion. "I am trying to uplift our community, and instead, I feel like I am fighting against our very traditions. It should not have to be this hard."

Javier nodded, but he hesitated before speaking again. "You know, it might not only be them. My family has been asking about us, and they are skeptical about my involvement with a woman who prioritizes her career. They worry I will not be supported in maintaining a traditional role if I am with you."

Isabella's heart sank. "What do your parents think? Do they think I am a bad influence?"

"They don't think you're a bad person, but they worry about how our paths may align," he admitted. "They've questioned whether I'll have the support I need to stand by you if it means stepping away from certain expectations."

"Expectations? What kind of expectations?" Isabella asked, a mix of anxiety and anger bubbling within her.

"Traditional views on gender roles. They believe a man should be the primary provider, and they have raised me to value family toward a different understanding of partnership. Your ambitions—while admirable—are a departure from what they had hoped for me," he confessed.

Isabella felt a mix of sympathy and frustration. "But our lives should not be dictated by outdated expectations. We are carving out our own paths!"

"I agree," Javier said, placing a hand on hers. "But we also cannot ignore the cultural weight of expectations. It is hard for them to see past norms, and it puts pressure on me to make a choice between supporting what I feel deeply and living up to family expectations.

Isabella sighed; the weight of his words settled over her like a heavy blanket. "I know it is not easy for you. I am proud of my efforts and contributions, but I also do not want to be the reason for friction between you and your family. We are both navigating this terrain in our own ways."

Days passed, and the tension between ambitions and traditional roles only intensified. The scrutiny Isabella faced weighed heavily on her spirits. Gossip circulating among community members began to twist her intentions, portraying her as a woman who sought public acclaim rather than community empowerment. She fought to hold onto her vision, yet with every passing gaze, the burden grew heavier.

It was one evening when she and Javier met again that she finally broke down. As they walked through a local market, the vibrant colors and sounds around them felt muted. "I am tired, Javier. I feel like I am constantly fighting for validation while trying to uplift others. There are days I question if it is worth it if it means I am alienating myself from our traditions."

Javier stopped, facing her, concern etched across his face. "It is worth it, Isabella. What you are doing has the potential to ignite change, but I see how much these external pressures are affecting you. We need to find a way to navigate these traditions while staying true to our beliefs.

"Easy for you to say," she replied, the bitterness creeping in again. "You are not facing the same scrutiny. You have the support of your family despite this friction."

He stepped closer, his voice low and steady. "I may not have your burdens, but I am here to stand by you. We cannot let other people's expectations dictate our lives or our relationship."

She looked up at him, their eyes locked, and in that moment, she felt a flicker of hope amidst the chaos. "You are right. I want to empower these women, which means learning how to meld our ambitions with our heritage. We can challenge those traditions without completely rejecting them."

Javier nodded, the tension in his face easing. "Exactly. We can demonstrate that support does not mean conforming. You lead through example, showing that women can pursue their ambitions and remain valuable members of our culture at the same time."

"Having you by my side gives me strength," Isabella said, finally allowing a small smile to break through her concerns. "Let us work on this together. How do we address both our community's needs and the expectations that weigh us down?"

Together, they began to brainstorm ways to foster dialogue between the younger generation and the elders, aiming to bridge the divide that had arisen from tradition. They organized community forums where women could share their experiences, emphasizing not just their ambitions but also how these contributions could benefit the entire community.

As they worked side by side, they discovered a shared resilience rooted in their understanding of the complexities they faced. They reached out to the elders with respect, acknowledging their perspectives while gently challenging outdated norms. By demonstrating the importance of women's leadership as essential rather than threatening, they began to garner support from unexpected allies within the community.

During this, they learned to lean on each other, their relationship strengthened by shared purpose. Even as they faced criticisms and doubts, they remained committed to navigating the path before them, determined to reshape traditional narratives into a more inclusive future—one where both their ambitions could thrive without fear of judgment.

And as they journeyed through the heart of their community, the weight of tradition grew lighter, replaced by a burgeoning sense of hope that told them that their love, united with their aspirations, could challenge the status quo and inspire those around them to reconsider what was possible.

The weeks rolled on, filled with both progress and mounting tension. Javier poured himself into his work, determined to shed light on the issues facing local farmers and women, and his passion culminated in a provocative article. It outlined not only the failures of the government but also praised Isabella's cooperative as a vital solution to the challenges that plagued the community. He portrayed her initiative as a beacon of hope, emphasizing the transformation that could come from empowering women.

When the article was published, the initial feedback was a mix of support and outrage. While many lauded Javier for bringing attention to critical issues, others took offense at the implication that established norms—and their keepers—had failed. Whispers spread like wildfire, and Isabella soon found herself in the eye of a brewing storm.

As she returned home after a long day at the cooperative, her heart sank upon hearing murmurs from her neighbors. She overheard them discussing the article, some whispering about how a woman should not be thrust into the spotlight, implying that Javier's support was unwelcome and misguided. The unease clung to her.

That night, over dinner, Isabella confronted Javier. "You didn't think about the repercussions, did you?" she asked, her tone tense. "Your article put me in a position where I'm being scrutinized even more than before!"

Javier looked taken aback. "I was trying to highlight the importance of what you are doing!

I thought you would appreciate that." "Appreciate it?" she retorted, frustration bubbling over. "I feel exposed, Javier! This is not just about my work—it is about our community's expectations of me as a woman. People are saying I am stepping out of line, and now your article has made it worse!"

"I had to draw attention to the issue!" he argued, his voice rising. "You think I enjoy ruffling feathers? But if we do not challenge the system, nothing is ever going to change. Your cooperative is critical to that change!"

Isabella shook her head, feeling the ground beneath her shift. "You do not understand the complexity of the situation. Yes, it is crucial to get the word out but doing that without considering how it affects me— how it makes me a target—shows me you do not see the full picture!"

"That's not true!" Javier shot back, clenching his jaw. "I do see the big picture, but it feels like you are afraid to take risks. You are focused on local change, and I am trying to connect it with something larger."

"Why is it that you can't see how these local efforts connect to the larger change?" she countered, her voice shaking with emotion. "I am not dismissing the need for systemic reform, but I am working with women who may not even feel safe engaging in those conversations right now! I am trying to give them strength!"

"Strength comes from standing up to power, not hiding behind it!" Javier replied sharply, his frustration palpable. "You are passionate, but it feels limited. I want you to have the same vision I do, one that includes mobilizing for change on all fronts!"

Isabella threw her hands up in exasperation. "And now, I am a target! I cannot just disregard tradition and the expectations of the elders that have been engrained in us. This is not just a personal journey for me; it is a community one! You have thrust me into the forefront without considering what that means!"

The intense argument escalated, each bargaining for understanding but fueling the flames of their insecurities. Isabella felt the walls closing in around her, battling to preserve her identity as a community leader while grappling with the expectations foisted upon her. Javier, in turn, was frustrated by what he perceived as her unwillingness to embrace the ambitious vision that could evoke real change.

Finally, they fell into heavy silence, the tension hanging thick between them. Javier turned his eyes away, staring at the wall as he tried to temper his anger. Isabella took a breath and spoke quietly, almost steadying herself through the words. "I want you to support me, Javier. But when you use my work to criticize the status quo, it feels like you are putting me at risk.

He looked back at her, his expression softening as he realized the burden she bore. "I wanted to shed light on what you are doing because I believe in it. I want you to have recognition. But I cannot ignore the larger problems we must address."

"Then let us find a way to harmonize our efforts without pitting each other against the expectations around us. We can work together to uplift the women while also advocating for systemic change," Isabella said, trying to rein in her emotions. "Your article could be part of that dialogue, but we need to tread carefully."

"Carefully," Javier echoed, nodding slowly. "I see that now. I assumed the community would rally behind your story, and I neglected the reality of entrenched beliefs. I did not mean to push you into a corner."

Isabella took a deep breath, her frustration easing as she saw the genuine concern in his eyes. "I appreciate your passion, but it must be balanced with an understanding of where we stand. We both want to uplift our community, but we need to navigate the complexities together rather than throwing each other into the fray."

He sighed, leaning back in his chair. "I agree. It is clear we have been pulling in different directions. I see that your focus is about empowering women one step at a time, and I need to respect that. But we also must find a way to show how that fits into a broader strategy."

The conversation shifted from confrontation to collaboration as they discussed strategies for addressing both their aims. They brainstormed how to engage the community rather than alienate it, envisioning forums where women could express their stories and needs safely while pinpointing how these local narratives could be woven into a larger call for action.

Isabella's heart eased as they worked through their ideas, feeling more aligned with Javier's passion to drive change. The collaboration would not be easy, but together, they could find common ground. They could advocate for the women in their community while presenting their stories as part of a larger tapestry, highlighting the intersections of personal and systemic challenges in a way that bridged gaps rather than deepened divides.

By the time they finished discussing, both felt a renewed sense of commitment to their causes and to one another. They realized that the intersection of their visions was no longer a conflict, but rather an opportunity to create meaningful dialogue, leading to change both for themselves and the community they cherished.

Days passed since their argument, and while they had reached a tentative peace, the storm outside their doors grew more tumultuous. Isabella began receiving anonymous threats regarding her work with the cooperative. Notes slipped under her door voiced concerns that she was overstepping her bounds, earlier whispers turning into veiled threats that hinted at dire consequences for challenging established norms.

The first note sent chills down her spine: "Women like you should know their place. Keep your ambition in check, or you will regret it." Isabella read it over and over, her heart racing. It was a stark reminder of the societal norms she was battling and the real danger that lurked for any woman who dared to deviate from those expectations.

As fear crept into her thoughts, she shared the ominous messages with Javier, her voice shaking. "They want me to back down. This is real, Javier. It is not just gossip anymore; these threats are serious."

Javier listened, his heart pounding in tandem with hers. "This is unacceptable. We need to take this seriously. Have you spoken to anyone about it?" he asked, concerned threading through his words.

"No," she admitted, shaking her head. "I do not want to be seen as weak or feeble. I am trying to be a leader here."

But Javier could see that Isabella was shaken to her core. "You are not weak. You are courageous for standing up, but this…it is not something you should face alone."

As he held her gaze, the conflict inside him heightened. These threats posed a stark dilemma: did he continue his pursuit of a broader agenda that might put them both at further risk, or should he prioritize Isabella's safety and the immediate efforts she was championing?

The weight of their ideals pressed heavily on his shoulders. He feared that if he stood firmly for his vision, he might inadvertently put Isabella in danger.

"Isabella," he started cautiously, "if this is unraveling your work and making you afraid, I may need to step back from my critique of the broader issues. My family might not understand my involvement, but your safety is paramount."

"No! You cannot just stop fighting!" she said, her voice rising. "That is not how change happens. I do not want to diminish our goals or shrink our vision! If we are going to make an impact, we need to challenge the status quo together."

"But at what cost?" Javier pressed. "You are confronting a system that is deeply ingrained, and the ramifications are severe. Your life matters to me more than any article or critique. What if this leads to something more dangerous?"

The tension grew thicker between them, both grappling with the possibility of sacrificing parts of themselves for the sake of love and safety. Isabella felt torn, realizing the fears Javier had for her were genuine, but at the same time, she knew they could not abandon their shared goals.

"Fear shouldn't dictate our actions," she said softly, emotions spilling over. "I do not want to fight separately, but the stakes are far too high for me to stand down now. I do not just have dreams; I have responsibilities for those women. If we are going to do this, we must confront these threats head-on—together."

As they stood there in the dim light of her home, the realization settled in. Their love, once a source of tension, could be a vehicle for strength. By combining their visions, they could challenge the fears and expectations surrounding them.

Javier took her hands, his lips pressed into a thin line. "Then let us fight together. But we need to plan this carefully. I will amplify your voice safely. We can use your cooperative as a platform to respond to threats rather than retreat. We will not hide; we will speak out against these injustices."

Isabella blinked back tears, hope returning to her heart. "Confronting the threats is one thing, but we need to navigate this with caution. We must empower our community to stand with us—to support us openly."

They spent the ensuing hours devising a strategy that intertwined their visions. Javier proposed using his platform to highlight not only the threats facing Isabella but also the larger systemic issues women faced throughout Dominica. Together, they would craft a message that underscored the importance of unity against oppression, urging the community to stand up—not just for Isabella, but for every woman striving for change.

As they finalized their plans, clarity washed over both. The fear that had once clouded Isabella's mind gradually dissipated, replaced by determination.

Javier pressed a kiss to her forehead, feeling the tension ease between them. "We will make our voices heard. We will show those who threaten us that their intimidation will only fuel our resolve."

With that, they rolled up their sleeves, ready to transform their fears into a rallying cry. They organized a community gathering at the cooperative, inviting women to share their experiences, reinforcing their collective strength. Recognizing how fear could be wielded as a weapon, they instead turned it into a symbol of resilience.

As the day of the gathering approached, the air was thick with anticipation. Isabella felt the weight of her leadership, but with Javier by her side, she felt emboldened. Together, they would not only stand against the threats but also illustrate how their shared ambitions complemented and strengthened one another.

When the gathering finally commenced and the community filled the cooperative, Isabella stood before them, Javier beside her. Speaking passionately, she shared the threats she had received and the importance of women's voices in shaping their futures. Her conviction resonated, and the room erupted with support, a chorus of affirmation that overshadowed the negativity.

Javier expertly threaded the dialogue into the larger conversation, emphasizing that this moment was about more than just Isabella—it was about every woman who faced the weight of tradition and the alive challenges they collectively faced.

As they left the gathering, the warmth of their community's support wrapped around them like a protective blanket.

Isabella turned to Javier, her eyes shining with gratitude. "I could not have done this without you. Your support made all the difference."

"And I didn't realize how crucial it was for us to align our dreams until now," he replied, taking her hand. "Together, we are a force—it is not just about you or me. It is about what we can become as a united front."

Through their challenges, they found an unwavering strength that was augmented by their love, rather than becoming a hindrance, it became the foundation upon which they would build their shared vision for change.

In that moment, they truly comprehended the depth of what they fought for: not just the ambitions for themselves, but the dreams they forged for every woman willing to rise against the tides of tradition. Together, they resolved to face whatever came next—confident that, hand in hand, they could confront the obstacles ahead and forge a path toward a brighter, more equitable future.

Weeks passed since the community gathering, and while it had been a significant turning point, the lingering tension between Isabella and Javier did not dissipate immediately. Although they had shared a powerful moment with their community, both felt an undercurrent of unresolved conflict that required attention.

With the dust settling from the outside pressure and their individual fears hanging heavy in the air, both Isabella and Javier spent time reflecting separately. Isabella, amid organizing workshops for the cooperative, pondered the weight of responsibility she carried, doubting if her vision alone was enough to lead meaningful change. Javier, on the other hand, found himself replaying their arguments in his mind, embarrassed about how he had prioritized his broader ambition over Isabella's immediate needs and safety.

It was a quiet afternoon when they both decided it was time to address their conflicts. Meeting at their favorite café, a small corner place surrounded by tall palm trees, they settled into a booth, seeking the solace of each other's presence. The air felt thick with unspoken words, both acutely aware of the gravity of the moment.

"Hey," Javier said, breaking the silence. "I've missed you."

Isabella's lips curled into a small smile, but the weight of their previous conversations lingered in her eyes. "I have missed you too. But we need to talk."

"Yeah, we do," he agreed, nodding slowly. "I have been thinking about everything—about us, and how our arguments have shifted the dynamic. I do not want these differences to come between us."

Isabella took a steady breath. "I do not want that either. I think we both let our fears guide our responses, and I am sorry if I pushed too hard. I was just overwhelmed."

He reached across the table, taking her hand in his. "We are both afraid—of failure, of the judgment from our community, and even of losing each other. That fear amplified everything we said."

She squeezed his hand, feeling warmth spread through her, grateful for his understanding. "Yes. I realize that I often focus on the immediate community, wanting to uplift those around me. I sometimes forget that there is a bigger fight we need to address. I know your broader aspirations matter, too." "And I understand how important your work is for the community," he replied, his voice earnestly. "I should not have been dismissive of your perspective. We both want to make an impact, but I need to remember that it needs to be rooted in our community first."

"I think we can find a way to intertwine our goals," Isabella suggested thoughtfully. "Your political aims do not have to overshadow my community initiatives. Instead, we can strengthen each other by merging our efforts."

Javier's eyes lit up with excitement at her proposal. "That is, it! We can amplify your work at the cooperative and use it as a platform to engage in political dialogue. We can build a network that connects women's issues locally with larger systemic changes."

"Exactly," Isabella said, her enthusiasm rising. "Imagine empowering the women in the cooperative to have a voice in political discussions. Your articles can highlight their stories as we push for broader reforms together. It creates a dialogue that allows their experiences to inform the political agenda."

"Let's strategize, then," Javier said, gripping her hand tighter. "We can organize workshops that not only train women in skills for the cooperative but also educate them on how to engage politically. We can give them the tools to advocate for themselves and their needs."

Their eyes met, and Isabella felt a rush of courage growing within her. "And by framing our work this way, we can show our community that we are fighting for a cause we both believe in. It is not just about the individual anymore; it is about collective strength."

As they exchanged ideas, the atmosphere lightened up. They spoke passionately, mapping out how they could combine Isabella's initiatives with Javier's political aspirations, blending their individual visions into something larger than either could have achieved alone.

"I want you to know that I see you—your strength, your resolve, and how much you care for our community," Javier said, his gaze unwavering. "We are better together. Your love fuels my ambition, and I want to support yours."

"And I want to be that source of support for you too," Isabella replied, her heart swelling with gratitude. "We can empower each other. Our dreams are not just compatible; they can be transformative."

When they finally finished mapping out their ideas, both felt a sense of readiness to face the world together. This conversation marked a significant turning point not just in their partnership but also in their approach to their ambitions.

Their reconciliations transformed conflict into a shared commitment, solidifying their bond in the process. They left the café with renewed purpose and energy, jointly envisioning the change they could enact as a unified front.

As they walked through the vibrant streets to the cooperative, the sun dipped low, casting a golden hue over everything. "Here's to new beginnings," Javier said, his eyes bright with determination.

"Together," Isabella affirmed, squeezing his hand as they stepped forward, ready to embrace their intertwined path of reconciliation and growth. They were no longer just fighting for individual dreams but were committed to blending their strengths, enabling a more profound impact for their community—and for themselves.

The intricate dance of love and conflict within Isabella and Javier's relationship had evolved significantly throughout their journey. Each clash revealed the depths of their ambitions and the resilience of their bond, forging an unbreakable connection that could withstand pressures from both inside and outside.

Their initial disagreements stemmed from deeply rooted fears, the fear of failure, societal judgment, and the potential loss of one another. Yet, through introspection and open dialogue, they discovered that those very fears could be transformed into catalysts for growth. Instead of allowing conflict to drive them apart, both Isabella and Javier learned to harness it as a tool for deeper understanding and connection.

Isabella's experience underscores the essence of a genuine partnership: one built on the foundation of empathy, active listening, and compromise. She realized that her strength lay not just in her ability to lead her cooperative but also in her willingness to embrace vulnerability and lean on Javier's unwavering support. By intertwining their individual ambitions, they created a powerful synergy that allowed them to pursue their dreams while uplifting their community.

Javier, likewise, recognized the importance of grounding his broader political aspirations in the individual stories of the women he sought to empower. He learned that his dreams were enriched when they aligned with Isabella's commitment to local action. Their reconciliation was not merely a resumption of romance; it was an evolution of their relationship, a mutual acknowledgment of their aspirations and a shared responsibility to nurture them.

Their love became a sanctuary, providing the strength necessary to confront external threats and internal doubts. It served as a reminder that ambition does not have to supersede romance; instead, it can enhance it, creating a more profound connection that embraces both the challenges and joys of life.

As they moved forward together, Isabella and Javier recognized that the complexities of their journey were not obstacles but steppingstones on the path to deeper intimacy. They stood united, ready to advocate for change while nurturing their love—a love that had grown resilient through understanding, compromise, and the courage to champion one another's dreams.

In the vibrant tapestry of their lives, Isabella and Javier exemplified that true partnership is not merely about coexistence but about making space for each other's ambitions, fostering growth, and celebrating resilience amid life's challenges. Together, they were not only crafting their future but also igniting a flame of hope and empowerment within their community, one that embraced authenticity and the power of collective action.

FIVE

SISTERHOOD AND SOLIDARITY

In the heart of Isabella's mission to establish the agricultural cooperative lies the concept of sisterhood—a bond that unites women in their struggles and aspirations. From the very beginning, Isabella understood that her dream could not be realized in isolation; it required the strength and support of those around her. She believed that true empowerment stemmed from collaboration, and she was determined to weave a fabric of solidarity among the women of her community.

As she ventured into the project, Isabella gathered the women at the local community center, a modest building adorned with peeling paint and memories of celebrations past. The air was thick with a mix of anticipation and apprehension. Many had come to share in her vision, but some hesitated, laden with doubts from their own experiences. Would they trust each other enough to embark on this journey together?

Isabella welcomed each woman, her voice warm and inviting, as she recounted her own story—an echo of struggle that resonated with many in the room. She spoke of her childhood, where she had witnessed her mother toil tirelessly to cultivate their small farm, ensuring that they had enough to eat. Yet, in those same years, Isabella had also seen her mother's dreams stifled by isolation, lack of resources, and the oppressive weight of societal expectations.

"We've all faced our own battles," Isabella said, looking around at the faces before her. "But imagine what we could achieve if we joined forces. Together, we can cultivate not only the land but also our dreams."

Soft murmurs of agreement rippled through the group. Among them was Rosa, whose family had been farming for generations. She stepped forward, her voice trembling at first. "After my husband passed, I felt lost and alone. I worked in the fields, but it was so much harder without him. I want to do more than just survive; I want to thrive, to honor his memory by building something lasting."

Her words struck a chord, igniting stories among the women. Maria, a single mother, spoke of the challenges she faced trying to balance work and parenting. Her voice sharpened with determination as she added, "I want my children to see their mother succeed. I do not want them to believe that our circumstances define us."

Tears glistened in several eyes, but with those tears came a sense of shared understanding. The weight of their stories began to lift as connections formed, each bond binding them closer together. Isabella recognized this as the spark of sisterhood—an understanding that in their unity, they were stronger.

In the coming weeks, the women met regularly, sharing not only their dreams but also their practical knowledge of farming, finances, and sustainable practices. They exchanged recipes, laughter, and strategies, turning their meetings into a whirlwind of energy. Each gathering felt like a celebration of their resilience, a testament to their strength as individuals and as a community.

Under Isabella's guidance, they began to organize training workshops. They brought in experts to teach them about crop rotation and organic farming techniques, equipping each other with the skills they needed to move forward. Each woman took on a specific role, relying on one another's strengths to fill in the gaps.

One of the most rewarding aspects of this process was the mentorship that naturally emerged among the women. Older members like Abuela Elena shared wisdom from years of experience, while younger women brought fresh ideas and enthusiasm. They learned everything from the best planting seasons to how to negotiate fair prices at the market. Together, they were creating a legacy of knowledge that would benefit future generations.

Isabella often reflected on the profound change taking place within the group. They were no longer just acquaintances; they were sisters in arms, united by a common purpose. Each woman's struggle felt less burdensome when shared, and victories, however small, were celebrated with equal fervor.

As the agricultural cooperative took shape, the physical manifestation of their sisterhood blossomed alongside a flourishing community garden. What had once been a neglected plot of land transformed into a vibrant patchwork of colors, strong vegetables mingling with fragrant herbs, nurtured by the care and love of its cultivators. This garden was not just a source of food; it was a symbol of their connection and the resilience they embodied.

One evening, gathered around a table filled with the day's harvest, Isabella looked at the faces illuminated by the soft glow of lanterns. "This is just the beginning," she announced with pride. "With our combined strength, we can expand beyond this garden. We can create a safe space for all women in our community, a place where we support one another, share our stories, and continue fighting for a better future."

The women nodded, hearts swelling with pride and hope. They were no longer just individuals fighting their battles; they were a cohesive force, a testament to the power of sisterhood and solidarity. They knew that if they stood together, their dreams were within reach.

This chapter of Isabella's journey not only set the foundation for a successful agricultural cooperative but also forged lifelong friendships and an unbreakable bond among women striving for a brighter future. As they toiled together, nurturing their garden and their community, they planted the seeds of empowerment, solidarity, and hope for generations to come.

As the weeks turned into months, Isabella's vision of creating a safe space began to flourish like the crops they tended to together. The community meetings at the local hall transformed into vibrant gatherings, each infused with warmth and camaraderie. The air buzzed with the energy of women who no longer felt alone in their struggles; they had forged connections that transcended mere acquaintance.

Isabella made it a point to initiate each meeting with an open heart, ensuring that every woman felt seen and heard. "Let's start our meeting by sharing a hope or challenge we're facing this week," she would say, her eyes encouraging. This simple invitation allowed women to express their thoughts freely, fostering an environment of mutual respect and understanding.

One Wednesday evening, as autumn leaves danced outside the hall, the atmosphere inside crackled with palpable emotion. Each woman brought with her not only her own worries but also triumphs gained from earlier meetings. Lidia, a quiet yet wise voice in the group, stood up to share her story of newfound confidence.

"I took the leap and applied for a loan to expand my farm," she announced, her voice trembling with a mixture of excitement and fear. "I have always held back, fearing I was not capable. But after our last meeting, I realized that if I wanted to chase my dreams, I needed to believe in myself.

A wave of applause erupted. Lidia's vulnerability served as a catalyst for others, emboldening them to voice their own aspirations. It was here, in these sacred spaces, that the line between individual struggles and collective strength blurred beautifully.

Encouraged by Lidia's courage, another woman, Marisol, spoke up. "I wanted to share something, too. I have had a tough relationship with my neighbor lately. We used to be friends, but lately, I have felt competitive with her over our crops. I realized it was all in my head. Thank you for allowing me to voice this. I want to mend that friendship."

Her admission prompted nods and murmurs of agreement among the group; many had faced similar feelings but had been too wary to speak out. This atmosphere of honesty resonated deeply as others chimed in, sharing their own struggles with comparison and snatched friendships.

With every story shared, Isabella noticed the weight of jealousy and competition lifted from the women's shoulders. They embraced their imperfections, recognizing that these feelings were part of their shared humanity. "Let this be a reminder," Isabella said, her voice unwavering, "that we can lift each other without diminishing ourselves. There is enough abundance for all of us; it is time we saw it that way."

To reinforce this notion, Isabella organized workshops on collaboration and community-building, teaching the women skills not just for farming but for fostering healthy relationships. They practiced negotiation techniques, learned about sharing resources, and established ways to celebrate each other's successes. Her goal was simple yet profound: to instill in them the belief that they could thrive together, cultivating not only their land but also their bonds.

One uplifting workshop featured a session on "Collaborative Gardening," where they explored how to plant companion crops. It was a fitting metaphor, as Isabella explained how different plants thrive better when grown together, benefiting from each other's strengths. "Just like the gardens we cultivate, our relationships can flourish when we understand and support each other," she said.

As they dug into the soil, laughter filled the air, punctuated by stories of crop failures and the lessons learned. The women shared tips and tricks, often discovering that the solutions they sought could be found in their collective wisdom. These hands-on experiences solidified their belief in collaboration, showing that support was not just theoretical; it was practical, tangible, and beautifully rewarding.

Through these fertile conversations, women began to form accountability groups. They would pair up and check in Regularly about their goals, ensuring that no one felt alone in their journeys. The stories they shared became a source of inspiration, reinforcing the idea that sisterhood was a living, active force among them.

As the weeks turned to months, Isabella could feel the changes deepening. Kindness and promotions of equality replaced suspicion, and women began to involve the younger generations in their practices, passing down knowledge that bridged the gap between experience and fresh ideas. They held intergenerational workshops where mothers and daughters learned together about gardening, cooking, and community resilience.

One evening, Isabella decided to invite the older women to share stories from their past with the younger ones, creating an oral history circle. As the elders spoke of their own trials and triumphs, the younger women listened mesmerized. The tales of struggle transformed into lessons of resilience and hope, binding the community across generations.

"Your generation paved the way for us," Nina, a teenager fascinated by the stories, said to Abuela Elena, who had just shared a particularly moving account of her journey through hardship. "I want to build something powerful too, like you."

"You will!" Abuela beamed, her eyes twinkling with pride. "Just remember, everything can flourish when it's watered with respect and love—especially relationships."

As winter approached, the gatherings at the local hall continued, and the spirit of togetherness illuminated even the coldest evenings. The women began to plan a community event to celebrate their accomplishments—a harvest festival that would showcase their efforts and honor the bonds they had forged.

On the day of the festival, vibrant colors adorned the hall. Tables overflowing with fresh produce, handmade crafts, and the delicious aromas of traditional dishes filled the space. Isabella stood proudly as she watched her vision come to life. The harvest festival was not simply a celebration of their produce; it was a testament to the community they had built.

Everyone, from the youngest children to the oldest matriarchs, joined in the festivities. Stories were exchanged like gifts, laughter echoed like music, and women danced together, a joyful burst of energy and unity.

In the heart of it all, Isabella felt a surge of gratitude for the journey they had shared. The envy that once threatened to divide them had transformed into sisterhood, and the safe spaces she had long envisioned were alive in every interaction, every shared meal, every embrace.

As the festivities continued and smiles lit up tired faces, Isabella knew this was just the beginning. They had created more than a cooperative; they had cultivated a sanctuary, a place where every woman could thrive and find strength in each other. United in their diversity, they were resilient, powerful, and ready to face whatever the world threw at them—together.

Central to the vibrant tapestry of sisterhood that Isabella was weaving was her friendship with Lydia. They were childhood companions, bound by shared memories and a deep mutual understanding that had withstood the test of time. Lydia was everything Isabella admired: unwaveringly supportive, fiercely loyal, and grounded in her beliefs. Where Isabella's ambitions soared high, pushing the boundaries of possibility, Lydia remained a steady anchor, reminding her to take a breath and appreciate the present moment amidst the whirlwind of challenges.

One rainy afternoon, as the sky released its pent-up emotions onto their village, Lydia arrived at Isabella's house, a warm, comforting presence carrying freshly baked bread. "I thought you could use a little pick-me-up," she said with a smile, her dark hair curling softly around her face, kissed by the steam of the oven. Isabella was busy writing plans for the cooperative's next steps, her brow furrowed with concentration.

"Thank you, Lydia," she replied, gratefully accepting the bread. "I've been so caught up in this planning that I hardly remembered to eat today."

Lydia plopped down on the couch, crossing her legs, and watching Isabella with concern. "You know, Isabella, you do not have to do it all at once. We are in this together. It is okay to lean on others—like me!" Lydia's voice was teasing, but the seriousness of her words lingered in the air.

Isabella sighed, running a hand through her hair. "I know, I know. I just feel this pressure to make everything perfect. To not let anyone down. Every day, there are new challenges, and I worry… what if I fail?"

Lydia leaned forward, her expression earnest. "You will not. And even if things do not go as planned, that does not mean you have failed. Remember that this is a journey, not a sprint. You are doing amazing things, but you do not have to carry everything on your shoulders alone. It is about the people who share the weight with you."

The warmth of Lydia's words wrapped around Isabella, and she felt a little lighter. "You always know how to ground me," Isabella admitted, a grateful smile breaking through her earlier tension. "Sometimes, I get so lost in my ambitions, I forget the importance of what's right here."

Together, they spent the afternoon discussing the cooperative, weaving in laughter and vulnerability. The open dialogue reinforced the essence of their friendship and reminded Isabella of the values she wanted to cultivate within the sisterhood she envisioned.

Later that week, as the inaugural harvest festival approached, Isabella felt a wave of anxiety crash over her. The vision she held for the festival was ambitious: there would be local produce, crafts, storytelling sessions, and music to celebrate their community's resilience. But the weight of it felt heavy, and doubts began to creep in. She called Lydia her compass in moments of uncertainty.

"Can you come over? I could really use your perspective," Isabella said, her voice shaky.

Lydia was at her side within minutes, her presence like the warm sun breaking through a gloomy sky. "What's going on?" she asked, immediately sensing Isabella's unease as she settled beside her on the couch.

"I am asking too much of everyone. What if no one shows up? What if I fail to deliver? What if..." Her words tumbled out, a mixture of frustration and fear.

Lydia placed a comforting hand on Isabella's arm. "Let us take a step back. Remember why you are doing this. It is not just about numbers or perfection; it is about connection. Focus on bringing people together, and they will respond. You have already created a safe space for women to share, support, and grow—this festival is just an extension of that," she encouraged.

Isabella took a deep breath, the knot in her stomach loosening under Lydia's reassuring gaze. "You are right. I have been so focused on everything that could go wrong, I forgot what this festival is truly about."

"Exactly. It is a celebration of our journey, our sisterhood," Lydia smiled, filling the room with a lightness that Isabella desperately needed. "And even if a few things don't go as planned, it will still be a success because we're all there for each other."

The festival arrived with a buzz of excitement. On the day of the event, Lydia was by Isabella's side, just as she had always been. They arrived early to set up, laughing as they arranged tables adorned with colorful tablecloths and the produce harvested from their fields. The sun shone brightly, casting warm light over the smiles of the women who had come together to support one another.

As the first guests arrived, Isabella scanned the crowd, her heart racing. But then she noticed Lydia weaving through the attendees, engaging everyone in animated conversations, inviting them to share their stories and their work. Watching Lydia uplift those around her brought a sense of calm to Isabella's nerves.

During the festival, Lydia took Isabella aside. "Let's take a moment to reflect," she suggested, guiding her to a quiet spot under a large oak tree overlooking the bustling gathering. The sounds of laughter and music drifted softly between the leaves, creating a melody both soothing and joyful.

"Look at what you've created," Lydia said, gesturing to the women milling about, sharing laughter, and embracing one another. "This is your dream coming to life. Each person here is a testament to your hard work, your determination, and your heart."

Isabella's chest swelled with emotion as she observed the connections forming around her. Women who had once been strangers were now engaging deeply, celebrating each other's achievements, and supporting one another in their aspirations. The embodiment of sisterhood she had long hoped for was manifesting right before her eyes.

As the sun dipped lower in the sky, painting the horizon in shades of pink and gold, Isabella and Lydia returned to the festival's heart to join the festivities. They danced, laughed, and even shared their own stories, illuminating the importance of the circle of support they had cultivated—one that encouraged vulnerability and empowered each woman to rise together.

That evening as the festival wound down, Isabella felt a sense of fulfillment settle in her heart. She grabbed Lydia's hand, drawing her into a warm embrace. "Thank you for believing in me, for reminding me of the importance of connection," she whispered, gratitude spilling over.

"In friendship and sisterhood, we find strength," Lydia replied, her eyes shining with sincerity. "You have created something beautiful here, and I am proud to stand beside you. Just remember, I am always in your corner—just like all of us."

As the stars began to twinkle in the night sky above their gathering, Isabella realized that the circle of support she had always envisioned was not only manifesting in her community but also in her cherished friendship with Lydia. Together, they had navigated the trials, celebrated the triumphs, and dismantled the barriers that kept women apart.

In the embrace of sisterhood, united by love and understanding, they had built a foundation that would last, nurturing not just the soil under their feet but the hearts of everyone around them. In that moment, Isabella felt an undeniable truth: when women support one another, they bloom together, growing into their fullest potential, strong and resilient—like the roots of a thriving garden.

As the cooperative blossomed and the spirit of sisterhood grew stronger, Isabella felt a deepening connection to the elder women in her community. Their wisdom, shaped by years of resilience and perseverance, offered her invaluable insight into the challenges she faced. Among them, Aunt Miriam stood out—a formidable matriarch with a wealth of stories etched into the lines of her face.

One sunny afternoon, Isabella invited Aunt Miriam to speak at one of their community meetings. The other women gathered in the local hall, buzzing with anticipation. The walls, adorned with colorful banners celebrating their harvest, seemed to vibrate with the energy of shared hopes and dreams. Isabella took a moment to introduce Aunt Miriam, her voice filled with respect. "We are honored to have Aunt Miriam with us today. She carries the stories of our past, and I believe we can all learn from her experiences."

Aunt Miriam, with her silver hair pulled back into a neat bun and her eyes sparkling with life, stood up slowly. "Thank you, my dear," she said, her voice warm and steady. "It is a joy to see so many young faces eager to learn. I have lived a long life, and I have seen a lot. I want to share some of my experiences with you, not just to recount the past, but to inspire you as you build your own paths.

As she spoke, the room fell silent, captivated by her presence. Aunt Miriam began to recount her childhood during a time of hardship, when women often had to fight against societal norms to protect their families. "I remember my mother," she said, her voice thick with emotion. "She worked tirelessly in the fields, often rising before dawn, and she did it all while caring for us. She taught me that resilience is not just about enduring; it is about standing firm in the face of adversity."

The women listened intently as Aunt Miriam shared stories of how her mother organized other women in the village to stand up against unjust practices imposed by local authorities. "We had to fight for our rights, for fair treatment, and for our dignity. My mother would say, 'When we stand together, we are unstoppable."

Isabella felt a rush of inspiration as Aunt Miriam's words resonated deeply within her. Here was a woman who had faced the same struggles they encountered today yet had forged a path through sheer determination and solidarity. The stories of resilience ignited a fire in Isabella's heart, reminding her of the legacy she was part of—a lineage of strong women who had fought for their families and communities.

As Aunt Miriam continued, she spoke of the importance of community support. "We did not just fight for ourselves; we fought for each other. When one of us was struggling, we rallied around her. That is the essence of sisterhood," she emphasized, her gaze sweeping across the room. "You young women have the power to create change, but you must remember to honor the legacy of those who came before you. We paved the way, and now it is your turn to carry that torch."

After Aunt Miriam finished her story, the room erupted in applause, a chorus of appreciation for the shared wisdom. Isabella felt a surge of responsibility wash over her. She understood that it was not only her duty to honor the past but also to ensure that the lessons learned were passed down to the next generation.

"Thank you, Aunt Miriam," Isabella said, stepping forward. "Your stories remind us of the strength we have within us and the importance of unity. We have a responsibility to uphold the traditions of our foremothers while also envisioning a future where we can thrive. Let us not just remember their struggles; let us embody their spirit in our actions."

Inspired by Aunt Miriam's tales, Isabella proposed a new initiative: a mentorship program where elder women would share their knowledge and skills with the younger generation. "We can create a bridge between our past and our future," she suggested. "Let's honor our legacy by learning from each other and building a community that supports growth and empowerment."

The idea met with enthusiasm, and soon, the cooperative was buzzing with plans for the mentorship program. Women of all ages began to pair up, sharing not only practical skills like farming techniques and traditional crafts but also life lessons that transcended generations.

One afternoon, Isabella watched as Aunt Miriam sat with a group of young women, her hands deftly demonstrating how to weave baskets from dried reeds. "This is how we create something beautiful from what we have," she explained, her voice filled with pride. "Just like our lives, weaving requires patience and care. Each strand represents a story, a connection, a lesson learned."

The young women listened intently, their hands mimicking Aunt Miriam's movements. They were not just learning a craft; they were absorbing the wisdom of resilience and creativity that had been passed down through generations.

As the weeks turned into months, the mentorship program flourished, creating a powerful bond of solidarity between the young and the old. The stories shared became a source of strength, and the younger women felt a profound responsibility to uphold the traditions of their foremothers while also forging their own paths.

One evening, as the sun dipped below the horizon, casting a golden glow over the village, Isabella gathered with her peers to reflect on their experiences. "We are the torchbearers of our legacy," she said, her voice steady. "Let us continue to uplift one another, honor our past, and create a future where we all thrive. Together, we can break down barriers and redefine what it means to be a woman in our community."

The group nodded in agreement, a sense of unity washing over them. They were not just individuals fighting their own battles; they were part of a larger movement, a sisterhood rooted in the lessons of the past and the promise of the future.

As Isabella looked around at the faces of her friends, each one a reflection of strength, resilience, and hope, she felt an overwhelming sense of gratitude. The connection between generations had become a powerful force, binding them together in a shared mission to honor their legacy while bravely stepping into the future.

In that moment, Isabella realized that the stories of Aunt Miriam and the elder women were not just tales of survival; they were blueprints for empowerment. With every lesson learned, every story shared, they were weaving a narrative of solidarity that would continue to inspire generations to come. Together, they would rise, uplifted by the strength of their past and the promise of a brighter tomorrow.

As Isabella poured her heart into promoting the cooperative, she came to realize that its success hinged not just on her vision but on the collective action of the women in her community. Inspired by the stories of resilience from elder women like Aunt Miriam, she

155

envisioned a movement that would empower each woman to take an active role in the cooperative's evolution.

Determined to build a strong foundation, Isabella set out to organize a series of workshops focused on sustainable farming techniques, financial literacy, and leadership skills. Her goal was to create a space where women could learn, share experiences, and support one another in tangible ways.

The first workshop kicked off on a warm Saturday morning, the sun shining brightly on the lush fields surrounding the village. Women of all ages gathered their faces alight with curiosity and anticipation. Isabella welcomed everyone, her voice brimming with enthusiasm. "Today, we embark on a journey together. By learning from one another, we can cultivate not just our land but also our potential."

Isabella invited local experts to lead the workshops. The first session focused on sustainable farming techniques, with a knowledgeable agronomist demonstrating organic methods that would optimize their crops while preserving the earth. As the women gathered around for hands-on training, a sense of camaraderie filled the air. They exchanged tips on watering, pest control, and soil enrichment, each contribution building upon another.

"Look, we can create a community garden right here," suggested Rosa, a spirited young mother. "We can share the harvest—and the labor!"

"Great idea!" Isabella responded, her heart surge with pride. "Let us make this a collaboration between all of us. We will work together and learn together!"

Throughout the afternoon, laughter mingled with hard work as relationships began to form. Women who once barely knew each other shared their hopes and concerns, breaking down barriers that had existed for too long. They found strength in their shared challenges— whether it was balancing family commitments, facing financial hardships, or battling societal expectations.

In the following workshops, Isabella introduced sessions on financial literacy. A local banker volunteered her time, eager to empower the women to manage their resources better. "It's vital to understand how to budget, save, and invest your money wisely," she taught. The women listened intently, taking notes and asking questions. Many had never had the opportunity to learn about finances in such a direct and supportive setting.

One day during a finance workshop, as the banker outlined the basics of savings accounts and budgeting, Sofia raised her hand. "What if we pooled our resources to create a community fund? We could help each other during tough times and invest in our collective goals."

Isabella's eyes lit up at the suggestion. "Absolutely! Imagine the possibilities if we worked together to support one another financially. We can build a safety net for our families and the cooperative." The room buzzed with excitement, and before long, the women began discussing the specifics of setting up their communal fund, demonstrating their commitment to collaboration.

As the weeks went by, Isabella continued to introduce leadership skills workshops, encouraging women to find their voices and take charge in their communities. Invited speakers shared their journeys—stories of stepping into roles they had never thought possible, of driving change in their neighborhoods. Empowered by these narratives, the women began to see themselves as leaders capable of enacting change.

During these sessions, Isabella made it a point to highlight each woman's unique strengths. She encouraged them to share their skills, creating a platform where each voice was valued. "You all have something important to contribute—whether it is in agriculture, art, business, or education. Let us celebrate our differences and use them to uplift each other," she urged.

Among the group, new alliances began to form. Clara, an accomplished seamstress, partnered with another woman who had a talent for marketing. Together, they launched a line of handmade crafts, showcasing their talents to the community and beyond. "We can sell our products at local markets," Clara proposed, sparking enthusiasm among the women. "This will not only keep us connected but also generate income for the cooperative."

Isabella watched as the cooperative transformed into a thriving hub of creativity and support. Women took pride in their individual contributions, and the workshops became a space for sharing triumphs and challenges alike. Together, they celebrated each success—no matter how small, understanding that even the smallest victory was a step toward their collective goals.

One evening, as they gathered for a workshop, Isabella could feel the sense of belonging emanating from her peers. It was evident that their collaboration was not just about farming techniques or financial advice; it was about creating a community rooted in trust, understanding, and shared purpose.

"Look at what we've built together," Isabella said, her voice filled with emotion. "We are stronger than ever. By supporting one another, we are not just cultivating crops; we are cultivating a future filled with possibilities."

Cheers erupted in the room as the women expressed their enthusiasm. They began brainstorming ideas for future initiatives: joint ventures, skill-sharing sessions, and community outreach programs. Each woman recognized that their empowerment was intertwined with that of others, creating a ripple effect that would impact their families and the larger community.

As the sun set over the horizon, casting a golden hue on their gathering, Isabella took a moment to reflect on the journey

they had undertaken together. The energy of collaboration and solidarity flowed through the air like a warm breeze, lifting their spirits.

It was no longer about the cooperative; it was a movement fueled by passion and unity. As the women chattered with excitement about their plans, Isabella smiled, knowing they were on the cusp of something truly transformative.

They had learned to mobilize for change, and together they would create a legacy of empowerment that would echo through generations. In their bond of sisterhood, they found purpose—bound to one another by shared dreams, resilience, and the unwavering belief that together, they could achieve anything.

As Isabella's dream for the cooperative took shape, excitement surged throughout the community. Yet, with ambition often comes opposition, and soon the winds shifted. Societal pushbacks began to surface, and whispers of discontent spread among those resistant to change. The same women who celebrated Isabella's vision found themselves confronted with threats and intimidation from individuals who saw the cooperative as a challenge to the status quo.

It started subtly—rumors circulated, and anonymous letters filled with veiled threats slipped under doors announcing that certain people would not tolerate "rebellion." Isabella felt the weight of these threats pressing down on her. Despite her determination, the reality of opposition sparked a flicker of fear within her. Late nights became filled with worry as she wondered if her ambitious plans would put her own safety—and that of the cooperative—at risk.

One evening, after receiving a particularly harsh note, Isabella gathered the women for an emergency meeting. The familiar community hall buzzed with anxiety, yet there was a shared determination in everyone's eyes. She stood before them, her heart racing but her voice resolute. "I need your support now more than ever. We have built something beautiful together, and I refuse to let fear silence us. But I cannot do this alone."

A hush fell over the room before Lydia, the irreplaceable friend by Isabella's side, stepped forward. "We stand with you, Isabella. No one should have to fight this battle alone." Her words resonated deeply, igniting a fire among the women. One by one, they voiced their unwavering support. "We're in this together," Clara affirmed. "You have inspired us all. We will not let this stop us."

Rallying around Isabella, the women decided to confront the fear and oppression head-on. They organized a community meeting, inviting everyone—supporters and skeptics alike—to discuss the cooperative and its vision. It was a bold move, but they understood that unity was their greatest strength. The following week, the hall filled with murmurs as villagers gathered, some curious, some hostile, and others supportive.

Isabella took a deep breath, feeling both anticipation and the weight of the moment. She stepped forward into the spotlight, flanked by her fellow women, their presence radiating solidarity. "Today, we stand together—a united front," she began, her voice steady. "Our vision for the cooperative is about more than just agriculture; it is about empowerment, community, and resilience. We have dreams for our families and our future, and we will not be silenced."

Her words reverberated through the hall, and for a moment, even the skeptics fell silent. The women beside her shared stories of their own struggles, recounting how the cooperative had changed their lives. They spoke of the strength they had found in working together, how the bonds of sisterhood had transformed their perspectives.

As the meeting progressed, some attendees joined in, expressing their own support for the cooperative. Over time, they turned hostile questions into productive dialogue, dismantling fears through open discussion. It became evident that unity was powerful; women were not just standing alongside Isabella—they were rising to face adversity together.

In the days following the meeting, a notable shift occurred in the community. The threats initially laden with fear gave way to tangible acts of solidarity. Women began arriving at the plantation in droves to lend their hands. Each morning, as the sun peeked over the horizon, groups of women gathered, eager to turn the rejuvenation efforts into a powerful statement against oppression.

With shovels, seeds, and smiles, they began planting new crops that would symbolize not just growth but resistance. Laughter and song echoed among the fields, a joyful counterpoint to the negative forces that sought to push them back. The work became a celebration of unity:

hands in the soil, hearts in harmony, and voices raised in defiance of those who wished to see them diminished.

Isabella watched in awe as the women formed a rhythm, working side by side. They exchanged jokes, shared stories of their victories, and encouraged one another through their labor. The physical act of planting became more than just agriculture—it transformed into an embodiment of their resolve. Each seed planted represented a commitment to not only their cooperative but also to each other.

During a particularly hot afternoon, Lydia paused to wipe the sweat from her brow. "This is what it means to be sisters," she stated, looking around at the sea of faces joined in purpose. "We're not just planting seeds; we're cultivating change!"

As the harvest approached, the atmosphere was electric with anticipation. The women rejoiced not just in the produce that would sustain them but, in the strength, they had discovered through their collaboration. They decided to host a community festival, inviting everyone—supporters and skeptics alike—to see the fruits of their labor, to understand that their unity could bring about meaningful transformation.

The festival day arrived, and the community hall was filled with vibrant colors, delicious smells, and sounds of celebration. Isabella and the women proudly displayed the produce they had grown together, their hard work visible in every basket and table.

They served food made from their harvest, mingling with guests, and sharing their stories. "This is what our unity can achieve," Isabella declared, her heart filled with gratitude as she looked at the gathered

162

crowd. "Together, we can create something beautiful that honors our heritage and cultivates a brighter future."

As laughter and music played into the night, Isabella realized that while adversity might have initially felt like a shadow threatening to overshadow their progress, it had brought the women closer together. They had faced fear and oppression not just as individuals but as a powerful collective, ready to stand against any challenge.

With arms linked and eyes shining with determination, Isabella and her sisters raised their glasses in a toast to resilience, solidarity, and the strength of togetherness. Here in this moment of joy and triumph, they had proven that nothing could diminish their spirit. Together, they would continue to sow the seeds of change, nurturing not just their dreams but a shared legacy built on courage, camaraderie, and the unwavering belief that in unity, there is strength.

As the cooperative blossomed under the strength of sisterhood, the women began to uncover the profound impact of their collective voice. United by a vision of empowerment, they recognized that their efforts could extend beyond the fields, reaching into the heart of the community and beyond.

Isabella and Lydia, fueled by the momentum of their recent successes and the support they had garnered, took the lead in organizing outreach initiatives. They understood that visibility was essential for their growth, so they set about developing relationships with local leaders, businesses, and organizations that could provide support and resources.

"Let's show them what we can do," Lydia suggested during one of their evening meetings. "If we want to thrive, we need to share our story with influential people in our area. They need to see not just our goods but the strong women behind them."

Isabella nodded, inspired by her friend's enthusiasm. "You are right. Our story is powerful, it is filled with resilience, hard work, and community spirit. We can highlight everything we have achieved and our mission to empower women. Together, we can create a campaign that captures that essence."

With renewed purpose, they planned a series of community meetings to invite local leaders, growers, and potential partners. The cooperative members came together, creating presentations that showcased their progress and future goals. They practiced their storytelling, honing how they would articulate their mission of empowerment and collaboration.

The day of the first meeting arrived, and nerves tingled in the air as Isabella stood at the front of the room, flanked by Lydia and several women from the cooperative. The faces of local leaders and business representatives filled the seats, many appearing skeptical but intrigued.

This was their moment to shine.

"Thank you all for joining us today," Isabella began, her voice steady despite her racing heart. "We are here not just to share our products but to tell you our story—a story of resilience, community, and the power of women standing together."

As she spoke, she watched the audience lean in with interest, captivated by the passion in her words. Each woman took turns recounting their journey, the challenges they had faced, and the triumphs they had celebrated through the cooperative. They shared not only their dreams for sustainable farming and financial independence but also the deep sense of belonging that their collaboration had fostered.

When they finished, applause erupted, and Isabella felt a wave of validation wash over her. The leaders who had once appeared distant were now engaged, asking questions, and expressing admiration for what the cooperative had achieved.

"Your story is inspiring," one local council member said, his tone shifting as he recognized their potential. "How can we help?"

With excitement and hope, Isabella and Lydia outlined their needs—ranging from seeds and tools to technical expertise and market access. By the end of the meeting, not only had they secured commitments for resources, but they had also ignited interest in their mission. Local leaders offered to connect them with potential sponsors and resources, looking to help elevate the cooperative's visibility.

Buoyed by the success of their outreach, the women felt empowered to take their message further. With the cooperative's first batch of goods nearing completion, they decided to launch a campaign that highlighted both the products and the story behind them. The women pooled their talents—some crafting social media posts, others designing flyers, and many preparing to share their story through local media outlets.

The campaign titled "Roots of Empowerment" aimed to showcase the cooperative's products while emphasizing the journey of the women who produced them. They featured images of women planting, harvesting, and working side by side, their faces glowing with determination. The accompanying text highlighted their commitment to sustainability, empowerment, and community support.

As they promoted their campaign on social media and in community spaces, the response was overwhelming. Local news outlets picked up their story, eager to share the inspiring narrative of women coming together to create something meaningful. The cooperative became more than just a source of goods; it evolved into a symbol of what was possible when women united for a common cause.

With each passing day, their campaign gained traction, and stories of their work spread like wildfire. People from neighboring communities reached out to support their efforts—some offering donations of seeds and supplies, while others expressed interest in joining the cooperative. Isabella felt a swell of pride as she and the women realized that their voices were resonating far beyond their own village.

"It's incredible to see how much attention we've garnered," Lydia remarked one afternoon as they reviewed orders pouring in from local markets interested in selling their products. "We are truly making a difference."

Isabella could not agree more. "This is just the beginning. Our collective voice can keep growing, and we can inspire others to join our cause."

The cooperative's visibility continued to draw support from various corners, transforming it into a hub of female empowerment. Workshops were organized not only for the cooperative members but also for women from other communities. They shared knowledge on sustainable practices, financial management, and entrepreneurship, empowering even more women to rise alongside them.

One sunny afternoon, as they prepared for another workshop, Isabella reflected on how far they had come. The cooperative, once a dream, had now become a beacon of hope and

possibility. The laughter and energy that filled the air reminded her of the bond that had formed through shared struggles and victories.

As the women gathered, Isabella stood before them, feeling a sense of gratitude wash over her. "Together, we have created something incredible. Let us remember that our voice carries every story we share, every product we sell is a testament to our strength. Let us keep advocating for ourselves and each other. We are just getting started."

With renewed determination, the women continued their work, knowing that through their unity and collective voice, they could challenge the status quo and inspire change in their community. The cooperative not only represented their achievements but also the potential to transform lives, proving that when women stand together, the possibilities are endless.

Isabella had a profound belief: every achievement, no matter how small, deserved to be celebrated. As the cooperative began to flourish, she instituted monthly gatherings where the women could come together, share their progress, and reflect on their journeys. These gatherings soon became a cornerstone of the cooperative, a time for connection, gratitude, and the celebration of their hard work.

The first gathering was a vibrant affair, filled with laughter, chatter, and the aroma of home-cooked dishes. Women arrived carrying baskets brimming with produce harvested from their fields, eager to share their bounty. The gathering was held at the community hall, transformed into a warm and inviting space adorned with colorful flowers and hand-painted signs that proclaimed, "Together We Thrive."

"Welcome, everyone!" Isabella announced, her heart swelling with pride as she looked around at the gathering of familiar faces. "Tonight, we're here not just to showcase our achievements but to celebrate each of you and the incredible work you've done."

After a hearty meal prepared from their combined harvest, the atmosphere softened, and stories began to flow. Each woman took turns sharing their successes over the past month. Clara spoke first, her voice bright with enthusiasm. "I started selling my handmade crafts at the local market, and I sold out within hours! I could not believe how supportive the community was!"

The women erupted into applause, embracing Clara's triumph. Inspired, others began to share their stories: Rosa expressed gratitude for learning new planting techniques, while Sofia shared her success in negotiating a better price for their produce with a local store. Each victory, big or small, was met with enthusiasm and encouragement, reinforcing the idea that all achievements contributed to the cooperative's collective strength.

As they shared their stories, Isabella could see how these gatherings fostered a deeper sense of belonging. The women were not just colleagues, they were friends. They laughed together, shared tears over challenges, and celebrated moments of joy, thus nurturing a bond that grew stronger with each passing month.

Realizing the importance of ritual in their celebrations, the women began to incorporate meaningful practices into their gatherings. They created a monthly tradition of honoring hard work by preparing a communal meal from their harvest—a reflection of their combined efforts. Each woman brought in dishes made from their ingredients, and together, they crafted a feast that showcased their labor and unity.

One month, they decided to experiment with new recipes: from hearty vegetable stews to savory pies filled with seasonal produce. The kitchen buzzed with excitement, and Isabella marveled at the teamwork as they chopped, stirred, and baked side by side. The laughter echoed through the hall, and the shared sense of purpose highlighted the joy of their collaborative spirit.

Before the meal, they held a small ceremony, inviting everyone to place an item from their harvest on a communal table. Each item represented the hard work and dedication put forth that month. Isabella pulled the women together in a circle, and they shared a moment of gratitude, acknowledging not just the food but the effort it took to bring it to the table.

"As we gather to share this meal," Isabella said, looking around at the smiling faces, "let us remember that each dish tells a story of our hard work, our passions, and our unity. This feast is not just about sustenance; it symbolizes what we can achieve together."

As they sat down to eat, the atmosphere exploded with joy and camaraderie. Conversations flowed easily, laughter punctuated the air, and for a few hours, their struggles faded into the background. In these moments of celebration, they became intertwined, their lives enriched by the shared experiences and dreams they were cultivating together.

The sense of celebration and gratitude soon transcended their gatherings, inspiring a culture of encouragement within the community. Word of their monthly celebrations spread, attracting more women to the cooperative. Some came to learn about sustainable farming; others were drawn by the sense of community and support that radiated from the cooperative's gatherings.

At each meeting, new women shared their stories—stories of seeking empowerment, overcoming obstacles, and the desire to be part of something bigger. Isabella and the founding members welcomed each newcomer with open arms, knowing that every additional voice would only strengthen their movement.

"You all inspire me," a newcomer named Elena said shyly during one gathering. "I've always felt alone in my struggles, but seeing how you uplift one another makes me feel like I can be a part of something meaningful."

Touched by her sincerity, the women gathered around her, offering words of encouragement and support. "You are not alone anymore, Elena. Welcome to our family," Lydia assured her, and the others echoed her sentiments.

With each passing month, their cause gained traction as they celebrated the lives they were transforming. The cooperative became a hub of empowerment, inspiring neighboring villages to initiate similar gatherings and support local women's endeavors. Women began echoing the sentiment of celebration in their own circles, fostering a ripple effect that encouraged even more to come together in unity.

As the year ended, Isabella felt a sense of fulfillment as she reflected on the progress they had made. Their gatherings had proven to be more than just a ritual; they had become a powerful mechanism for growth and empowerment. Each shared meal, each story told, and each hand clasped strengthened their resolve to uplift not just themselves but the entire community.

At their end-of-year gathering, the mood was festively charged. Women dressed in bright colors, adorned the hall with handmade decorations that celebrated poured, toast was made, and stories were shared, marking the successes and challenges of the past months.

In her closing remarks, Isabella stood once again before her friends, gratitude flooding her heart. "Tonight, we celebrate not just our achievements but the bonds we have formed. Each of you has contributed to our growth—together, we are powerful. Let us carry this spirit of celebration into the new year and continue to uplift one another as we pursue our dreams.

With cheers echoing through the room, the women felt an unbreakable bond flowing among them, one forged by hard work, love, and unwavering support. They knew that whatever challenges lay ahead, they would face them together united by a culture of celebration that would inspire others and bring even more women into their growing movement. Together, they were unstoppable.

SIX

CHALLENGES AND BETRAYAL

As Isabella embarked on her ambitious plan to revive the sugar cane plantation and establish the cooperative, she quickly found herself facing immense challenges that tested her resolve. The vision she had nurtured for so long was not only a dream of economic empowerment but also a radical departure from the traditional roles expected of women in her community.

From the very beginning, Isabella was acutely aware of the societal expectations that loomed over her like a heavy fog. In her village, many believed that a woman's place was in the home, tending to family and managing household duties, rather than pursuing ambitious projects that required leadership and risk-taking. This sentiment was particularly pronounced among the older generations, who often dismissed Isabella's dreams as overreaching and unrealistic.

At community gatherings, Isabella often felt the weight of judgment in the air. While she passionately discussed her plans for the cooperative, she could see the skepticism etched on the faces of some of the older women. "Why would you want to take on such a burden?" they would whisper among themselves. "What about your family? What will your husband think?"

These questions echoed in Isabella's mind, fueling her insecurities, and amplifying the fear of societal judgment. She braced herself against criticism, constantly preparing for the onslaught of doubt that followed her every move. Each time she proposed a new idea, she felt as if she was stepping onto a precarious ledge, balancing the hopes of her community against the weight of traditional expectations.

One afternoon, as she met with a few members of the cooperative to discuss their upcoming plans, the tension in the room was palpable. Clara, usually one of her strongest supporters, hesitated as she spoke. "Isabella, I believe in what we are trying to do, but…what if we fail? What if the community turns against us?"

Isabella's heart sank at Clara's words. She understood the fear that lay behind them, but it stung, nonetheless. "We can't let fear dictate our actions," Isabella replied, her voice firm. "If we do not take these risks, we will never know what we can achieve. We owe it to ourselves to try."

Despite her determination, doubts crept into her mind. The older generations' voices echoed louder with each setback. The fear of judgment loomed large, and she found herself questioning whether her ambitions were too grand, whether she was destined to fail in a world that was not ready for her vision.

As the weeks turned into months, the challenges intensified. The cooperative struggled to secure funding, and logistical issues began to pile up. The initial excitement that had fueled their efforts started to wane, and Isabella sensed a growing hesitance among the women. Rumors circulated, fueled by

those who disapproved of her aspirations. "She's trying to change everything," they would say, their voices dripping with disdain. "What does she know about running a plantation?"

The whispers reached Isabella's ears, and each comment felt like a weight added to her already burdened shoulders. The very people she sought to uplift were now questioning her leadership, and the betrayal stung deeply. She had poured her heart into the cooperative, and now it felt as if the ground was shifting beneath her.

One evening, after a particularly challenging day, Isabella sat alone in her small home, the flickering candlelight casting long shadows across the walls. The isolation felt suffocating. She had fought so hard for her vision, yet the fear of failure and the weight of others' expectations threatened to crush her spirit.

Determined to confront the challenges head-on, Isabella called for a special meeting with the women of the cooperative. She wanted to address the growing doubts and reaffirm their collective commitment to the vision they had built together.

When the day arrived, Isabella stood at the front of the room, her heart racing. "I know that some of you have concerns about our direction," she began, her voice steady but tinged with vulnerability. "I want us to have an honest conversation about what we are facing. We are a team, and it is crucial that we communicate openly."

As the conversation unfolded, tensions flared, and emotions ran high. Some women expressed their fears about the risks involved, while others voiced their support for Isabella's vision. The discussion grew heated, but Isabella remained calm, encouraging everyone to share their thoughts without fear of judgment.

Eventually, Clara spoke up, her voice wavering. "We are all scared, Isabella. We want to support you, but we also fear what will happen if we fail. We have never done anything like this before."

Isabella nodded, understanding the weight of their concerns. "I know this is uncharted territory for us. But remember, every great achievement comes with risk. We are not just building a cooperative; we are breaking barriers and redefining what is possible for women in our community."

As the meeting continued, Isabella felt a shift in the atmosphere. The women began to express their fears openly, and through this vulnerability, they found common ground. They acknowledged the challenges they faced, but they also recognized the strength that came from their unity.

By the end of the gathering, a renewed sense of purpose filled the room. The women agreed to work together to address concerns, establish clearer communication channels, and support one another through the challenges ahead. They understood that while the road would be difficult, they were committed to standing together against societal expectations and doubts.

As Isabella left the meeting, she felt a mixture of relief and determination. The challenges ahead were daunting, but she knew that with the support of her sisters, they could navigate the treacherous waters together. The betrayal she had felt would not define them; instead, it would serve as a catalyst for growth and resilience.

In the days that followed, Isabella found herself more motivated than ever. She focused on strengthening the cooperative's foundation, fostering an environment of encouragement and collaboration. She organized workshops to build skills and confidence among the women, empowering them to embrace their roles as leaders in their community.

Despite the challenges that lay ahead, Isabella remained steadfast in her belief that they could overcome societal expectations and carve out a new path for themselves. With each small victory, she felt the weight of doubt begin to lift, replaced by the unwavering strength of their collective spirit. Together, they would rise, challenging the norms that sought to confine them and proving that women could indeed thrive as leaders, visionaries, and changemakers.

As Isabella embarked on her mission to establish the cooperative, the weight of financial challenges bore down heavily on her. Each day felt like a tug-of-war between her dreams for the plantation and the harsh reality of funding obstacles. Securing the resources needed to breathe new life into the old estate became a daunting quest that tested her resolve.

Banks were hesitant to lend money to a young woman with an untried vision. Despite her well-prepared business plans and passionate proposals, she faced countless rejections. The stark truth was that many local investors preferred to support established male counterparts, choosing to invest in those whose success seemed more assured. Each rejection stung deeply, amplifying her doubts and fears, but Isabella refused to let despair take root.

Determined to find alternative funding sources, Isabella turned her attention to grants and sponsorship opportunities. She spent hours researching various foundations and organizations that supported women-led initiatives and community development projects. By day, she would draft persuasive proposals, while by night, she networked tirelessly, attending community events and meetings aimed at raising awareness about her vision.

In addition to seeking external funding, Isabella organized community fundraising events. Bake sales, donation drives, and local artisan fairs soon filled her calendar. She rallied her friends and neighbors to join the cause, not only to support the cooperative but also to foster a sense of collective ownership in the project. The community's enthusiasm buoyed her spirits, reminding her that she was not alone in this fight.

However, despite her relentless efforts, the financial strain often felt insurmountable. There were days when her budget seemed impossibly tight, and setbacks came in waves. Unexpected expenses associated with the property restoration—a leaky roof here, a broken piece of equipment there—combined with dwindling resources left her feeling overwhelmed. Each obstacle felt like a loud reminder of the uphill battle she faced.

Isabella often found herself pacing through the dusty halls of the plantation, her mind racing with worries. Would she ever find the funding needed to turn the cooperative into a reality? Would the community support her vision long enough to see it through? In these moments of doubt, she would close her eyes and picture the vibrant cooperative she dreamed of—a thriving hub for local women to share resources, learn new skills, and foster entrepreneurship. That vision kept her grounded, even amidst uncertainty.

One afternoon, driven by frustration and the weight of setbacks, Isabella sought solace at her favorite spot under the old banyan tree on the plantation grounds. It was a place where she could collect her thoughts and admire the beauty of the estate that held so much potential. As she closed her eyes, she could almost hear the laughter of children who would one day play in the gardens, the murmur of women sharing stories, and the clinking of glasses celebrating their successes. Suddenly, she felt a hand on her shoulder. It was Javier, who had come to offer support. "Hey," he said softly, sensing her distress. "I thought I might find you here. What is on your mind?"

Isabella opened her eyes, grateful for his presence. "I am just feeling overwhelmed. The financial obstacles keep piling up, and I am not sure how much more I can handle."

Javier sat beside her, in a comforting presence. "You are doing more than most would in your position. It is hard when the odds feel stacked against you, but I believe in your vision. Together, we will find a way."

Encouraged by his words, they sat in companionable silence for a moment before Isabella spoke again. "I just wish I could find one investor willing to take a chance on me. Someone who sees the potential beyond my gender or my age."

Javier nodded thoughtfully. "What about reaching out to local women's organizations? They might have resources or connections to people who would be interested in supporting a women-led initiative. Plus, you could leverage social media to share your story and garner support from a broader audience."

Isabella's eyes brightened at the suggestion. "That could work! If I create a campaign that highlights our mission and the impact this cooperative could have on the community, it might resonate with others. I will need to showcase real stories from the women involved. We need a narrative that draws people in."

"Exactly," Javier replied. "You have a powerful story to tell. And remember, building a network can be just as important as securing funding. You will build relationships with others who share your vision, and they may help you connect with potential investors.

Inspired by their conversation, Isabella felt a renewed sense of purpose. It was true; she had to get the community involved and create a narrative that showcased the transformative impact the cooperative could have. She realized that by creating a sense of collective ownership and involvement, she could turn the tide of support in her favor.

Returning to her planning, Isabella began drafting a strategy for a community outreach campaign. She envisioned workshops where women could share their experiences and aspirations, showcasing the potential the cooperative held for them. Rather than solely focusing on the money needed, her focus shifted to building a cohesive community that would stand behind the cooperative.

As the days turned into weeks, Isabella's efforts began to bear fruit. Emboldened by her new approach, she started to gather stories from local women about their aspirations, using these narratives to craft compelling messaging around the cooperative. The sense of urgency around their mission was palpable, and she felt the tide slowly turning in her favor.

Embracing the collaborative spirit, Isabella involved the women from the cooperative in her fundraising initiatives. They brainstormed ideas, held consultation meetings, and harnessed their collective talents to create events that celebrated their skills. Each step taken fortified their commitment to the cooperative while providing visibility and fostering community support.

Although the financial obstacles remained, Isabella now faced them with a sense of hope and determination. With each small success, she proved that her vision could ignite a movement, one rooted in shared purpose and resilience. She understood that while the road ahead might be challenging, the bonds forged within her community would empower her to overcome adversity.

Guided by love, support, and shared dreams, Isabella knew she was not just fighting for funding but for a movement that would change lives— for herself and others. And that, she realized, was worth every struggle.

As Isabella threw herself into the foundation of the cooperative, she soon discovered that external financial challenges were not the only hurdles she would face. Within the supportive circle she had worked so hard to build, internal conflicts began to surface, threatening the fragile unity among the women involved.

While many of the women shared Isabella's vision for empowerment and solidarity, a palpable tension soon emerged among them. What had initially begun as a collaborative effort quickly revealed varying motivations and expectations that each woman brought to the table. In discussions about the cooperative's direction, differing visions clashed, leading to friction within the group.

One individual at the center of this turmoil was Clara, a charismatic and ambitious member with a talent for persuasive arguments. While her enthusiasm was infectious, Clara's intense ambition sometimes overshadowed the cooperative's core values. She advocated for a more aggressive, profit-driven approach, suggesting they pivot their focus toward maximizing revenue rather than nurturing the community aspect that Isabella held dear. Clara's insistence on a more competitive stance often left the group at odds, polarizing opinions and sparking debates that felt as promising as they were divisive.

"Isabella, we cannot afford to be gentle about this! If we want to be taken seriously, we need a concrete plan that prioritizes profitability," Clara argued during one particularly fraught meeting. Her voice echoed in the small room, her gaze intense as she looked around at the other women, gauging support for her ideas.

Isabella felt her heart sink at these words. "But we cannot lose sight of what makes this cooperative unique—our commitment to uplift one another and create a supportive community. Profit should not be our only focus. We need to build trust and solidarity among ourselves if we want this to last."

Clara's response was swift, laced with heightened emotion. "Trust and solidarity are important, Isabella, but if we do not make money, there will not be anything left to trust! We must position ourselves to compete in the market—otherwise, we will just be another failed initiative."

The room was charged with tension as Clara's words hung heavily in the air. Some women nodded in agreement with Clara, while others shifted uncomfortably, torn between the two perspectives. This growing schism began to manifest as jealousy and competition among members, a stark departure from the cooperative's original intent.

Isabella was caught in the crossfire. On one hand, she wanted to encourage the ambition and drive that Clara embodied; on the other hand, she feared that compromising their core values would undermine the very essence of the cooperative. The spirited discussions—once filled with ideas and camaraderie—had morphed into contentious arguments that complicated decision-making processes and hindered progress.

In quiet moments, Isabella found herself reflecting on the leadership role she had embraced. Was she too lenient? Should she take a firmer stance against Clara's push for a more aggressive business model? Questions churned in her mind, leaving her feeling uncertain and increasingly isolated.

After one particularly tense meeting, she sought solace by walking through the plantation grounds, searching for clarity in the familiar sights. The fields were still and eerily quiet, a stark contrast to the chaos of her thoughts. That is when she spotted a small group of women gathered around the kitchen garden, their laughter drifting through the air like a soothing balm.

Realizing how critical it was to reconnect with the community's foundational spirit, Isabella approached them. As she listened to their lighthearted banter and shared recipes, it felt as if a weight began to lift from her shoulders. It became clear that the cooperative's heart beat strongest when they were united in their values and camaraderie, beyond profit margins and business strategies.

With renewed determination, Isabella decided to address the internal conflicts directly. In the following weeks, she organized a series of workshops focused on collaboration and team building. The aim was to foster open discussions about individual motivations and collective aspirations. She invited women to share their personal stories, hopes for the cooperative, and what they envisioned for their futures.

During these workshops, something remarkable began to happen. Women who had previously held back from sharing began to open, revealing not only their ambitions but also their fears and vulnerabilities. It became evident that many felt the pressure to prove themselves, influenced by societal expectations and past experiences. Clara, too, revealed her struggles to break free from the stigma placed on women in business, a reality that resonated deeply with others.

As the workshops progressed, Isabella emphasized the importance of a shared vision—one that combined aspiration with community-driven values. "We can strive for success while remaining committed to one another. Let us redefine what success means for us," she urged, her voice steady with conviction.

By creating a space for dialogue and understanding, Isabella helped pave the way for healing within the group. Slowly, the divisive energies cooled, replaced by a commitment to work together collaboratively. Clara, while still ambitious, began to see the value in a balanced approach that intertwined profitability with community welfare. "I see now that our strength lies in our unity. If we can support each other, we can also become a force in the market," she admitted during a follow-up meeting.

As the women began to collaborate more effectively, they harnessed their diverse strengths. Decision-making processes became more fluid, and they discovered innovative ways to weave together their differing visions. Together, they reframed their goals—not as isolated ambitions but as collective triumphs founded on mutual respect and support.

Isabella felt a newfound sense of purpose and clarity. The experience taught her that leadership was not just about steering the ship; it was about listening, fostering an environment where every voice was valued, and ensuring that ambitions could coexist with a shared mission.

With tensions eased and a sense of unity restored, the cooperative began to forge ahead with renewed momentum. The vision that had sparked the initiative transformed into a mosaic of ideas, talents, and aspirations, empowering each woman to contribute her uniqueness toward a common goal.

In the months that followed, dynamism surged through the cooperative, breathing life into their plans. They devised community workshops that not only built skills but also celebrated the stories and contributions of each member. Fundraisers became vibrant events, filled with laughter and collaboration, the very spirit Isabella had envisioned from the beginning.

As Isabella worked alongside her fellow women, the weight of internal conflicts gradually lifted. They were not merely a group working toward a goal; they had grown into a supportive community, proving that through honesty, understanding, and collaboration, they could rise above challenges, turning obstacles into steppingstones for success.

What began as a fractured unity evolved into a harmonious and empowered collective—one that exemplified the true strength of women rising together in solidarity. Isabella's journey through these internal conflicts sharpened her leadership and deepened her commitment to nurturing not just the cooperative but the very women at its heart, ensuring that every voice mattered in shaping their future.

In the serene silence of the plantation once more, Isabella knew they were on the cusp of something beautiful legacy of empowerment, resilience, and hope.

Just when Isabella believed she had forged a strong foundation for the cooperative, a storm began brewing within their ranks. Clara's ambition and desire for success turned into fixation, creating an unanticipated rift between them. The once supportive camaraderie began to fracture, and a wave of betrayal would soon challenge everything Isabella had worked for.

Clara's discontent with Isabella's more cautious approach grew increasingly apparent. After several heated discussions, Clara concluded that the only way to jumpstart their venture was to secure funding from influential local businessmen who were willing to sacrifice community values for profit. Disregarding Isabella's vision of a sustainable and community-oriented cooperative, Clara resolved to take matters into her own hands.

Without confiding in the group or Isabella, Clara reached out to Mr. Dorian, a wealthy local businessman known for his involvement in corporate development projects. Under the guise of seeking partnership opportunities, she proposed selling the plantation land for a development project that promised immediate profits—a notion that enticed her with the allure of quick success. Clara believed that aligning with male power players would be the shortcut she needed to achieve their goals, even if it meant jeopardizing their core mission.

When Isabella learned of Clara's secret dealings, her heart plummeted. It was the greatest betrayal she had ever experienced; it felt like a knife plunging into the very fabric of the sisterhood they had labored to build. In the days that followed, fear and confusion gripped Isabella as she struggled to come to terms with the reality of the situation. The revelation sent a shockwave through the cooperative, igniting whispers and uncertainty among the women.

"How could she do this?" Isabella whispered to herself, staring out over the fields, her thoughts racing. Anguish hung in the air as memories of laughter and shared aspirations dulled under the shadow of betrayal. This moment threatened not only Isabella's dream but also the fragile trust she had nurtured among the women.

As news of Clara's intentions spread across the community, many began to question their allegiance to Isabella and the cooperative. Comments like, "Is it worth investing so much time when profits are at stake?" and "Maybe Clara has a point; success can come faster with the right partnerships," pierced Isabella's heart. Doubts regarding her leadership surfaced, and whispers of discontent permeated the air.

Isabella felt the weight of the world on her shoulders. Memories of the collaborative discussions and the bonds forged began to haunt her thoughts. How had it come to this? Clara, who had once stood beside her, was now a potential destroyer of the very dream they had fought for together. The doubts and fears spiraled in her mind, clouding her sense of purpose.

One evening, the tension reached a breaking point during a gathering meant to discuss upcoming community events. When Isabella attempted to address the matter delicately, Clara cut her off, a defiant fire igniting in her eyes. "You are being too sentimental, Isabella! This is not just about feelings; it is about creating real opportunities. I am simply trying to open doors that you seem too afraid to walk through!"

The room fell silent, the air heavy with tension. Isabella's heart raced, torn between betrayal and the need to uphold the cooperative's integrity. "Clara, this dream was never about making money—it was about building something sustainable and empowering for our community. Selling the land would betray everything we stand for."

A ripple of murmurs echoed through the group as the weight of Isabella's words settled. Some women shifted uneasily, caught between their loyalty to Isabella and the tempting allure of Clara's proposition. The conflict intensified as Clara's ambitions came to the forefront, igniting debates that felt less like discussions and more like battles. This was no longer just a disagreement; it was a fracture in their sisterhood, and Isabella felt the persistent ache of vulnerability.

Facing Clara meant confronting not only the betrayal but also the fracture it introduced in the unity they had cultivated. In moments of deep reflection, Isabella wondered how to guide her sisters back to solid ground. She understood that this was not merely about Clara; it posed fundamental questions about their mission, values, and the future of the cooperative.

Determined to reclaim their narrative, Isabella called for a community meeting to address the growing unrest. She wanted to create a space for open dialogues and to reestablish trust. As the women gathered, their expressions mirrored a tangle of confusion, curiosity, and concern. Isabella took a deep breath, her heart pounding as she began to speak.

"Thank you all for coming. I know we are facing a difficult moment, and that is okay. I want us to be transparent about what is happening and to discuss our feelings and thoughts openly," she began, her voice steadier than she felt.

Clara interrupted, "Isabella, these women are here to hear solutions, not just feelings. Let us get to the point."

Isabella acknowledged Clara's urgency, but she pressed on. "I want to hear from each of you. This cooperative was built on the foundation of support and understanding. We must not allow fear or doubts to cloud our values or tear us apart. What do we want for ourselves and for our community?"

As Isabella spoke, she gazed around the room, her eyes meeting those of the women she had come to value dearly. One by one, they began to share their thoughts, fears, and frustrations. The weight of Clara's betrayal hung in the air like a heavy fog, but slowly, it began to lift as the women articulated their hopes and aspirations.

Several women voiced their commitment to the community-focused vision that Isabella had championed. "I believe in empowering each other," said Marisol, her voice steady. "That's what drew me to this cooperative in the first place."

As more women chimed in, the bond that Isabella had nurtured began to reemerge amidst the conflict. They expressed their frustration at the prospect of abandoning their mission, recognizing that while success was desirable, it could not come at the expense of their values.

With each voice that rose in support of her vision, Isabella felt a renewed sense of strength. Clara's ambitious pursuits had drawn the group into conflict, but it also illuminated their shared desires for empowerment, accountability, and standing together against external pressures.

Finally, Isabella turned to Clara, who remained poised yet defiant. "Clara," she said with calm determination, "your ambition can be a powerful force. But I cannot lead this cooperative down a path that veers too far away from our original intent. Our success depends on us standing together, trusting each other, and honoring the bond we have built."

After a long silence, Clara crossed her arms, the fire in her eyes flickering as she considered Isabella's words. Finally, she said, "Maybe I was too focused on the fast track. I just want to succeed for all of us, but I see now that we define success differently."

While tension remained palpable, a glimmer of reconciliation emerged. The women began to forge pathways toward understanding and collaboration, realizing that each of their visions added unique elements to the mosaic of their future.

In the days that followed, Isabella and Clara worked side by side, albeit cautiously, striving to integrate their ideas into a cohesive plan. Clara would focus on seeking out partnerships that complemented the cooperative's values while remaining open to new ideas from others.

The cracks forged by betrayal slowly began to heal, but the scars remained as a reminder of the fragility of trust and the complexities of ambition. Isabella learned that while betrayal could threaten sisterhood, it could also serve as a catalyst for deeper connections and reinvention.

As the weeks intensified, unity continued to blossom among the women. With Isabella and Clara embracing their roles—one as visionary nurturers of communal values and the other as a driven advocate for progress, the cooperative began to emerge stronger than ever. They rekindled their commitment to one another, working together to build a resilient foundation that would withstand future challenges.

While betrayal had tested Isabella's resolve, it enriched her understanding of the dynamics within their circle. It instilled in her an unwavering commitment to prioritize transparency, trust, and fragility in all future dealings. In her heart, Isabella believed that together, they could transform the darkness of betrayal into a landscape of renewed hope—a testament to the unbreakable bonds of sisterhood amid adversity.

As they ventured forward, Isabella understood one essential truth: unity was not the absence of conflict but the commitment to navigate through it together, reaffirming the strength that came from their shared dreams and aspirations. The future lay ahead, illuminating a path forged by resilience, collaboration, and the unwavering spirit of the women of the cooperative.

As the dust settled from the turbulent community meeting, Isabella felt an urgent need to confront Clara directly. The weight of betrayal pressed heavily on her chest, propelling her to seek clarity amidst the chaos that had unfolded. The tension between them simmered, and it was clear that they could no longer dance around the issue.

With a deep breath, Isabella found Clara in the garden, her back turned and shoulders tense as she worked alone. The sun dipped low on the horizon, casting a golden hue over the plantation, but for Isabella, that warmth felt distant.

"Clara," she called softly, approaching cautiously.

Clara turned slowly, surprise flashing across her face, which quickly faded into a guarded expression. "What do you want, Isabella?" Her tone was sharp, laden with the remnants of indignation.

"I want to talk about what happened," Isabella replied, her voice steady but her heart racing. "I want to understand why you didn't trust me enough to share your thoughts beforehand."

"Trust?" Clara scoffed. "You mean your idealism? I am trying to save this cooperative while you cling to naïve dreams! Change is necessary for survival." The anger in Clara's voice cut through the air, sharp and unyielding.

Isabella felt the fire rise within her, emotions swirling like a tempest. "Naïve?" she echoed incredulously. "What is naïve is abandoning our

190

values for the sake of profits! We have an obligation to each other and to our community. This is not just a business; it is about building something meaningful together!"

The confrontation escalated, their voices rising in passionate exchange. Clara's frustrations exploded as she gestured emphatically. "Do you seriously think we can make a difference clinging to outdated ideals? Corporations do not care about dreams; they care about results! You are risking everything by being stubbornly idealistic!"

"Stubbornness? This place was built on trust and solidarity, both of which you seem willing to throw away!" Isabella shot back, emotion tightening her throat. "I believed you understood that!"

The air crackled with tension, and for a heart-stopping moment, it felt as if the world hung between them. Clara's eyes narrowed, and for a brief second, Isabella saw a flicker of uncertainty within her. "I just want what's best for all of us," Clara muttered, her defensive posture wavering slightly.

"It's easy to equate what's best with what's easiest, Clara," Isabella replied, softer now. The fight seemed to dissipate for a moment, replaced by the shared hurt. "But if we buckle at the first sign of difficulty, what does that say about our dreams? We can achieve success on our own terms, but we must do it together."

The silence that followed was deafening. Clara's expression shifted, revealing a mix of frustration and conflict. "You can't expect everyone to share your vision," she said quietly. "Ambition can breed jealousy and fear."

"Maybe," Isabella admitted, her heart aching as she recognized the truth in Clara's words. "But that does not mean we have to turn against each other. Trust is everything, Clara. I need to trust the women in this cooperative, and I need to trust myself as a leader. This betrayal cuts deeper than I expected."

In the end, Isabella left the garden with a swirl of emotions—hurt and disappointment intertwined with a strengthened resolve. It was a confrontation that underscored their divergent paths, forcing her to reevaluate her relationships with other women in the cooperative.

In the days that followed, Isabella found herself lost in reflection. The betrayal had unleashed a torrent of insecurities, and she began to question her ability to lead. Each decision she made felt heavy with doubt, casting shadows on her instincts. Every encounter with her fellow women stirred unease within her, as if every smile concealed the potential for betrayal.

Was she too trusting? Had their shared dreams ignited envy instead of the sisterhood she longed for? The weight of these questions bore down on her, challenging the very foundation she had sought to build.

One night, as she stared out at the stars twinkling overhead, Isabella felt vulnerable and exposed, grappling with the complexities of leadership. She recognized that ambitious dreams could invoke jealousy and fear, compelling individuals to act in self-interest rather than in unity. It was a painful lesson, underscoring the reality that the road to collective success was fraught with obstacles, both external and internal.

With each passing day, though, Isabella developed a deeper understanding of her role. The betrayal, while painful, became a catalyst for growth. She realized that it reinforced her responsibility to foster an environment of transparency and support among the women.

It was a reminder that leadership required vigilance and an unwavering commitment to trust-building, even in the face of adversity.

In her heart, Isabella still clung to the belief that their shared mission could triumph over personal ambitions. But she also understood that such a path required honesty and accountability—of herself and others. This experience had opened her eyes to the nuanced dynamics of sisterhood and leadership.

While the branches of her dream no longer felt ironclad, Isabella remained committed to nurturing the roots of trust and collaboration. This required acknowledging vulnerabilities while remaining steadfast in her vision. She would not allow betrayal to extinguish her dreams; instead, she would rise stronger, resolved to protect the sisterhood she had fought so tirelessly to create.

With each reflection, Isabella reaffirmed her dedication to the cooperative and its women. She understood that true leadership was not just about embracing ambition but also about balancing dreams with integrity, ensuring that every voice was honored, and nurturing an environment where collaboration flourished.

Thus, while the shadow of Clara's betrayal lingered, it also illuminated a path forward—a reminder that through the struggle, the cooperative could still unite, transform adversity into strength, and inspire a legacy of resilience and hope for generations to come.

With Clara's betrayal still fresh in her mind, Isabella felt an escalating tension with another member of the cooperative—Lottie. Known for her pragmatic approach and sharp intuition, Lottie had always been an advocate for change, but her intentions began to feel increasingly at odds with Isabella's vision. Determined to address the growing rift,

Isabella sought out Lottie, needing to confront the simmering discord between them.

Isabella found Lottie in the kitchen, meticulously preparing a meal for an upcoming community gathering. The scent of spices filled the air, but the warmth of the kitchen felt muted amidst the rising tension.

"Lottie," Isabella began, her voice steady but strained. "Can we talk for a moment?"

Lottie paused, wiping her hands on a dishtowel. "About what, Isabella? More ideals and dreams?" Her tone was teasing yet tinged with sarcasm, a clear indication that she was on the defensive.

"It's about the cooperative," Isabella replied, taking a deep breath to steady her resolve. "I feel like we are drifting apart in our vision for what this should be. I need to understand where you stand."

Lottie crossed her arms, her posture instantly guarded. "Where do I stand? I stand for progress, Isabella! You have been so focused on your idealism that you are blind to the fact that we need to adapt, or we will fail. It is the real world out there; you cannot stick your head in the sand and expect everything to magically work out!"

Isabella's heart raced, her instincts flaring. "So, your answer is to abandon everything we have built? To sell out for a quick profit? What happened to the community we aimed to empower, the sisterhood we have fought so hard for?"

"Empowerment doesn't pay the bills!" Lottie shot back, her voice rising. "Change is necessary for survival. Do you think Clara was wrong in seeking support from Mr. Dorian? This is not just about you and your dreams; it is about all of us trying to create something that lasts. Your idealism is naïve!"

Hurt surged through Isabella. She felt the sting of Lottie's words cutting deep, but she knew she could not back down now. "No, Lottie! What is naive is thinking we can achieve anything meaningful while sacrificing our values. We owe it to ourselves and our community to uphold what we believe in! The moment we compromise our integrity, we lose everything!"

The tension between them was palpable, and they stood locked in their shared disappointment. "I wish you could see that without change, there is no hope. The world will not wait for our ideals! You must be realistic!" Lottie asserted, her passion igniting an urgency in her words.

"This cooperative was built on trust and sisterhood, not compromise of our beliefs!" Isabella shot back, her heart now pounding with a mix of frustration and sadness. "If we lose sight of that, we will become just like the corporations we're trying to stand against."

The confrontation left both women breathless. Lottie, typically composed, was visibly shaken, and Isabella felt the weight of the conflict settle into the pit of her stomach.

After an uncomfortably long silence, Lottie turned away, her shoulders tense. "Maybe I don't fit into your perfect picture as much as I thought," she muttered under her breath, making it clear she had no intention of furthering this argument.

Isabella, shocked by Lottie's retreat, felt a profound sense of loss wash over her. Loss not just for her friendship with Lottie but for the ideals they had shared. This intense exchange of emotions pushed Isabella to reflect deeply, forcing her to consider the vulnerabilities within her leadership and the fragility of the relationships she had worked tirelessly to cultivate.

The days following the confrontation were heavy with contemplation. Isabella found herself questioning not only her relationships with Lottie and Clara but also her very capacity to lead. Could she effectively balance her dreams for the cooperative with the need for practical change? Did her idealism have any place in a world that seemed increasingly pragmatic and ruthless?

Lying awake one night, Isabella faced the tumult within her. Doubt began to creep in, a shadow cast over her resolve. She realized that ambition could invoke jealousy and fear, a reality she had previously ignored. She had believed in the power of sisterhood, of shared aspirations uniting them, but now she understood that the pursuit of lofty dreams could sometimes drive wedges between even the strongest bonds.

The experience weighed heavily on her heart, yet amidst the turmoil, it also sparked a newfound strength within her. She contemplated what leadership truly meant. It would require more than just nurturing an ideal; it demanded the ability to navigate complex emotions, foster open dialogue, and embrace the inevitable conflicts that would arise.

As she reflected, Isabella recognized that while betrayal had shattered some aspects of her trust, it also reinforced the necessity for clarity in her mission. True leadership involves being transparent about dreams and aspirations while also being willing to listen and adapt in the face of differing perspectives.

While ambivalence lingered in her heart, Isabella steeled herself to confront these uncertainties. She chose not to allow the betrayal and

196

discord to define her path forward. Instead, she would view them as moments of growth—a way to cultivate resilience and deepen her commitment to accountability and support within their cooperative.

In the days that followed, Isabella resolved to engage more deeply with her fellow women, encouraging honest conversations about their fears and ambitions while reaffirming the core values that had brought them together. She would strive to create an environment where all voices could be heard, where differing visions could coexist, and where collaboration could flourish.

In doing so, she hoped to mend the fractures that had threatened their sisterhood while remaining steadfast in her commitment to the cooperative's mission. Isabella understood that the journey ahead would not be easy, but it was necessary for the survival of their dreams and for the growth of their community.

Through the struggles of confrontation and reflection, Isabella emerged with a renewed sense of purpose. Navigating the complexities of leadership would be an ongoing endeavor, but she was ready to embrace it, inviting her sisters to join her in shaping a future built on unity, understanding, and an unwavering shared hope.

In the wake of her confrontations with Clara and Lottie, Isabella found solace in the realization that she was not alone in her struggle. While betrayal had splintered some alliances, it had also illuminated the unwavering support of other women within the cooperative who still believed in her vision. They shared her commitment to building a nurturing community grounded in trust, and Isabella knew that together, they could overcome the challenges ahead.

Isabella called upon these women, gathering them for an informal meeting in the common room of the cooperative. The energy in the air was different—thicker, charged with both uncertainty and an eagerness to come together as a united front. The room filled with warmth as they settled into a circle, reflecting the sense of solidarity that Isabella hoped to cultivate.

"Thank you all for being here. I know times are tough, and recent events have shaken us," Isabella began, her voice steady. "But it is crucial that we do not lose sight of why we started this cooperative. We have a shared vision that can still thrive if we work together."

Several women nodded in agreement, with Marisol speaking up first. "We have built something beautiful here, Isabella, and it is worth fighting for. I believe in what we can achieve together."

Encouraged by Marisol's words, Isabella continued, "I want to create a space where we can openly discuss the challenges we are facing— together. We cannot let fear or mistrust dictate our actions. We need transparency and collaboration to move forward."

As the meeting unfolded, women began to share their thoughts and feelings openly. They voiced concerns about the future and the impact of the recent betrayals but also reaffirmed their commitment to the cooperative's ideals. The conversation flowed freely, encouraging mutual respect and understanding.

In the spirit of rebuilding trust, Isabella introduced a series of community meetings where they could confront issues head-on. "Let us gather regularly, not just to discuss problems, but to celebrate our successes, too. We need to uplift one another and reinforce our bonds," she suggested, her passion igniting a spark in the room.

Lottie was not present that day, but her absence was felt. Regardless, Isabella chose to focus on the connections that remained strong, recognizing that mending the skeletal cracks of their sisterhood required patience and consistent effort.

As days turned into weeks, the community meetings became a cornerstone of their cooperation. The discussions illuminated a range of perspectives, revealing the unique challenges each woman faced in her journey. They brainstormed ideas, shared experiences, and celebrated small victories together, fostering a sense of belonging and empowerment.

One evening, Marisol proposed a creative workshop to involve the entire community, integrating their talents while reinforcing their sisterhood. "Let us organize a craft fair! We can showcase our skills and share our stories. It could also bring in some income to support our cooperative," she suggested excitedly.

"Great idea!" Isabella replied, feeling a renewed sense of hope. "This will highlight our strengths and build connections not only among ourselves but with the broader community as well."

They set to work, pouring their hearts into the craft fair planning. The enthusiasm was palpable as each woman contributed her unique talents—some crafted beautiful textiles while others whipped up delicious treats or created artwork to display. Conversations flowed as they collaborated, each laughter and shared experience knitting them closer together.

As the day of the fair approached, Isabella watched in awe as the women transformed their energy into an event that weaved their dreams into reality. They hung colorful banners and set up tables adorned with their handcrafted goods, each corner of the venue bursting with creativity and camaraderie. The overall atmosphere radiated something Isabella had fought to preserve: a spirit of unity.

When the event finally unfolded, the support of the local community was overwhelming. Neighbors, families, and friends flocked to the fair, celebrating the women's resilience and talent. It became a platform not just for showcasing their crafts but for storytelling, connecting them with a shared purpose that extended beyond individual ambitions.

Throughout the fair, Isabella observed the connections forming between women who had previously felt isolated or uncertain. Bonds that had been fractured began to heal as they shared not only their triumphs but also their challenges. Isabella felt a surge of pride within her, the realization that their collective vision was anything, but naivety was rooted in the very values they were nurturing together.

As night fell on a successful day filled with laughter and joy, Isabella stood outside under a canopy of stars, her heart full. She knew that the road ahead would not be easy, and the undercurrents of jealousy and fear might always linger, but she was no longer fighting alone. With the support of her loyal sisters, she could remain steadfast in her ideals and help them navigate the complexities of their journeys.

In the days that followed, they faced new challenges, some logistical, some emotional. Yet each conversation, each meeting, and each collective action reaffirmed their commitment to one another and their mission. They began to rebuild not only trust but also a shared foundation upon which they could grow.

While Isabella knew that Clara and Lottie's perspectives were valid and necessary for the evolution of the cooperative, she also understood that the essence of their community lay in valuing all voices, fostering inclusivity, and remaining true to their core beliefs. It was a delicate balance but one worth maintaining.

Isabella's experience had transformed her understanding of leadership. She recognized that it was not simply about guiding others but about cultivating an environment where authentic conversations could flourish, where dreams could thrive while still accounting for reality. As challenges arose, she committed to facing them head-on, reminding herself that vulnerability was not a weakness but a strength that opened pathways for deeper connections.

Through the support of her sisters and the bonds they were reforming, Isabella felt an indomitable spirit. Together, they would navigate the complexities of their cooperative, transforming every obstacle into an opportunity to connect, grow, and fulfill their shared vision. As they ventured forward, Isabella's heart swelled with hope, determined to champion the cooperative's ideals, and ensure that their journey was a testament to the power of unity, resilience, and sisterhood.

Isabella stepped off the small bus at the bustling terminal in Roseau, the capital city, alive with energy and movement. The air was thick with a blend of savory spices from nearby food stalls and the rich aroma of fresh coffee from street vendors calling out to passersby. It wanted to step into another world a sharp contrast to the serene landscapes of her island home, but invigorating, nonetheless.

As she navigated through the crowded streets, the sounds of laughter, shouts of merchants selling their wares, and the distant clanging of a steel drum parade enveloped her senses. Colorful awnings decorated the narrow streets, where lively shops brimmed with handcrafted goods, vibrant textiles, and local produce. The diversity of the city reflected the energy of its people, each face a story waiting to be told.

Isabella took a deep breath, feeling a rush of excitement mixed with determination. Today was significant. She had come to Roseau not only to experience its vibrancy but to seek allies for her cooperative— leaders and activists who could help her navigate the political landscape and amplify her vision for empowering women in her community.

Making her way toward the Roseau Market, a hub of activity and a meeting point for locals and tourists alike, she felt a growing sense of purpose. The market was alive with voices, colors, and sights, where vendors showcased everything from fresh tropical fruits to intricate handmade crafts. Isabella paused at a stall selling watermelon and exchanged pleasantries with the vendor, absorbing the warmth of the interaction.

As she pressed on, she spotted a group of activists gathered near the government buildings, their passionate voices rising above the din of the market. A banner reading "Empower the Women, Enrich the Nation" fluttered in the breeze, drawing Isabella closer. Her heart raced as she joined the crowd, inspired by the fervor of those around her.

One of the speakers, a seasoned activist named Rosa, was addressing the group with a voice full of conviction. "Women are the backbone of our communities! When we empower them, we empower our entire nation!" This resonated deeply with Isabella, igniting a fire within her. She had come here to seek connections, but now she felt called to contribute to the conversation.

Rosa's speech ended, and Isabella stepped forward, raising her hand to gain the speaker's attention. "Excuse me! My name is Isabella Philogene, and I am from the Colihaut community where I am working to establish an agricultural cooperative to empower local women." She paused, feeling the eyes of the crowd on her. "I believe that by joining forces, we can make a real difference."

A murmur of interest rippled through the crowd, and Rosa smiled encouragingly. "Every initiative matters, Isabella. Collectively, our voices will create the change we seek. Let us hear more about your vision."

As Isabella shared her story—the struggles of local women, her plans for sustainable agriculture, and her dreams for the cooperative—the energy in the crowd shifted. Heads nodded in understanding, and faces lit up with enthusiasm. Afterward, many approached her, eager to offer support and share their own experiences, creating a palpable sense of solidarity in the air.

Later, as the sun began to dip toward the horizon, casting golden hues across the sky, Isabella and her new allies gathered at a nearby café. They discussed strategies for outreach and advocacy, brainstorming ways to connect her cooperative with broader networks of support. Isabella felt a surge of hope as she realized the potential of their collaboration.

"I believe we can create a coalition that not only supports your cooperative but also amplifies the voices of women across the region," Rosa suggested, her eyes sparkling with excitement. "Together, we can advocate for policies that prioritize women's empowerment and sustainable practices."

Isabella nodded vigorously, her heart swelling with gratitude. "That is exactly what I envisioned! I want our cooperative to be a model for others, showing that women can lead and succeed in agriculture without relying on external influences."

As they exchanged ideas, Isabella felt the weight of her mission lighten. The collective energy of the group fueled her ambition, and she realized that she was no longer alone in her fight. Their discussions ranged from organizing workshops to create awareness about women's contributions in agriculture to planning community rallies that would draw attention to their cause.

As they wrapped up their meeting, Rosa reached out to Isabella, placing a reassuring hand on her shoulder. "You have a powerful vision, Isabella. Remember, the journey may be challenging, but you have allies now. Together, we will pave the way for change."

With her determination strengthened and new connections forged, Isabella left Roseau with a renewed sense of purpose, her heart set on returning home to rally her community with the knowledge and support she had gained. The journey ahead would be challenging, but she felt ready to take on the fight for the women she cherished, armed with the power of unity and shared vision.

As she boarded the bus back to her village, Isabella reflected on the vibrant city and the passionate individuals she had met. Roseau, with its thrumming pulse of life and activism, had become an unexpected ally. She felt invigorated, ready to channel the energy she had experienced into her cooperative, knowing that she was part of a larger movement for change.

The road ahead was still fraught with challenges, but Isabella was no longer daunted. She had transformed her visit to Roseau into a powerful catalyst for her mission, and she was determined to lead her community forward, one step at a time.

Determined not to let Clara's actions derail their efforts, Isabella returned from her empowering visit to Roseau with a renewed sense of purpose. The connections she forged with local leaders and activists—especially Rosa—had equipped her with the inspiration and tools needed to protect her cooperative from external threats. She realized that they needed to approach their mission not only with resolve but with a strategic plan that would defend their vision and strengthen their ties.

Isabella gathered the women of the cooperative to discuss their way forward. "We cannot let betrayal define us or our mission," she began, her voice steady. "Instead, we will turn this setback into strength. Our resolve to support one another must be stronger than ever."

She outlined her strategy: they would engage in active outreach to local activists and allies who shared their vision for empowerment. Leveraging the relationships she had cultivated in Roseau; Isabella knew they could build a coalition that would counter the prevailing narrative suggesting women could not succeed without the influence of powerful men. Together, they would showcase the strength of their cooperative and the remarkable achievements of its members.

"We will reignite the spirit of unity in our community," Isabella declared, her passion igniting a fire in the hearts of the women gathered. "Let us launch a campaign that highlights our successes and the value of women-led enterprises. We will show them that we can achieve greatness on our own terms."

In the days that followed, Isabella, alongside her allies, organized a series of workshops and collaborative projects. They focused on sustainable agricultural practices and skills training, inviting women from all backgrounds to participate. The cooperative soon became a rallying point for women from neighboring communities looking to empower themselves through shared knowledge and resources.

Rosa, passionate about grassroots activism, encouraged Isabella to implement advocacy efforts that would elevate their voices beyond the confines of the cooperative. "Let's hold a community rally where we can share our stories and success," she suggested eagerly. "We need everyone to see that the achievements of one woman represent the strength of all of us."

Isabella loved the idea and expanded it further. The Women's Empowerment Rally would not only highlight their collective achievements but also serve as a platform for women to speak about their journeys, emphasizing the importance of self-sufficiency and collaboration. They set a date, and excitement swept through the cooperative as they began preparations.

The rally attracted attention from various media outlets, amplifying their message across the region. As Isabella worked tirelessly to organize the event, she invited women from different backgrounds— small business owners, artists, educators, and activists—each bringing their unique stories and successes to the forefront.

As the day of the rally approached, the cooperative pulsed with energy and anticipation. Women poured their hearts into their preparations, creating banners and logos that represented their mission. They shared ideas for speeches and performances, ensuring that the event was a true celebration of their collective strength.

On the day of the rally, the atmosphere was electric. The community center was adorned with colorful decorations, and the air was filled with the sounds of laughter, chatter, and music. Isabella stood at the entrance, welcoming participants, her heart swelling with pride as she witnessed the outpouring of support.

As the rally commenced, Isabella took the stage alongside Rosa and other women from the cooperative. Each speaker shared personal stories of resilience, how they had navigated challenges and embraced their strengths. Their words resonated deeply with the audience, sparking conversations that would ripple beyond the event.

"We are here to prove that we are capable," Isabella passionately addressed the crowd. "We are building a future where women can thrive independently, without the shadow of someone else's influence. Each one of us has a role to play, and together, we are a force to be reckoned with!"

The crowd erupted in applause, a chorus of voices lifting her spirit higher. In that moment, Isabella realized that they had already begun to rewrite their narrative. Clara's betrayal had initially threatened to fracture their mission, but instead, it had galvanized them, creating a stronger bond among the women of the cooperative.

As the sun dipped below the horizon, casting a warm glow over the gathering, Isabella watched as women celebrated not only their successes but also their potential for growth. The rally had transitioned into a celebration of unity, resilience, and hope. Conversations flowed freely, with women exchanging ideas and opportunities for collaboration, fueling the energy of the movement they were building together.

In the following weeks, the cooperative flourished under the momentum of the rally. With newfound confidence, they expanded their outreach efforts, directly supporting women in their community and beyond. Workshops on entrepreneurship, leadership, and self-advocacy empowered participants to take charge of their futures.

Isabella's vision had evolved; she now recognized that their cooperative was more than just a business model—it was a movement. Together, the women transformed their achievements into a tapestry woven with tales of empowerment, challenge, and solidarity. They centered their focus on cultivating an environment where each woman's success was celebrated and valued.

The cooperative had indeed become a rallying point for women's empowerment, and Isabella felt a deep sense of fulfillment as she reflected on how far they had come. They had turned betrayal into strength, showing the world that through determination, unity, and resilience, women could thrive together—independently and powerfully. As Isabella looked ahead, she knew the journey was just beginning, but she felt ready to embrace whatever lay ahead, knowing that she was not alone. Together, they would continue to dismantle narratives that limited them, proving that empowered women truly could change the world.

SEVEN

THE TURNING POINT

The turning point in Isabella's story unfolded dramatically during a pivotal community meeting that had been convened to discuss the future directions of the cooperative. The hall was filled with expectant faces, women radiating hope and determination as they gathered to celebrate their progress and strategize the next steps in their journey of empowerment.

Isabella stood at the front, her heart buoyed by the passion and energy around her. "Together, we have built something incredible," she began, noting the enthusiasm radiating from the women who had rallied around their cooperative. "By supporting each other, we have created a foundation for lasting change in our community. Our next steps will help solidify our purpose and expand our impact."

As she spoke, she noticed Clara lingering near the back. Clara had been a significant part of their efforts, her charisma and persuasive nature often drawing others into their cause. However, doubt loomed over Isabella as she caught glimpses of Clara's distracted demeanor. Just days before, Isabella had sensed something was amiss, but she had chosen to trust in their shared vision.

Just as she was about to outline the plans for their upcoming initiatives, Clara stepped forward, her expression unreadable. "Excuse me, everyone. It is time to share something important," she said, a hint of defiance in her voice. The murmurs of the crowd quieted, all eyes turning to her.

Isabella's stomach knotted. This did not feel right.

Clara's gaze swept over the room, locking onto Isabella for a moment before she continued, "I've made a decision that I believe will benefit our community." She paused, letting the tension build before revealing her startling news. "I'm partnering with Mr. Dorian to sell the land for a new commercial development project."

The air in the room turned electric, a collective gasp echoing off the walls. Isabella felt as if the ground had shifted beneath her feet. "What? Clara, you cannot be serious!" she exclaimed, her voice tinged with disbelief and hurt. "This land is our future, our cooperative! We have been working so hard to establish something meaningful here!"

Clara's demeanor hardened. "We're in a crisis!" she shot back. "The community needs economic growth now, and Mr. Dorian's project will bring jobs and investment. We need to open our eyes to reality! The cooperative is just a dream without substantial backing."

Isabella felt a wave of betrayal crashing over her. This was not the Clara she had trusted, the Clara who had stood beside her in meetings, who had raised her voice for women's empowerment. "But what about the sisterhood we have built? The trust we have established. You are jeopardizing everything!" Isabella's voice trembled with sorrow and disbelief.

The room erupted into a chaotic mix of protest and confusion.

The women, who had stood united in their mission, were now thrown into disarray at the revelation of Clara's plans. Those who had looked to Clara for leadership now felt a deep sense of betrayal, their eyes darting between Clara and Isabella, uncertainty clouding the meeting.

"I can't believe you'd do this to us, Clara," Rosa interjected, her voice a blend of anger and disappointment. "This is not just about you; it affects all of us! We built this together, not just to sell it off to the highest bidder!"

Clara's expression shifted to one of irritation and resolve. "I am doing what I believe is necessary for our community's survival. You are being naive, thinking your dreams can sustain this place. Change is hard, but it is real. I am not backing down."

The crisis spiraled from there. Isabella felt as if the very foundation of sisterhood and the solidarity she had worked tirelessly to cultivate was crumbling before her eyes. Each woman's face reflected the hurt and confusion. Whispered conversations erupted as leaders confronted Clara, questioning her motives and the reality of her plans. Clara's attempt to frame her actions as a "necessary evil" only deepened the chasm between her and the women who had trusted her.

In that moment, Isabella knew she had to take a stand for what she believed in. "We fought hard to create a vision that empowers us, that respects our land and our values," she declared, her voice rising above the tumult. "We must stand together against this betrayal. We cannot let Clara's actions define us or our future!"

But Clara remained defiant. "You cannot stop progress, Isabella. I am making the necessary deal for all of us, whether you choose to see it or not." Her words hung heavy in the air, a threat that cut deep and left Isabella gasping for air in disbelief.

The truth weighed heavily on Isabella's heart: Clara was not just a friend but also a formidable opponent. Her betrayal resonated beyond the immediate shock; it threatened to tear apart the very fabric of the cooperative and destroy everything they had fought to create.

In the days that followed the meeting, Isabella faced the crisis with undeniable resolve. She convened emergency gatherings with the cooperative members, emphasizing the need to confront the threat and protect their vision from what Clara had initiated. They strategized counterarguments to highlight the importance of community-led initiatives that prioritized women's empowerment over short-term profits.

Isabella sought to galvanize support not only among the women of the cooperative but also within the larger community. "We must remind them what is at stake," she urged. "If we let Clara's actions go unchallenged, we risk losing our land, our heritage, and the very foundation of sisterhood that has united us."

As they rallied together, Isabella understood that the path ahead would not be easy. Clara's betrayal, while painful, also fueled a fire within them—a determination to fight back and defend their cooperative at all costs. The struggle for the plantation had transformed into a battle for their unity and vision.

Facing the unfolding crisis, Isabella vowed not to let Clara's betrayal be the end of their story. With renewed vigor, she dedicated herself to reclaiming the narrative, drawing strength from her sisters and the community around her. They would prove that women could succeed on their own terms, working together to reclaim the future they had fought to create.

The urgency of the moment pressed upon them, and with each passing day, Isabella felt the push of destiny guiding her forward. She was prepared to take a stand, to challenge betrayal with unity, and to protect not just the land, but the dreams of every woman who had dared to believe in a brighter future.

As news of Clara's actions spread throughout the community, the fracture within the cooperative deepened. The initial shock of her betrayal crystallized into an undeniable division, drawing lines that pitted sister against sister. Isabella watched helplessly as some women rallied behind her, reaffirming their commitment to her vision of empowerment and sustainability, while others seemed tantalized by the prospect of immediate financial gain heralded by Clara.

"What Clara is proposing is a lifeline," those in favor of her plan asserted during heated discussions. "We cannot ignore the fact that our community is in a crisis. Businesses are closing, jobs are scarce. We need this development!" Their voices, infused with desperation, echoed around the room, pressing against Isabella's heart.

Clara's arguments about adapting to a changing economic landscape resonated with women who felt the weight of their financial struggles. The allure of quick profits and new employment opportunities painted a tempting picture, enticing those who worried about their families' futures.

"It's about survival, Isabella," one member urged, her eyes glistening with unshed tears. "We cannot be idealistic when so many around us are suffering. This will help us build a better tomorrow now!"

Isabella stood before the gathered women, feeling as if the ground was crumbling beneath her. Why couldn't they see the long-term consequences of Clara's proposed partnership? "Each of us has fought so hard to establish this cooperative," she implored. "We are not just building a business; we are building a legacy for future generations. If we sell out now, what will that mean for our daughters and the community we serve?"

But the atmosphere in the room was charged with tension, uncertainty hanging over them like a storm cloud. Some women furrowed their brows, torn between loyalty to Isabella and the seductive promise of prosperity. Others crossed their arms, their expressions hardened, unwilling to sway.

In the days that followed, the rifts became sharper. Informal alliances formed, creating factions that pitted some women against each other. They no longer gathered to celebrate achievements or seek inspiration; instead, meetings devolved into intense arguments where trust was replaced by accusations.

As the leader, Isabella felt the weight of responsibility crush her. Was she failing them? On nights when the moon cast shadows over the land, she lay awake questioning her decisions, fearing that she had not been strong enough to hold them together. Self-doubt crept into her thoughts, whispering that her vision was too ambitious, that she had misjudged Clara all along.

Feeling increasingly isolated, Isabella turned to Rosa, her steadfast ally. "I don't know how to move forward," she confessed one evening, her voice barely above a whisper. "Every time I speak, it feels like I am shouting into a void. I thought we all shared the same dream, but now… it is falling apart."

Rosa listened intently, her expression a mixture of empathy and determination. "You cannot lose faith now. Yes, the division is painful but think about those who stand with you. They believe in what you are fighting for. We need to remind everyone of what we have built together."

"Remind them?" Isabella echoed, feeling a flicker of hope ignited within her. "But how do we reach those who have been swayed by Clara's promises?"

Rosa's eyes sparkled with determination. "We hold a gathering— something to celebrate our victories and share our stories. We can shine a light on the true impact of our work,

showing how far we have come. If we help them remember why they trusted us in the first place, we can bridge the divide.

With renewed energy, Isabella agreed to plan an event that would showcase the cooperative's achievements and the strength of their mission. They aimed to create a safe space where women could express their fears and aspirations while feeling supported by their shared experiences.

As preparations began, Isabella felt a pulse of purpose return. She reached out to women who remained loyal, inspiring them to share their own stories of empowerment and growth. Together, they crafted an agenda that highlighted their shared values, emphasizing not just the potential for economic growth but the importance of building a sustainable community where everyone could thrive.

However, Isabella knew Clara would not back down without a fight. As the day of the gathering approached, Clara's influence grew ever more evident. Her supporters felt increasingly emboldened, believing they were making the right choice for their families and the community.

The tension reached a peak on the day of the event. As Isabella prepared to welcome everyone, she felt a knot of anxiety in her stomach. Women began to arrive, some wearing expressions of hope, others still clouded with uncertainty. Upon entering the cooperative space, Clara and her supporters stood off to the side, sparking whispers and side-eye glances.

Isabella took a deep breath, preparing herself before addressing the gathering. "Thank you all for being here today," she began, her voice steady despite the turbulent emotions swirling within her. "We stand at a crossroads not just for ourselves, but for the generations to come. Our choices today will affect how we define our community in the future."

Clara stepped forward, her eyes glinting with determination. "Isabella, I respect what you are trying to do, but you must face the reality of our situation. The world is changing, and we must adapt. Selling to Mr. Dorian is not selling out; it is seizing an opportunity. Why hold on to an ideal that is only keeping us in stagnation?

The air crackled with tension as Isabella responded, "But what kind of future do we want to build? One that benefits a few at the cost of our home and sense of community.

Our strength lies not in short-term gains but in the bonds we create."

The battle of ideals was palpable. Tension hung heavy as the women chose sides, some clapping in agreement with Isabella, while others quietly nodded along with Clara's arguments. The uncertainty of how the community would emerge from this turmoil loomed larger than ever.

Just when it appeared that the divide might deepen further, a woman from the back spoke up—a soft voice filled with clarity. "What if we could find a way to challenge Mr. Dorian's proposal while still seeking a path to economic growth? We have built a cooperative based on collaboration and shared values. Why can't we innovate together?"

Silence enveloped the room as Isabella felt a surge of hope. The idea of collaboration, the very essence of what they stood for—could bridge the division. "That's exactly it," Isabella said, her enthusiasm revitalizing her spirit. "Let us use this moment to brainstorm options that honor our values while finding pathways for growth. We do not have to choose one over the other!"

With that, a dialogue emerged, creating an atmosphere where doubts began to subside. Women across both factions engaged openly, exploring ideas that combined sustainable practices with economic strategies. The discussion flourished as suggestions flowed, reinvigorating their shared mission.

By the end of the gathering, though the divide remained, a glimmer of hope and unity sparked within the cooperative. Isabella realized that although challenges lay ahead, they had laid the groundwork for a future rooted in collaboration rather than conflict.

As she stepped outside, the weight on her shoulders felt lighter. They may have been divided, but together, they could navigate the difficult terrain ahead. The journey toward healing and redefining their community had only just begun, and Isabella felt a sense of renewed purpose. Together, they would find a way to honor their dreams for a future that embraced resilience, sisterhood, and empowerment.

The rhythmic sound of leaves rustling in the gentle breeze accompanied Isabella as she made her way through the winding path of the dense forest. Sunlight dappled the ground, creating a mosaic of light and shadow that danced around her feet. This serene trail, one she had walked many times, led her to the tranquil haven known as Emerald Pool—a hidden gem nestled deep within the lush greenery of her island.

As she stepped out of the forest and into the clearing, Isabella paused, breathless at the sight before her. The pool shimmered like a jewel, its water a deep emerald hue reflecting the vibrant flora that surrounded it. Tall trees draped their branches protectively over the pool, their leaves whispering secrets to the wind. The air was rich with the scent of damp earth and blooming wildflowers, creating an intoxicating perfume that enveloped her senses.

Isabella approached the water's edge, her sandals slipping off as she sank her toes into the cool, smooth stones. She closed her eyes, allowing the sounds of nature—a distant birdcall, the gentle lapping of water against the rocks—to wash over her like a soothing balm. Here, in this sacred space, the burdens of her daily life began to dissolve, replaced by a profound sense of peace.

Sitting on a large, flat rock, Isabella gazed into the clear waters, reflecting on her dreams for the cooperation. She thought about the land she had worked so hard to secure, the plans she had devised to empower local women, and the vision of a flourishing community that had kept her awake at night. Despite the obstacles she faced—radical opposition and moments of self-doubt—her resolve remained unyielding.

As she stared into the depths of the pool, Isabella allowed her mind to wander. She pictured the cooperative bustling with women sharing laughter and stories, planting crops that nourished their families and the earth. She envisioned classrooms filled with young girls eager to learn, their eyes bright with curiosity, their futures no longer limited by societal expectations.

"What do you want, Isabella?" she whispered to herself, the sound of her voice startling in the stillness. "What do you truly want for your community?"

In the reflection of the water, she saw not just her face but a tapestry of the women she wished to uplift—their struggles, their dreams, their potential. Suddenly, she felt an overwhelming surge of determination. She wanted to create something lasting; a legacy that would empower generations to come, a cooperative that would stand as a testament to the strength and resilience of women.

With newfound energy, Isabella picked up a small, smooth stone from beside her and tossed it into the water, watching as ripples radiated outward, distorting her reflection. Just as the stone disrupted the calm surface, she realized her actions too could create waves of change in the community.

In that moment, the weight of her fears began to lift, replaced by a profound sense of purpose. She understood that her journey would not be easy, but the beauty and serenity of Emerald Pool reminded her of the importance of hope and perseverance. This place was not just a refuge; it was a source of inspiration, grounding her in her mission to uplift others.

Standing up, rejuvenated, and fueled by her discoveries, Isabella took a deep breath and let the fresh forest air fill her lungs. As she turned to leave, a soft smile played on her lips. She would return to the challenges awaiting her, armed with the clarity and resolve she had gained from this visit. Emerald Pool would forever remain her sanctuary—a place where she could always come to find solace, inspiration, and the unwavering spirit to pursue her dreams.

The atmosphere in the cooperative's gathering space was thick with tension as members filled the seats. Conversations buzzed like angry bees, and the air was electric. Women stood in clusters, their expressions reflecting the division that had seeped into every corner of their community. At the front of the room, Isabella felt her heart race as she prepared for a confrontation that had been brewing beneath the surface for weeks.

Clara stood at one end, her posture confident, exuding the air of someone who was accustomed to being in control. Isabella could see the smirks and nods from her supporters, and for a moment, doubt crept into her mind. Could she really face Clara and articulate the fears that were tearing at her heart?

Taking a deep breath, Isabella stepped forward, her head held high. "Thank you all for gathering here today," she began, trying to find her footing amidst the swirling emotions. "I know that tensions have been high lately, and I appreciate everyone's willingness to come together and discuss the future of our cooperative."

Before she could continue, Clara interjected, her voice cut through like a knife. "You are talking about the past, Isabella. We need to focus on the now! Our community is struggling. We cannot cling to outdated ideals while the world changes around us!"

Isabella's pulse quickened, but she pressed on, fueled by a sense of urgency. They had to confront the chasm that had formed between them. "Clara, I hear your concerns, but what I am proposing is not about nostalgia—it is about our future! Our cooperative is built on ideals that matter deeply to us: unity, empowerment, and sustainability. These are not just words; they represent our values and our dignity."

A murmur of agreement rippled through the room, but Clara remained unyielding. "Unity does not pay the bills, Isabella. We need to make pragmatic choices for the sake of survival. Mr. Dorian's offer could provide us with the means to uplift our families right now!"

Feeling the weight of the moment, Isabella gathered her courage. "And at what cost, Clara? What are we sacrificing for that immediate gain?" Her voice trembled slightly, betraying her internal struggle, but she pressed on.

"Are we willing to trade our community's heritage and the integrity of our cooperative for a quick fix?"

Isabella's eyes darted across the crowd, noticing the uneasy shifts in some of the women's expressions. She took a breath and continued, driven by raw emotion. "When I joined this cooperative, it was not just for economic benefits; I believed in a dream of empowerment that would uplift every single woman and child in our community. Facing failure scares me to my core—not just for myself, but for all of you who believed in this vision. If we abandon our principles now, what message does that send to our daughters? What are we teaching them about sacrifice and solidarity?"

Her voice cracked, and as the tears threatened to spill over, Isabella felt a wave of vulnerability wash over her. "I am terrified that if we choose this path, we are saying that profit matters more than each other, that our dignity comes second to economic pressure. We have the power to create a future that values our heritage and our dreams—one that does not prioritize immediate financial rewards at the expense of our collective identity!"

Silence enveloped the room as the weight of Isabella's words lingered in the air. She could see some women nodding, their faces softening in response to her impassioned plea. Clara's confident facade began to crack, and Isabella sensed the shift.

"This is not just about our financial state. It is about who we are and who we want to be as a community," Isabella said, her voice steady now. "We have the power to shape our destiny collectively. We owe it to ourselves, to our daughters, and to the generations to come to fight for a future that is rooted in shared values. We must choose a path that honors our integrity and our vision for a better tomorrow!"

After a moment that felt like an eternity, Clara finally spoke, her voice quieter but still defiant. "You make a compelling argument, Isabella, but vision without action does not get us anywhere. We need to find a middle ground—something that pays today while still hoping for tomorrow."

Isabella nodded, her heart racing. "Yes! A middle ground is precisely what we should be seeking. But it must come from a place of unity, with regard for everyone's well-being and the legacy we want to leave behind. We can create practices that ensure financial stability without sacrificing the values we hold dear."

The atmosphere in the room began to shift from one of division to potential resolution, hope igniting in the eyes of the women who had once felt torn. Yet many remained skeptical, and Isabella knew the path ahead would not be easy. However, the emotional weight of her confrontation had sparked something deeper—a flame of determination and collective purpose.

"Let's discuss how we can create sustainable initiatives that bring income into our community without compromising our beliefs," Isabella proposed. Her voice resonated with conviction; the strength of vulnerability having transformed the atmosphere. "We can think creatively and harness our unique strengths. Together, we can rise to this challenge!"

Clara maintained her stance but seemed less combative now. "I am willing to listen. We can brainstorm ideas that accommodate both our concerns."

As the meeting progressed, the conversation became more constructive, moving from the heated confrontation to exploring collaborative solutions. Isabella felt a torrent of emotions wash over her—relief, exhaustion, and a new sense of hope.

In that moment, she knew the power of vulnerability had illuminated the path toward healing. Though the divide still existed, a bridge of understanding had begun to form. The cooperative was not just a group of women with a common goal; it was a sisterhood capable of weathering storms and emerging stronger on the other side.

As the meeting ended, Isabella felt the warmth of camaraderie rekindling within the room. Together, they had faced the tempest of conflict, and though challenges lay ahead, she was confident that they would navigate their way through, united in their fight for a brighter future built on shared values, dignity, and the promise of empowerment for all.

After the stormy confrontation in the gathering hall, Isabella sought refuge by the river near the plantation—her sanctuary since childhood. The gentle rush of water, the rustle of leaves in the wind, and the sweet scent of earth grounded her, reminding her of the connection to the land that had nurtured generations of women before her.

As she settled onto a smooth stone, the worries of the day began to fade. The sun dipped towards the horizon, casting a golden hue over the river, and Isabella allowed herself to breathe deeply, savoring the serenity surrounding her. It was a stark contrast to the emotional turmoil she had just faced with Clara and the fracturing community.

In this moment of solitude, she was flooded with memories of her journey—how she had built the cooperative from the

ground up, infused with her dreams of a better future for the women in her community. But the path had not been easy. She had faced doubt, resistance, and now, betrayal. Each hurdle had tested her resolve, and today's confrontation amplified the weight of those challenges.

Isabella closed her eyes and focused on the sound of water flowing, letting it wash over her anxieties. What did it truly mean to lead? The question echoed in her mind, demanding an answer she had long buried under the responsibilities of leadership.

As she reflected, thoughts turned to the women who had come before her. The elders—strong, wise women who toiled under the sun, their hands calloused, their faces lined with stories of resilience. They had sacrificed everything to lay the groundwork for future generations, including Isabella herself. Their unwavering spirits and fierce determination were woven into the fabric of her own dreams.

Tears pricked at the corners of her eyes as she recalled the stories shared around the fire, the lessons learned through hardship, and the whispers of their hopes for her—hopes that she would continue their legacy and empower those who would follow her. It was her duty to honor that legacy, to fight for the women who believed in her vision and values, just as those elders had fought for her opportunities.

A surge of determination coursed through her. Today had tested her spirit, but it also reaffirmed the importance of her mission. She was not just fighting for the cooperative; she was fighting for the memory of every woman who had ever stood strong in the face of adversity. The vision she articulated was not solely her own; it was a culmination of generations of aspirations and sacrifices woven together into a tapestry of hope.

Isabella opened her eyes and gazed at the river rushing past, its waters relentless and powerful, shaping the landscape even in the face of obstacles. Like that river, she too could carve a path forward, flowing around the challenges without losing her essence.

With this clarity, her purpose crystallized: to foster a community built on unity and shared strength, to inspire those around her to see the collective beauty in their struggles. She envisioned initiatives that merged economic stability with the values they held dear. The confrontation with Clara had ignited a spark; instead of division, she would lead them toward collaboration.

As the sun dipped lower and shadows lengthened, Isabella stood up, feeling renewed. She would not abandon her vision or the legacy of the women before her. Drawing strength from their sacrifices, she would navigate the turbulent waters ahead with resilience, determination, and heart.

With a final glance at the flowing river, Isabella made her way back to the community, every step infused with purpose. She would not allow doubt to extinguish the fire within her; instead, she would rally her sisters to embrace the challenges ahead, ensuring that their shared dreams could become a reality rooted in dignity and respect. Together, they would create a future that honored their heritage while paving the way for generations to come.

With renewed determination coursing through her veins, Isabella returned to the heart of the cooperative, resolved to act. The confrontation with Clara had set the stage for an important battle—not just for the cooperative's future, but for the very soul of their community.

That evening, she gathered the women who had remained steadfast in their belief in her vision. With each woman who arrived, Isabella felt her spirit lift. Together, they represented the foundation of everything she wanted to revitalize—a shared commitment to their values and a collective spirit that had once brought them together.

As the sun began to set, casting a soft orange glow through the windows, Isabella stood before them. "Thank you for coming tonight. I know things have been difficult and tensions are high, but we have the power to reshape our narrative—together."

The women, some still weary from the strife of the past weeks, leaned in closer, the spark of hope igniting in their eyes. Isabella felt a warmth within her, sensing that they were ready to reclaim their voice.

"I have witnessed your strength, your resilience," she continued, her voice steady. "Each challenge we face is not a roadblock; it is an opportunity for us to unite and push forward. We have let individual fears create rifts among us, but now is the time to remind ourselves why we came together in the first place.

She paused, allowing her words to sink in. "We have a legacy to uphold—one that prioritizes community over individual gain. We are not just about surviving; we are about thriving, and we can do that through sustainability and empowerment!"

A murmur of agreement rippled through the crowd. Isabella could see the women connecting with her message, their faces lighting up with the possibility of change. Encouraged, she pressed on.

"It is time for us to organize a community assembly—a gathering where every woman, every member of our cooperative, can bring their voices, their ideas, and their dreams to the table. We will brainstorm sustainable initiatives that benefit us all, not just a select few. Let us craft a future that reflects our values instead of abandoning them for quick profits!"

The energy in the room began to shift, enthusiasm bubbling over as the women exchanged glances filled with renewed purpose. Isabella knew, however, that it would take more than just words to unite them—they needed to create a space where every voice felt heard and valued.

"This assembly will not just be about discussing plans. It will be a call to arms reminder that our strength lies in our diversity, in drawing upon the unique gifts each of us brings into this circle. We must stand together and reaffirm our commitment to each other and our principles," she said, her voice rising with conviction.

With each added word, she felt the atmosphere become electric. Women began to nod, some even standing up in support. The energy grew palpable as one woman shouted, "Yes! We need to reclaim our story!"

Isabella smiled, invigorated by their growing momentum. "Exactly! We will write the next chapter together. Let us think of innovative solutions that not only bring financial stability but also honor our heritage. We can launch initiatives that focus on sustainable farming practices, products crafted by our hands, and educational programs for our children that empower them to dream big."

As the excitement swelled, Isabella took a moment to absorb the scene before her. It was a tapestry of bond and determination woven from the threads of each woman's story—stories filled with hardship, dreams, and a desire for a brighter future.

"Let us come together for the assembly this weekend. Bring your ideas, your talents, and your passion. Let us remind ourselves of who we are and what we can achieve when united.

The room erupted in applause, the sound of clapping hands blending with the muffled hum of excitement swirling around them. Isabella knew that their journey would not be easy, but she felt certain of one thing: they were ready to reclaim their narrative.

As the meeting concluded, Isabella could see the shared spirit rekindled in their eyes. The cooperative's future was being rewritten, fueled by their collective strength. Standing among them, Isabella felt a kinship—a sisterhood bound not just by the cooperative but by shared dreams and a common purpose.

As they dispersed, chatter filled the air with ideas blooming, and Isabella could not help but smile. The tide was beginning to turn;

together, they would ignite a movement rooted in resilience and empowerment.

With her heart full, she walked home under the starlit sky, feeling like a beacon of hope for her community. They would face the challenges ahead—not as isolated individuals but as a force united in purpose, determined to pave the way for their daughters and for the generations to come.

As Isabella stood at the front of the hall, feeling the weight of the moment pressing on her shoulders, she looked out at her community—faces painted with anticipation, curiosity, and a hint of apprehension.

She took a deep breath, collecting herself, ready to share her vision for a united cooperative.

"Thank you all for gathering here today," she began, her voice steady and clear, resonating with the strength of shared purpose. "We stand together at a pivotal moment. It is time for us to reaffirm our commitment to one another and reignite the dreams that brought us together in the first place."

The audience shifted, eyes brightening as they listened. Isabella continued, her passion spilling forth. "We have faced struggles that would break many, but we are not merely survivors—we are thrives. And that is because of our solidarity. When we support one another, we uplift not just ourselves but the entire community."

A low murmur of agreement rippled through the crowd, encouraging Isabella to push forward. "Our journey has not been without its scars, but those scars tell a story of resilience. The challenges we face now are not insurmountable; they are calls to action for a movement rooted in dignity and empowerment."

Her words hung in the air, igniting flickers of recognition amongst the women. Many leaned forward, eager to engage. Isabella could see growing interest and determination reflected in their eyes. It was time to remind them of the ideals that had forged their cooperative shared dream of equality, support, and mutual growth.

"We must restore our vision for this cooperative," Isabella emphasized. "This is a fight against not just external pressures, but an opportunity to elevate every woman within our walls. A movement for dignity that honors our past and envisions a brighter future for our daughters."

As she spoke, one woman rose tentatively from her seat. "I remember when we first came together," she said, her voice trembling but firm. "We dreamt of a cooperative that would not only support us financially but also nurture our spirits. I have struggled through hard times, but I find strength in this community." Her words resonated deeply, and an encouraging murmur of agreement swept through the hall.

"Exactly!" Isabella responded warmly, emboldened by the support. "Each of our stories builds the foundation of this cooperative—your experiences illuminate the urgency of our cause. We uplift all women when we stand together. Who else would like to share?"

Another woman rose, her voice stronger this time. "I worked the fields alone for years, struggling to make ends meet. But when I joined this cooperative, I found my voice and my community. I refuse to go back to feeling isolated. We need this for all our sisters—no one should have to face their battles alone."

The energy in the room began to shift. What started as subdued skepticism was transforming into passionate solidarity. The assembly became a powerful exchange of stories—each woman amplifying the others' voices, weaving a tapestry of shared struggles and triumphs.

A ripple of stories continued to flow—experiences of hardship, dreams deferred, and the resilience each woman cultivated in her heart. Voices rose higher, speaking of the joy found in collaboration and the pain of living in isolation.

"I fought for my family's future," called a woman from the back. "I faced challenges in silence, thinking I had to bear it all alone. But we do not have to endure this struggle in isolation.

Together, we can thrive!"

The more they spoke, the more the atmosphere shifted from uncertainty to urgency. The room crackled with a sense of purpose, empowering each woman to share her truth and reinforcing the collective vision.

Isabella looked around; her heart swelled with pride. "This is what I envisioned for us! Together, we are stronger. This cooperative must be a space where every woman feels seen, heard, and empowered to chase her dreams."

As the assembly continued, the group began brainstorming tangible ideas—plans for workshops, community outreach, and sustainable practices that could rely on their strengths without compromising their values. Isabella facilitated the conversations, ensuring each voice had the chance to contribute, reinforcing their bond.

The energy pulled through the hall, an undercurrent of excitement building. They were transforming the assembly into a call to arms—a unified front ready to chase their dreams, reclaim their narrative, and support one another in a manner never seen before.

As Isabella wrapped up the assembly, she glanced around the room, her heart full. "Let us take this momentum and create action! Together, we will build a cooperative that stands as a beacon of hope and empowerment for all women in our community."

As the audience erupted into cheers and applause, Isabella's spirit soared. She understood that their collective dreams were not just her dreams, they were woven together, strengthened by their voices rising in unison.

In that moment, the assembly had become a beautiful tapestry of solidarity, binding them together with an unwavering commitment to uplift, empower, and thrive. Isabella knew that together, they could confront any challenge that lay ahead, fueled by the strength of community and a shared vision of dignity for all.

The air buzzed with renewed energy as the assembly concluded. The women of the cooperative suddenly felt like a force to be reckoned with, empowered by shared stories and the collective determination to uplift each other. Their initial hesitations began to fade, replaced by a resolute spirit willing to act.

During the discussions, Isabella sensed an urgency growing among them—a palpable desire to protect what was rightfully theirs. And as the topic of Clara's plans for the commercial development came to the forefront, a wave of steadfast resolve surged through the room.

One woman rose, her voice trembling with emotion but filled with conviction. "We cannot let Clara's vision destroy what we have built! This plantation is not just land; it is our history, our home, a source of sustenance for our families." Her sentiment resonated deeply, igniting a chorus of nods and murmurs throughout the crowd.

"Yes! It is time to stand up!" shouted another woman, her fists clenched as if ready to fight for their cause. "We cannot let her betrayal go unchallenged!"

With each passing moment, Isabella felt the thunderous unity building around her. The women were not just speaking of resistance; they were embracing it as a collective purpose—a commitment to protect their heritage and the livelihoods embedded in the soil they tended.

In a powerful gesture of solidarity, the group began to formulate a plan. "Let's create a petition," Isabella suggested, her heart racing with excitement. "A statement that articulates our collective stance against development and emphasizes the significance of the plantation in our lives. This is not just about preserving land; it is about safeguarding our values and our community's future!"

Cheers erupted in response, and the energy shifted from discussion to action. The women gathered into smaller groups, brainstorming the language they wanted to use, ensuring every voice was heard in crafting their petition. Amid laughter and serious debate, ideas began to take shape on brightly colored posters and sheets of paper.

"That land represents our heritage," one woman said passionately. "It's where our ancestors toiled, where we found community, where our children play and learn."

"Exactly," another added. "It is a representation of our survival and our culture! We need to emphasize the sustainable livelihoods it provides for our families."

Isabella watched with pride as the women passionately expressed their sentiments, transforming their individual concerns into a collective voice that would resonate far beyond their community. The simple act of writing became a galvanizing force, echoing their commitment to one another and to their shared future.

After several hours of brainstorming, the women finally turned their attention back to Isabella, their faces flushed with excitement and determination. One woman held up a completed draft of the petition, and the crowd erupted in applause.

"We stand as one! Together, we will make it clear that we will not allow this commercial development to overshadow our legacy," Isabella affirmed, her heart swelling with pride. "This petition will remind everyone of the significance of our plantation, of our dreams, and of the community we cherish. This is our chance to reclaim our narrative!"

Soon, bright-blue pens filled the hall as each woman signed the petition, their names becoming part of a unified stand against Clara's plans. The act of signing fueled their commitment and fortitude, weaving a stronger bond among them all. Each signature carried with it a story of its own—a testament to their struggles and their collective hope for a sustainable future.

With the petitions collated, the group planned a rally for the upcoming weekend to publicly present and advocate for their cause. They would gather not just to resist Clara but to share their vision for a cooperative that honored their heritage and uplifted their voices. Isabella could already envision the day unfolding women standing shoulder to shoulder, united against adversity, reclaiming their place in the narrative of their community.

"This isn't just about us," Isabella reminded them, her voice ringing clear in the charged atmosphere. "It is about the generations to come. It is about ensuring our daughters and granddaughters inherit a community that values them, just as we have. Our fight is for dignity, for empowerment, and for the future of women everywhere."

A hush fell over the room as her words sunk in, each woman reflecting on the immense importance of their cause. With renewed energy and purpose, they began to organize the details of their rally, determined to make their voices heard in every corner of their community and beyond.

As they worked side by side, laughter and conversation flowed freely, replacing the earlier tension with camaraderie. The betrayal of one had transformed into the unyielding spirit of sisterhood among them. The unity they formed in that hall not only signified a turning point for the cooperative but reignited a deep-rooted bond that would guide them through the challenges ahead.

Isabella felt the spirit of their ancestors surrounding them, whispering words of encouragement. Together, they would rise, united against adversity, ready to reclaim their narrative and ensure that their heritage would thrive in a world that often sought to silence them.

With the petition in hand and the rally planned for the weekend, Isabella felt a surge of determination coursing through her. The sense of unity among the women of the cooperative was palpable, and she knew they needed to channel this resolve into actionable steps. It was time to transform their collective passion into tangible resources to support their cause and strengthen their cooperative.

Standing before the group once again, Isabella shared her vision. "We have made great strides in standing up for our rights, but we need to mobilize our resources effectively to truly empower ourselves. Let us establish committees that focus on different aspects of our cooperative—this way, we can ensure every voice contributes, and every woman could take on a leadership role."

The crowd buzzed with enthusiasm at the idea of taking ownership of their cooperative. Hands shot up as women expressed interest in various committees—food production, marketing, education, and community outreach. Isabella smiled as she observed the eagerness in her sisters' faces, knowing this was a pivotal step toward strengthening their cooperative.

"Let's focus our efforts on community farming events," Isabella suggested enthusiastically. "They will not only enhance our production but also bring us together. By preparing the land, planting crops, and nurturing our vision together, we can foster a sense of ownership and pride in our cooperative."

The women erupted into applause, excited about the prospects of hands-on involvement. "We can set aside specific days for communal work—where everyone brings their skills and labor," said one woman, her energy infectious. "It'll be a chance to teach each other and ensure everyone knows how to tend to the land!"

"Yes, and we can celebrate our hard work with small gatherings afterward!" another woman added, her eyes sparkling. "Cooking and sharing our harvest will create even stronger bonds between us."

With shared ideas flowing, Isabella guided the women as they formed committees aimed at organizing the upcoming community farming events. They established roles for each committee, assigning coordinators and inviting everyone to participate based on their strengths and interests. Women began to voice ideas for the types of crops to plant, focusing on plots that could yield both sustenance and economic support for their cooperative.

"Let's grow not just enough for our families but also for selling at local markets," proposed a woman experienced in agriculture. "This way, we can create more revenue for the cooperative while promoting sustainable practices!"

There was a clear, vibrant energy in the room as the plans solidified. The committees delegated tasks such as securing tools, organizing transportation to the plantation, and even creating schedules for the farming days. The atmosphere buzzed with newfound purpose, every woman feeling an empowered sense of responsibility.

Over the following weeks, the cooperative vibrantly transformed. The community farming events commenced, drawing women of all ages to the plantation. They gathered, wearing their sturdy shoes and wide-brimmed hats, ready to dig into the earth and bring forth new life. The sight of women working side by side—laughing, sharing stories, and learning from one another—was a powerful testament to their bond.

Isabella moved through the rows of women, offering encouragement and support. She watched a skilled farmer teaching younger women the intricacies of planting seeds, sharing long-held traditions and techniques that had been passed down through generations. Each plot they nurtured became a symbol of their resilience and commitment to their vision.

As the crops began to sprout and flourish under their collective care, the sense of ownership only deepened. Each woman took pride in her work, celebrating small victories and learning from challenges. The spirit of collaboration ran deep, with women freely sharing tools, seeds, and advice—fostering a true sense of community.

The aroma of fresh food filled the air during their post-work gatherings, where they cooked together and shared their meals in a joyful celebration. Laughter echoed as they broke bread, filling their spirits with the energy of camaraderie. Through their labor, they not only cultivated the land but also sowed the seeds of sisterhood and support.

These farming events became a ritual, reaffirming their shared commitment to the cooperative and its values. They nurtured the crops but equally tended to each other's hearts, creating a nurturing environment where each woman's dreams were recognized and valued.

As summer brightened the landscape, Isabella felt a profound sense of achievement in what they had created together. The camaraderie and empowerment budding among the women transformed them into a powerful collective force, ready to tackle the challenges ahead.

With every crop that blossomed, every flower that unfurled, and every shared moment of joy, they not only fortified their livelihoods but built an unshakeable foundation for the future of their cooperative. As the women continued to labor with love and unity, Isabella knew they were on the path to crafting a legacy of dignity, resilience, and empowerment that would echo through generations to come.

As the community farming initiatives flourished, the women of the cooperative knew that their work extended beyond the fields. With renewed confidence and a sense of purpose, they decided to take their message to a broader audience, demonstrating that their cooperative was more than just a means of survival; it was a beacon of empowerment and sustainability, ready to inspire other communities.

Isabella gathered the committees once more, her eyes glimmering with determination. "We have made significant strides on the ground, but now we need to advocate for our cooperative publicly. We should approach local leaders and organizations to secure funding through grants tailored towards women-led enterprises. This will allow us to amplify our efforts and create a lasting impact."

The idea resonated deeply with the women, many of whom had previously felt sidelined in their community. Now, they were ready to step into roles as advocates, representatives, and leaders. They began brainstorming potential sources of support, identifying local government initiatives, NGOs focusing on women's empowerment, and even corporate sponsors who might be interested in aligning with their mission.

"Let's draft a proposal that highlights our achievements and outlines our plans for the future," one woman suggested, her enthusiasm infectious. "We can show how our cooperative not only supports our community but also embodies a sustainable model that can be emulated by others."

Energized by this vision, they formed a special committee focused on outreach and advocacy, meticulously crafting a powerful proposal. They emphasized their community farming achievements, the growing sense of unity among the women, and the potential for scalability. The aim was not just to secure funding but to foster relationships that could potentially transform their cooperative into a model for other women-led initiatives.

Next, Isabella proposed a new approach to showcase their efforts—a social media campaign. "We need to tell our story far and wide," she explained. "Let us create an online platform to share our journey, our successes, and the challenges we face. This will help us gain attention, allies, and supporters beyond our village."

The women eagerly agreed, and soon the outreach committee set to work developing a social media strategy. They began by documenting their farming initiatives—capturing the vibrant colors of their crops, photographs of women working together in the fields, and uplifting moments of laughter during their gatherings.

As they shared their journey, they also highlighted their advocacy efforts, informative posts about women's empowerment, and sustainability practices. They used hashtags thoughtfully to connect with broader movements and like-minded individuals, creating a network that extended beyond their geographic borders.

As the campaign gained momentum, the response was overwhelming. Comments of support flooded their posts, and people began sharing their stories with friends, family, and networks. Stories of resilience and empowerment struck a chord with many, and soon, local media outlets began to take notice.

One afternoon, a reporter arrived at the plantation to cover their story. Isabella welcomed her and guided her through the fields, showcasing the women at work and sharing their successes. The reporter captured the essence of their cooperative journey, highlighting the mission to

240

empower women and reclaim their narrative, showcasing not only their immediate efforts but also their commitment to inspire change in similar communities.

The article, published shortly thereafter, reached a wide audience, drawing support from various quarters—local leaders expressed admiration for their work, and several organizations reached out with offers of collaboration and funding opportunities. Encouraged by this newfound attention, they secured meetings with local policymakers, advocating for policies and resources that would benefit women-led enterprises.

With every step, their vision began to expand beyond the confines of their village. The women realized they were not just nurturing their cooperative but planting seeds of change that could ripple through their region and beyond. By pioneering a model of sustainable practices and community empowerment, they aimed to inspire other women's groups to find their strength and reclaim their voices.

Isabella felt a profound sense of possibility as their efforts blossomed. The challenge was now about creating a future where women could stand united, confident in their roles as leaders and community builders. She envisioned workshops and training sessions that could be offered to guide others in establishing similar cooperatives, nurturing a network of empowered women ready to embrace their strength.

Through this broader outreach, the women encapsulated the very essence of their cooperative model—a commitment to sustainability, empowerment, and advocacy. With every grant applied for, every social media post shared, and every conversation held with local leaders, they were rewriting the narrative for themselves and for generations to come.

As the cooperative continued to thrive and gain recognition, Isabella kept her focus on the bigger picture. They were sowing the seeds of change not only for their own community but for women everywhere proving that when united, their voices could rise to challenges, create sustainable futures, and inspire others to take bold steps towards empowerment. The journey ahead was vibrant and promising, and with each passing day, the women of the cooperative grew more confident in their ability to shape their destiny.

EIGHT

A FIGHT FOR THE FUTURE

As the sun began to rise on the day of the community meeting, a mixture of excitement and nervous anticipation filled the air. Isabella stood outside the meeting hall, taking a moment to gather her thoughts before this pivotal announcement. The cooperative's momentum had built steadily over the past few months, and today was the moment to officially unveil their vision and proposals to the community.

She clutched her notes, filled with statistics and heartfelt stories that illustrated their journey, the successes they had achieved, the challenges overcome, and the dreams that lay ahead. Today, she would present their partnership proposal with local agricultural organizations aimed at strengthening the cooperative's resources, seeking mentorship, and securing funding for sustainable farming practices.

"Today, we will show everyone how far we've come together," Isabella whispered to herself, grounding herself in the spirit of the women who had worked so hard alongside her.

As the hour approached, women from the cooperative gathered in the hall, their faces a mixture of determination and trepidation. The atmosphere was charged; many felt the weight of what was to come, aware that this meeting could determine the future of their efforts. Isabella moved among them, exchanging encouraging words and reassuring smiles.

However, beneath the excitement, Isabella sensed the simmering tensions among a few individuals. Clara's betrayal still lingered in the shadows, casting doubt on their mission for some. A small group of women voiced concerns about the viability of the partnership with larger organizations, fearing they might lose their autonomy or be sidelined once more.

"I just don't know if we can trust these big players," one of them remarked quietly, her brow furrowed. "What if they take over and push us out?"

Isabella could feel the weight of those words, echoing the distrust that had snaked its way through the community in the past. It was vital to address those concerns while fostering hope in her vision and the promise of what their collective strength could achieve.

"Let's remember why we started this," Isabella said, gathering the women close. "We are not looking to lose ourselves; we are seeking partnerships that can enhance our autonomy, provide resources, and empower us to make our own choices. The more we collaborate, the stronger we become! We are here to uplift each other."

The room nodded slowly, a flicker of resolve igniting in their eyes. Isabella felt relieved her, knowing that she needed to be the anchor in this storm of emotions.

Finally, the time came for the meeting to begin. The hall filled with both cooperative members and local community leaders, creating an eclectic mix of voices and perspectives. Isabella took a deep breath, stepping onto the makeshift stage before the crowd, her heart racing with a blend of excitement and apprehension.

As she opened the meeting, she acknowledged the journeys of her fellow women, emphasizing their collective achievements. "Today, we stand together not just as individuals but as a powerful cooperative—a symbol of resilience and hope," she proclaimed, her voice steady with conviction. "Together, we have already accomplished so much, but to foster true sustainability, we need to expand our resources and seek mentorship from those who have navigated these waters before us."

She shared stories of the community farming events, with friendships forged, skills learned, and the crops sprouting from the fertile land they nurtured together. With each word, the energy in the room shifted from uncertainty to enthusiasm. As Isabella laid out the proposal for partnerships with local agricultural organizations, she was met with rapt attention.

"We are seeking not only funding but mentorship to help us develop sustainable farming practices that honor our heritage and empower our women. Together, we can build a model that showcases how collective action leads to tangible results," Isabella emphasized, making her passion clear.

However, as she continued, she noticed the uneasy shifts among a smaller group of women sitting at the back. Clara's absence from the gathering was palpable, and the fear of her influence still loomed large. Isabella had to navigate this tension without losing the momentum so carefully built.

"I understand there may be concerns about our direction and the partnerships we seek. It is crucial that we build trust and ensure that our voices remain at the forefront of these decisions. Our cooperative is ours to shape!" Isabella declared, looking directly at those expressing doubt. "This isn't just about funding; it's about paving a path for our future, one defined by our values and our dreams."

As she opened the floor for discussion, the atmosphere became charged with a mix of support, skepticism, and hope. Questions were raised, and Isabella listened intently, acknowledging each concern while also reinforcing their collective vision. The women shared both supportive remarks and cautious critiques, but Isabella remained resolute, understanding that this dialogue was essential to their future.

"Let's prioritize our community's needs and ensure that every decision we make is in the spirit of collaboration and empowerment," Isabella replied to a concerned woman who spoke about potential risks involved with external partnerships. "Our strength lies in our unity and our ability to navigate these challenges together."

As the discussions unfolded, Isabella noticed a gradual shift; the bonds among the women solidified with shared learning and views. The conversations began to pivot toward possibilities rather than fears, and Isabella felt the atmosphere lighten as hope rekindled.

By the end of the meeting, there was an unmistakable sense of purpose in the air. The women voted overwhelmingly to pursue the partnerships, united by a common goal: to create a sustainable future that honored their community while embracing new resources and opportunities.

As the meeting ended, Isabella could not help but feel a mix of relief and pride. The tensions that had once threatened to derail their initiatives had given way to a stronger sense of purpose and community. The cooperative was not just preparing for a fight for their future, it was carving a new path together, empowered by their shared commitment to rise above adversity.

Together, they were ready to face whatever challenges lay ahead, armed with their unity and unyielding spirit, determined to shape a future that would inspire generations to come. The bond they nurtured today would be the foundation of their cooperation, resilience, and their success.

As Isabella stood before the gathering, the energy in the room surged with anticipation. She shared her heartfelt vision for the cooperative, framing it as a pivotal opportunity for economic independence and empowerment. Her words painted a picture of community women taking control of their destinies, working together not only for survival but for strength and unity.

"By coming together," she proclaimed, "we can create a sustainable model that allows us to thrive. We have the power to change our circumstances, support each other, and build a brighter future!"

The reaction was overwhelmingly positive from many women in attendance. They nodded eagerly, eyes bright with hope. As the meeting progressed, several women stood up to voice their enthusiasm, proclaiming how they felt inspired by Isabella's vision. They shared stories of the community farming events and the pride they had felt when planting seeds together, reinforcing the feeling that the cooperative was about much more than agriculture was about reclaiming their voices and autonomy.

However, the optimism in the room was soon met with a chilling interruption. Clara, accompanied by a small contingent of influential male landowners who had previously aligned with Mr. Dorian, strode into the meeting. The shift in atmosphere was palpable as whispers of confusion and surprise swept through the attendees. Clara radiated a confidence that immediately caught the attention of the audience.

As the collective energy shifted, Clara took the floor, her presence casting a long shadow over Isabella's earlier proclamations. "Isabella," she began, her tone laced with challenge, "your dreams are noble, but they are unrealistic. We live in a world that demands financial backing to succeed—without strong corporate alliances, this cooperative will not survive!"

The reaction was electric, with mixed whispers spreading through the hall. Clara's followers nodded in agreement, their skeptical expressions contrasting sharply with the enthusiasm that had previously filled the room.

"We need to secure investments from established players like Mr. Dorian," Clara continued. "Only then can we expect to thrive. This talk of independence will lead us to failure—it is time to be practical and form partnerships that bring real capital. We cannot afford to romanticize this process when survival is at stake!"

Several women in the audience began to murmur in objection, torn between their trust in Isabella's vision and the fear of Clara's warnings. Yet, Clara pressed on, rallying her supporters to rise against the tide.

"Look around you," she urged, her voice rising. "Do any of us believe we can compete without the assistance of powerful investors? Let us not lose sight of reality here—we need immediate backing if we want to make anything of this cooperative!"

Isabella stood momentarily stunned, parsing Clara's words amid the rising tension. The intensity of the situation surged as Clara's supporters—primarily those who had long held positions of power in the community—joined in, voicing concerns that resonated with others.

"Clara's right!" shouted one of the landowners, his tone steeped in authority. "This is naive. We need to align ourselves with those who can propel us forward, not keep them at arm's length."

The room buzzed with uncertainty, and Isabella felt her heart race as she faced this loud opposition. She knew she had to respond, to reassure her fellow women while addressing the fears being voiced.

"While I understand where you're coming from, I believe true empowerment lies in our community's hands," Isabella responded, raising her voice with calm determination. "We can cultivate sustainable growth on our terms—our cooperative can be a model of what collective strength looks like. We do not just have to rely on those with the deepest pockets; we can prioritize our values and grow our resources through our collective efforts! It is time to change the narrative!"

Isabella's words ignited a passionate response among the women who had been supporting her, some standing and voicing their agreement. "We've already seen the results of our unity!" one woman shouted. "We must harness our power and show that we can thrive without becoming dependent!"

Yet, amidst this show of support, Clara and her followers were relentless, working to drown out those voices. They dismissed the community's accomplishments and continued to advocate for a reliance on powerful investors, creating a divide that deepened the rift within the crowd.

The tension reached a boiling point as accusations flew back and forth, and the atmosphere became charged with hostility. Isabella felt caught in the storm of emotions, doubt and fear nested in some corners, while determination and hope thrived in others. It was a fight not just for the cooperative but for the very soul of their community.

Looking around at the faces of the women who believed in her vision, Isabella realized she needed to appeal to their shared experiences, their common dreams, and the trust they placed in each other.

"Let's remember that to empower ourselves means taking risks and challenging the status quo," she urged, her voice steady. "If we constantly align ourselves to powerful interests, we risk losing the very essence of what we stand for. We are not just fighting for survival; we are fighting for a future that embodies our aspirations, our autonomy, and our values!"

With that, Isabella took a deep breath and called for a moment of reflection. "I urge all of you to think about what kind of legacy we want to build for our children. The fight for our future is not just about immediate gains—it is about laying the groundwork for something lasting and meaningful."

As the tensions continued to simmer, the discussion gradually shifted, with some women recognizing the importance of Isabella's message. A few more voices joined in, echoing her sentiments, and slowly, the whispers of support began to build once again.

In that moment, Isabella knew the battle was far from over, but she felt the surge of solidarity that many still believed in. The fight for their future was just beginning. As she scanned the room, she resolved to work harder to bridge the divide and remind everyone that together, they could turn their dreams into reality—if only they remained true to themselves and their community's values.

As the debate escalated, the air in the meeting hall crackled with tension. Clara, emboldened by her alliance with Mr. Dorian, stood firm in her opposition, using every tactic she could muster to stoke fear among the attendees. "Many cooperatives have crumbled just like dry leaves in the wind," she declared, her voice ringing strong. "They thought they could survive without backing from powerful corporate partners, and they were wrong!"

She gestured emphatically, recounting stories of cooperatives that had once thrived but failed due to disagreements among members, lack of resources, and the absence of experience mentorship. "They faced insurmountable challenges because they chose independence over pragmatism. My friends, do you want that to be our fate? Think about your livelihoods—your families' futures!"

Her comments hung thick in the air, inciting polarization within the community. Friends who had stood shoulder to shoulder in solidarity just moments before now glanced at each other uncertainly. The fear that Clara sowed began to blossom in nervous whispers, sparking doubt and division as the women grappled with conflicting visions for their future.

As tempers flared and voices rose, Isabella felt a swirl of concern mixed with determination. She realized this was more than a mere debate; it was a critical test of her leadership and the resilience of their cooperative spirit.

"Clara, I appreciate your concern for our future, but we cannot let fear dictate our choices!" Isabella asserted, stepping forward with purpose. She felt the weight of her words, understanding that the stakes had never been higher. "True empowerment does not come from relying on patriarchal structures that have perpetuated our powerlessness; it comes from us—our agency, our cooperation, and our collective resilience!"

Some women within the audience began to cheer, their voices rising to meet Isabella's passion. "Yes!" one woman called out. "We control our destinies!" Others, however, shifted uncomfortably as fear still clouded their judgment.

Isabella continued, her heart racing as she spoke, "We are not naive; we know that building something new requires trials and tribulations. But history has shown us that when we work together, lift each other up, and stay true to our values, we not only survive, but we thrive!"

The energy in the room shifted slightly as Isabella's fervent words started to resonate. She drew on the stories she had shared earlier—the women who had come together during communal planting, laughter shared during long hours in the fields, and the powerful friendships forged amidst the struggle. "A cooperative formed on trust and collaboration can weather any storm; we have what it takes to create something meaningful!"

As her voice rose with bravado, she caught the eyes of those who had once stood behind Clara. "Are we to be defined by fear? Or are we courageous women, determined to reclaim our futures?"

In that moment, a few women stood to voice their support. "Courage is our strength!" one proclaimed, her fist raised. "We can build it together!" Isabella's heart soared with renewed hope, but she could still feel the weight of uncertainty from others.

Clara was unfazed, her eyes narrowing at the shift in mood. "But what if it fails? What about the jobs that will be at risk?

If you are serious about this cooperative, you must face reality," she pressed, pushing back against the tide of support. "I urge you to think carefully before fairy tales of success sweeps you away! I do not want to see any of you suffer because of misplaced trust!"

The room hummed with anxious energy once again, and Isabella felt the tension gripping her heart. She had to find a way to cut through the anxiety and reach those who were wavering, caught in the whirlwind of fear and urgency. She took a deep breath and steadied herself.

"I understand the fear because I share it," she said, her voice softer now. "We all want security for our families. We cannot dismiss that concern. But see this for what, truly is a chance to redefine our struggles. This journey will not be easy, but every step we take together will be one we choose for ourselves!"

With each word, she painted a clearer vision of what their future could look like if they indeed chose the path of unity and strength. "If we lean into our community and draw on our unique strengths, we can work to secure the resources we need on our terms. We will craft our own story! If we do not invest in ourselves, who will?"

Isabella's voice reverberated against the walls as more women began to nod in agreement, their resolve visibly rising. For every woman expressing doubt, it seemed at least one more leaned into her message of hope and empowerment.

"I challenge each of you to channel your fears into action. Let us collectively seek the guidance we need without sacrificing our power! Together, we can forge contracts with local organizations on our terms. We can partner with those who respect our autonomy. But it starts now—with us standing together!"

The energy in the hall shifted as murmurs of agreement floated through the gathering. Women began to speak with excitement, pitching in with their ideas, sharing their hopes for collaborative projects that celebrated their strengths.

Yet, Clara remained unbowed. "You are in over your head, Isabella. Do you think you can change the world with lofty aspirations? Without real-world support, you will lead all these women to despair!"

Isabella felt the tension tighten again but pressed on. "You may believe in limited horizons and dependency, Clara, but I choose to believe in our power as women. And I invite you all to take part in this journey with us. We can redefine what it means to be strong and sustainable. We must harness our collective strength rather than shrink into what has been comfortable! The fight is ours!"

As Isabella stepped back, the room sat in a heavy silence that felt pregnant with possibility and tension. She had spoken from her heart, bearing her convictions openly. The moment was crucial, eyes were upon her, and she sensed she would either galvanized the group or risked deepening the divide.

Slowly, a few brave women began to clap, their hands coming together in support. Others joined in hesitantly at first, then with more conviction. The sound began to swell, filling the hall with a cacophony of hope and solidarity, drowning out the remnants of Clara's influence.

"Together!" one woman shouted. "We can make it work!"

As the applause grew louder, Isabella felt tears prick her eyes. She had witnessed a transformation, however fragile. Together, they were igniting a fire that could propel them forward, but Clara's presence still loomed large, and Isabella knew that the fight for their future was far from over. This battle was only just beginning, and as she glanced around the room, she understood that the resolve of the cooperative still needed nurturing in the days ahead. Together, they would rise to face whatever challenges lay on the horizon.

The atmosphere in the meeting hall crackled with tension as Isabella and Clara faced off. Passionate voices filled the air, echoing the division that had rapidly escalated between the two women. Despite the expressions of solidarity that had begun to bloom, the rift was growing dangerously wide, threatening to tear the community apart.

As Clara stepped forward, her demeanor was sharp and confrontational. "You're living in a dream world, Isabella!" she exclaimed, her voice slicing through the murmurs of the crowd. "Your ideals are commendable, but you are being reckless. Do you believe that these women can thrive operating independently? You are leading them straight to ruin!"

Isabella felt her heart pound in her chest, the weight of Clara's accusations crashing down on her. "And you think pawing at corporate interests will protect us?" she shot back, her voice strong yet shaking slightly with the heat of the exchange. "Your vision would only lead to our community's exploitation! We cannot keep relying on outside investors who do not care about our lives or our struggles. They will swallow us whole, and like others before us, we will become a casualty of their greed!"

The intensity of the confrontation escalated not just between the two women but within the entire room. The supporters who had rallied behind Isabella began to exchange anxious looks, while Clara's followers sneered at the perceived naivete of Isabella's beliefs.

Clara raised her hand, bringing it down sharply as she retorted, "Isabella, this is not just about ideals! This is about survival. You speak of empowerment, but you are putting these women at risk! What happens when the reality of your 'independence' makes it impossible to put food on the table?"

Each word clawed at Isabella's confidence, and she felt a momentary crack in her resolve. This was no longer just a debate about differing philosophies; it was a raw confrontation, a battle for the very future of their community. Every moment felt charged as eyes turned to both women, waiting for a resolution that now seemed further away than ever.

As Clara pressed on, her tone shifted, growing sharper and more personal. "How long until your cooperative fails? I assure you, the moment it starts to crumble, people will whisper about your shortcomings, Isabella. We have seen it before—leaders who cannot deliver become demons in their own lands. Are you ready to shoulder that blame?"

The ferocity of Clara's words swept through the crowd, causing Isabella's supporters to shift uncomfortably in their seats. Frustration, fear, and despair began to replace the hope they had felt earlier. They looked at Isabella for reassurance, but as Clara's provocations hovered in the air, Isabella felt herself grasping for solid ground.

"Clara, these women are not pawns for you to manipulate. They are our friends, our sisters!" Isabella insisted, though her voice trembled a bit. "Just because you align with those who would use us does not mean we have to acquiesce to that oppression. We can—"

"Can what?" Clara interrupted, a mocking edge creeping into her voice. "You can waste a lot of time for no reason while we starve? You cannot simply wish for change without having the means to support it. Look around you! You are risking your futures for an illusion!"

In that critical moment, Isabella froze momentarily, feeling a deep frustration welling up inside her. She saw the slide in some faces around her—conflicted expressions painting doubt where there was once vibrant support. The words Clara used were sharp enough to pierce her growing confidence, and for a fleeting second, doubt began to creep in.

But then something inside her ignited. "It isn't an illusion!" she declared, raising her voice to be heard amidst the growing chaos. "This is our opportunity to forge a path that respects who we truly are! It is true I cannot promise smooth sailing or a risk-free road, but I promise that together we can build something resilient and grounded in our values.

Yet Clara's accusations felt like a storm looming overhead, casting shadows of uncertainty over Isabella's vision. "What do you think happens when our cooperative has no resources, no backing? Do you think those ideals will feed our families? You are setting this entire community up for failure, and I will not stand by while you push that dark path forward!"

Tears pricked at the corners of Isabella's eyes as Clara's words twisted in her stomach. The tension was boiling, emotions spilling over, and she could feel the weight of her vision teetering precariously. Despair began to seep into the hearts of some women around her, and Isabella knew the stakes had never been higher.

"I understand the risks," Isabella asserted, trying to sound steadier, forcing her chin up. "But I refuse to let fear dictate our actions. What will we tell our daughters? That we bowed down to fear instead of pursuing a future where we could forge our own destinies?"

A silence fell over the crowd, thick and suffocating, as Clara's assertions hung in the air. Some supporters offered quiet affirmations, but the echoes of doubt lingered heavily around them.

The atmosphere had shifted again, no longer simply a meeting of ideas. It had become a battleground, with friendships and futures hanging in the balance. With every word exchanged, alliances were being forged or broken, and the outcome of this confrontation could reshape their community for years to come.

Isabella knew she had to find a way to redirect the emotions swirling around her. "I'm asking for your trust," she pleaded, her voice hoarse yet hopeful, as she turned to her supporters. "We may stumble along the way, but if we choose this journey together, we can create a network that fosters true independence! We deserve a future defined by us—by our choices, not by the fears that seek to control us."

Yet Clara was not ready to relent. "And when those future collapses, who then will be there to lift you up?" she challenged fiercely. "Think long and hard about this choice, ladies. Because this is not just about today—it is about every tomorrow and whether you want it to be one marked by regret!"

The heated exchange left the group at a precipice, and Isabella could sense the division permeating throughout the room. But deep down, she also felt a flicker of hope amid the rising tension. This was a critical moment, and she had to seize it.

"Together we can weather any storm!" Isabella shouted, her voice ringing with urgency. "We must choose courage over fear! How do we want our community story to unfold—through unity and strength or through division and despair? I am here for our future, and I hope you will join me!"

As she stood there, her heart racing, and uncertainty swirling around her, Isabella felt the urgency of the moment. She still believed in the power of their cooperation, and she was determined to rally those who shared that vision before it was too late. It was a tipping point, and now more than ever, she had to fight for the future they all longed for.

As the heated exchange raged on between Isabella and Clara, the tension in the meeting hall became almost unbearable. Voices escalated, friends were turning against one another, and fear began to overshadow the initial spark of hope that Isabella had ignited. It was a pivotal flashpoint that could either solidify their community's resolve or plunge it into chaos.

Javier, who had been observing the fierce debate with concern, felt an urgent call to step in. With his background in journalism, he understood the power of words to clarify and connect, and he believed it was essential to shift the tone of the meeting. Taking a deep breath to center himself, he approached the front of the room.

"Everyone, can we take a moment to breathe?" he said, his voice steady and commanding. "This conversation is turning into a battleground, but we can't forget that we're all here for the same reason: to support our community."

The crowd quieted slightly at his request, the noise diminishing as they shifted their attention toward him. Javier gestured for Isabella to join him at the front, standing alongside her to show solidarity. "Isabella has a vision for the cooperative that is rooted in our shared values, and while I understand that change is difficult and scary, we need to talk about it respectfully and openly," he continued.

He moved confidently through the crowd, making eye contact with as many individuals as he could. "What we are witnessing today isn't just a disagreement about ideals. It is a struggle against the systemic barriers that have oppressed us for too long—a push for independence versus the allure of external investors who may promise quick financial gains but threaten our autonomy."

Javier's words began to reach the audience, evoking soft murmurs of agreement. He pointed out how their struggle was not just about one cooperative but about a legacy that would impact generations to come. "Think back to our discussions about values. We have put a lot of effort into the foundation of this cooperative values rooted in our community's strength, resilience, and shared commitment to uplift each other. Is it not our responsibility to honor those principles as we navigate this path?"

With each statement he made, Javier articulated the peril of blindly pursuing financial support from corporate entities that could exploit their labor and resources. "Choosing a path that risks our independence means sacrificing our ability to make choices for ourselves. We have seen the pitfalls of that approach too many times already. When we rely on others for our livelihoods, it opens the door for exploitation."

He paused, allowing his words to sink in, watching as a few nods of agreement spread through the crowd. Clara, visibly frustrated, attempted to interject, but Javier continued, his voice unwavering. "Isabella is not being reckless; she is fighting for an opportunity to redefine our future. Empowerment means owning the decisions that affect our lives. We have a chance to create something sustainable, something that reflects who we are and what we stand.

Javier's firm yet compassionate tone soothed the escalating emotions in the room. "Ladies, I urge you to consider the long-term vision of our cooperative. This is not just about today; it is about building a foundation that will serve our children and their children. We owe it to ourselves and to them to invest in a future that we shape together."

He shifted his focus momentarily to Clara, who was visibly seething. "And Clara, I want to acknowledge your concerns as well. They come from a place of wanting to protect our community, just as many of us here do. But let us focus on constructive dialogue instead of confrontation. We can recognize the risks without losing sight of our goals and the strength we possess when we unite."

Javier's approach added an unexpected layer of civility to the conversation, gradually softening the hostility that had permeated the air. More women began to lean in, listening intently as Javier framed the discussion around the larger impact of their choices.

"What is at stake is not just our cooperative," he continued. "It is our ability to determine our destinies, our reflections of strength, and our relationships within this community. Can we really afford to put that in the hands of those who see us merely as a financial opportunity?"

Another round of murmurs spread through the crowd; this time more thoughtful. Javier could see the tide slowly changing; doubts began to ease, and a few faces softened as his words resonated.

"Let's remember why we formed this cooperative," Javier said, raising his voice a little to punctuate his point. "It is about community, empowerment, and independence. We cannot let fear drive us apart. Rather, we should harness that fear to fuel our determination. We stand at a crossroads. We have the power to decide how we want to move forward."

Isabella, emboldened by Javier's intervention, felt her own resolve returning. With renewed energy, she spoke up alongside him. "Together, we can shape our own narrative. It is a journey that will not be without obstacles, but one we must embark upon to reclaim our community's voice!"

A ripple of energy surged in the room as the audience began to shift in sentiment. More hands lifted in agreement, and the initial chaos began to morph into hopeful affirmations.

Javier's clear articulation of the issues had started to bridge the divide. Faces brightened with the recognition that their struggles were shared and that together, they could confront the challenges ahead—not in opposition, but as a unified front.

"Let's discuss how we can strengthen our cooperative," Javier suggested, inviting everyone into a more open conversation. "What resources can we tap into collectively? How can we support one another in this pursuit?

As he spoke, enthusiasm grew, and women began to share their hopes and ideas for collaboration. The hostility that had threatened to tear them apart was gradually being replaced with a sense of community recognition that the fight for their future would require them to come together in new and profound ways.

While Clara still stood on the sidelines, her influence weakened, Isabella felt lighter, bolstered by Javier's intervention and the renewed support from the group. Together, they could navigate the road ahead, united in their commitment to their cooperative and each other. It was a turning point, and at that moment, hope flickered brightly once more.

After the meeting, Isabella felt a mix of relief and determination. The confrontation had been intense, but thanks to Javier's intervention, she could see the seeds of unity starting to take root. As the crowd began to disperse, she and Javier moved to a quiet corner of the hall, ready to strategize the next steps in their journey.

"First things first," Javier began, his tone pragmatic. "We need to build on the momentum we created today. Clara will not back down easily, and we must prepare not only to defend our cooperative but to actively showcase its value to the community."

Isabella nodded, her mind racing with ideas. "What do you suggest? I want to provide everyone with a clear understanding of what our cooperative stands for and how it can benefit them.

"Let's organize a follow-up event," Javier proposed, leaning forward with enthusiasm. "We can invite successful cooperatives from other regions to share their experiences. Show the community real examples of what is possible. Hearing success stories will inspire them and help them visualize the potential of our own cooperative."

"That sounds like a solid plan," Isabella agreed. "We could also incorporate workshops and discussions that emphasize sustainable practices and local empowerment. Engaging local leaders and agricultural experts would lend credibility to our message."

"Absolutely," Javier said, taking out a notebook and jotting down ideas. "Workshops could cover everything from organic farming techniques to financial literacy. We can emphasize the importance of keeping resources within our community and how our cooperative can be a model for others to follow."

Isabella felt her spirits lift as the vision for the event began to take shape. "If we can gather a diverse group of voices, it'll illustrate that what we're trying to build isn't just a fleeting ideal, but a sustainable framework for our future."

As they continued brainstorming, Javier reminded Isabella of the importance of community relations. "We need to reach out to those who may still be on the fence. A friendly and transparent approach will go a long way. Invite them to participate and voice their concerns—this will show that we are listening and open to collaboration.

"Right," Isabella said, her mind working quickly. "We could set up informal gatherings in different neighborhoods, allowing people to discuss their worries and ideas. I want everyone to feel included and empowered."

"Exactly. And while we do this, it is crucial for you to present a unified front," Javier advised. "Share clear, consistent messaging about the strengths of our cooperative model, while also acknowledging the community's concerns. It is all about balanced demonstrating how we can address those concerns while moving forward.

Isabella appreciated Javier's insight. "That makes sense. I tend to get swept away in the passion for what we are building, sometimes at the expense of addressing people's fears. I can work on presenting the positives while reassuring everyone that we will not ignore their needs.

"That's the spirit," Javier encouraged, smiling. "Your passion is inspiring but combining it with a strategy will maximize its impact. And remember, you have supporters who want to help you amplify this message. Engage your network—tap into the stories of those who have experienced empowerment through cooperatives."

They began drafting a comprehensive plan, outlining goals for the upcoming event. They mapped potential dates, topics for discussion, guest speakers, and strategies for outreach to the community. With every detail, Isabella felt her confidence grow.

"Also, consider social media as a way to showcase the preparations for the event," Javier suggested. "Share updates about the cooperative's progress and upcoming workshops. Create a sense of excitement— make the community feel like they are part of something bigger."

"That's a great idea!" Isabella exclaimed. "I have been meaning to utilize social media more effectively. I want to create a buzz about our cooperative—show the community the benefits and the real-life impact we can make together."

As they wrapped up their planning session, Javier turned more serious. "Just be prepared for pushback from Clara and her supporters. They may try to undermine your efforts, and we need to be ready to respond with calm and collected messages. Focus on facts and community benefit."

Isabella nodded, feeling a sense of resolve wash over her. "I will not let their negativity sway me. This cooperative is for our community, and I will not back down in the face of opposition.

Javier placed a reassuring hand on her shoulder. "And you will not have to do this alone. I will help you every step of the way. Together, we can show Clara and everyone else of what we are capable."

As they concluded their meeting, a feeling of hope blossomed in Isabella's chest. She was no longer just reacting to Clara's challenges; she was actively shaping the narrative for her community's future. With Javier by her side and their strategic plan in place, she felt empowered and ready to lead the charge toward a sustainable cooperative that bolstered their collective strength.

It was time to turn their vision into action, to navigate the political landscape with purpose and clarity, and to cultivate a sense of unity that would defy any adversary that dared to threaten their cause.

As weeks passed and their plan began to take shape, Isabella and Javier's partnership deepened. Their initial strategy meetings transformed into a dynamic collaboration, blending Javier's political acumen with Isabella's unwavering passion for the cooperative's mission. Together, they were creating more than just a framework for workshops and outreach programs—they were laying the groundwork for a movement.

The first workshop, titled "Empowering Our Future: Sustainable Practices from the Ground Up," was a resounding success. Held in a community center decorated with local artwork and vibrant fabrics, the atmosphere buzzed with anticipation. Women from all levels of society gathered, eager to share their knowledge and connect with one another.

Isabella facilitated the session, encouraging participants to discuss their experiences and expertise in various sustainable practices. The conversations were rich and lively, filled with stories of triumphs and challenges faced in their individual gardening and farming endeavors. One by one, women stepped up to share their ideas, from crop rotation techniques to innovative methods of organic pest control.

"Every person here holds a piece of the puzzle," Isabella reminded them, her voice bursting with enthusiasm. "This cooperative thrives on our collective wisdom! The more we share and learn from one another, the stronger we will become."

As the workshop progressed, Javier took detailed notes, capturing key ideas and valuable insights shared by the attendees. He had also invited a local agricultural expert, Maria, to speak on sustainable farming techniques. Maria captivated the audience with her practical advice, providing resources that would benefit everyone involved in the cooperative.

The sense of camaraderie and empowerment was palpable, fostering a growing sense of ownership and pride among the women. They left the workshop invigorated, exchanging phone numbers, and agreeing to meet regularly to continue their discussions and share resources.

"Today was incredible," Javier noted as they wrapped up the event, watching the women chat animatedly in groups. "You have inspired them to take ownership of this journey. They are not just followers; they are becoming leaders."

Isabella smiled; her heart swollen with pride. "I can see it too! It is more than I ever hoped for—we are really building something special here."

With the workshops creating a solid foundation of knowledge and inspiration, Javier saw their opportunity to build alliances with local officials who championed women's empowerment and community resilience. He reached out to a few sympathetic figures, including Councilwoman Elena, a tireless advocate for local initiatives.

During a meeting with Councilwoman Elena, Javier eloquently outlined their vision and the potential impact of their cooperative on the community. He emphasized how it aligned with the city's goals of fostering resilience and sustainability.

"I want to help amplify what Isabella and the women in her cooperative are doing," Javier explained passionately. "By supporting them, we can create a model that can be replicated throughout the region."

Elena leaned forward; her eyes bright with interest. "I love what I am hearing. This community needs initiatives like yours to flourish. I can help connect you with resources and funding opportunities that can elevate your work."

With newfound encouragement, they left the meeting energized. Collaborating with local officials not only provided vital resources but also lent credibility to their efforts, reinforcing the cooperative's vision.

As they continued to host workshops and outreach events, Isabella's infectious passion began to resonate with others in the community. Slowly but surely, skeptics were transformed into supporters. The cooperative became a focal point of pride and collaboration, attracting young women who had previously felt marginalized.

During one particularly impactful gathering, a young woman named Rosa, formerly hesitant to participate, boldly stepped forward to share her vision for the coop's future. "I want to start a mentorship program where we can teach younger girls about sustainable agriculture," she proposed, her voice steady and filled with determination. "Let's inspire them, just like we've been inspired here!"

Isabella beamed at Rosa's initiative, feeling a wave of joy as she realized that the cycle of empowerment was unfolding before her eyes. "That is a fantastic idea, Rosa! Together, we can create a program that fosters the next generation of leaders."

The cooperative began to gain a reputation for collaboration and innovation, drawing attendees from neighboring communities who sought to learn from their successes. The workshops evolved into community celebrations where women showcased their projects, swapped seeds, and shared recipes—every event reinforcing their bonds and furthering their collective vision.

Amidst the growing enthusiasm, Clara's influence continued to dwindle. While she still attempted to rally opposition, many community members had witnessed the positive changes emerging from the cooperative and were unwilling to overlook its achievements. They began to publicly share their own testimonies of empowerment, forming a supportive network that countered Clara's narrative.

One evening, at a gathering focused on sharing their stories, an older woman named Luz spoke, her voice steady despite the years of hardship she had endured. "I have watched this community rise and fall so many times. This cooperative is our chance to break that cycle. It is a path towards a future where we all thrive together, not just struggle apart.

The room erupted in applause, and Isabella felt tears pricking her eyes. The once-divided community was now coming together, recognizing the strength they possessed as a collective. They were rewriting their narrative, firmly establishing their cooperative as a vital part of the community's growth and resilience.

Isabella turned to Javier, her heart swelling with gratitude. "I could not have imagined this journey without your support. Thank you for believing in us."

Javier smiled; his pride evident. "This is your vision, Isabella. You are the heart of this movement. Together, we are showing what community can achieve when we unite."

As they immersed themselves in their work, collaborating with local leaders, fostering community spirit, and educating others, Isabella realized their journey was just beginning. There were still challenges ahead, including navigating the political landscape Clara continued to influence, but she felt more prepared and emboldened than ever.

With the strength of purpose and a united community, Isabella knew they could weather any storm that arose. They were no longer just fighting for survival, they were building a legacy and this time, they would do it together.

The day of the farmer's market arrived, and excitement buzzed in the air. The cooperative had set up a vibrant booth, showcasing their produce, handmade goods, and the fruits of their labor. Colorful banners adorned their space, proclaiming messages of empowerment and sustainability. Isabella felt a swell of pride as she observed the community coming together, but a shadow loomed on the horizon.

Clara had been quiet for a while, but Isabella sensed that this event would be her stage for a final push against the cooperative. Sure enough, as the crowd began to gather, Clara made her entrance, her demeanor confident and poised. She was flanked by a few of her supporters, all wearing expressions that suggested they were ready for battle.

"Ladies and gentlemen!" Clara called out, her voice cutting through the chatter. She climbed onto a makeshift platform, commanding attention. "I know many of you are excited about this cooperative but let us take a moment to consider the implications of this movement. Are we really prepared to gamble our livelihoods on untested ideas? What about the risks?"

Isabella's heart raced as she recognized the familiar tactics Clara employed fear and uncertainty wrapped in a veneer of concern. She exchanged a glance with Javier, who nodded, reassuring her that they would face this challenge together.

Clara continued, her tone dripping with condescension. "I am not against progress, but we must be cautious. The truth is many of these women may not have the experience needed to run a successful cooperative. We could end up jeopardizing our community's future!"

The crowd shifted uneasily, and Isabella could sense the doubt creeping in. Clara's words were designed to sow discord, and Isabella knew she had to act swiftly. Taking a deep breath, she stepped forward, her voice steady and clear.

"Clara," Isabella called out, drawing the crowd's attention back to her. "I appreciate your concerns but let us talk about the real impact we have had as a cooperative. This is not just about ideas; it is about action, growth, and community empowerment.

Isabella's heart pounded as she continued. "Over the past few months, we have worked tirelessly to build something meaningful. We have hosted workshops where women have shared their knowledge and experiences. We have created mentorship programs for young girls, ensuring that the next generation is equipped with the skills they need

271

to succeed. This cooperative is not just about farming; it is about creating a sustainable future for all of us.

She paused, scanning the crowd. Faces that had once been uncertain now reflected hope and determination. "Together, we have transformed fear into empowerment. We have shown that when we unite, we can overcome challenges and uplift one another. This is not just my vision; it is OUR vision!"

The crowd began to murmur in agreement, and Isabella felt a surge of energy. "We are not just individuals trying to survive; we are a collective force. We are women who have faced adversity and risen above it. We are the voices of our community, and we will not be silenced by fear tactics or half-truths!"

Clara stepped forward, her expression a mix of frustration and disbelief. "But what about the risks?

What if this cooperative fails? We cannot afford to take that chance!"

Isabella's voice rang out, unwavering. "What if it succeeds? What if we create a model that empowers us all? What if we redefine what it means to be resilient? The only way we can fail is if we allow fear to dictate our choices!"

With every word, Isabella illustrated the potential of their collective strength. She highlighted the stories of women who had taken leadership roles, the successes they had achieved, and the support they had garnered from local officials. She spoke of the relationships they were building, not just within their cooperative but throughout the community.

"This is not about opposing ideologies," Isabella declared, her voice rising with passion. "It is about solidarity versus exploitation. It is about choosing to invest in ourselves and our community rather than relying on external forces that may not have our best interests at heart."

The crowd erupted into applause, and Isabella felt a wave of encouragement wash over her. Clara's facade of authority was crumbling, and the community was rallying behind Isabella's vision. The energy shifted, and the atmosphere transformed from one of uncertainty to one of unity and purpose.

Javier joined Isabella on the platform, standing beside her as a symbol of their partnership. "We are here to support each other," he said, addressing the crowd. "This cooperative is a testament to what we can achieve when we work together. We have seen the power of collaboration, and together, we can create a future that reflects our values.

Isabella turned to Clara, her expression earnest. "I understand your concerns, Clara, but we must choose to move forward together. The strength of our community lies in our ability to support one another, not tear each other down. Let us focus on what we can achieve as a united front."

Clara hesitated, her confidence wavering as the crowd responded with cheers and claps of support for Isabella. The realization that her tactics were failing began to sink in. The community was no longer divided; they stood together, recognizing the power they held as a collective.

As the applause echoed around them, Isabella felt a sense of triumph. This was more than just a confrontation; it was a turning point. The cooperative had become a beacon of hope and empowerment, and the community was ready to embrace it fully.

In that moment, Isabella knew they had not only defended their vision but had also ignited a movement that would resonate for years to come. The final showdown had transformed into a celebration of solidarity, and together, they were ready to forge ahead into a brighter future.

NINE

VICTORY AND TRADITION

After months of relentless effort, Isabella stood on the brink of a monumental victory. The struggles against external pressures and the internal divisions that had once threatened the cooperative now seemed like a distant memory. With unwavering determination, Isabella had dedicated herself to advocating for the cooperative, leveraging every relationship she had built in the community.

The day of the critical community assembly arrived with an atmosphere thick with anticipation. Residents filled the town hall, their faces a mix of eagerness and apprehension. As Isabella prepared to speak, she took a moment to survey the room, noting how strongly the community had rallied around their cause. Javier stood nearby, offering silent support, his presence a comforting reminder of how far they had come together.

When the time came for her to address the assembly, Isabella stepped to the front, her heart racing. She could feel the weight of expectation pressing down on her, but she also felt a surge of strength from the many women whose dreams were tied to this outcome.

"Thank you all for being here today," Isabella began, her voice steady. "Today is not just a vote on land; it is a decision about our future, our heritage, and our collective identity. It is a chance for us to redefine what it means to be a community, rooted in values of sustainability and empowerment."

She paused, looking around at the familiar faces, their hopes and struggles echoing in her mind. "This land represents not only economic opportunities but also our connection to the earth, to our history, and to each other. It is a space where we can cultivate not only crops but our dreams for a better tomorrow."

Isabella shared stories from the workshops, highlighting the resilience and ingenuity of the women in her cooperative. She recounted how they had come together to share knowledge, resources, and support, transforming their little pieces of land into vibrant havens of sustainability. "Each of us brings unique skills and experiences to this cooperative. This land reflects our collective spirit—a place for our children, our daughters, to inherit the aspirations we have fought so hard for."

Her voice rose with emotion as she continued. "We have faced doubts and pressures, but we have also witnessed the strength we gain when we come together. The decisions we make today will echo through generations. Let us choose to stand united in our commitment to this land and our mission."

As she spoke, Isabella could see the shift in the room. Skepticism began to melt away as she appealed to the shared values and dreams of the community. She could sense the empowerment blossoming—a shared recognition of the importance of their collective vision.

When she finished, the hall was filled with applause, and she felt the energy in the room crackle with optimism. The community members exchanged glances, murmuring their agreement as they considered the implications of the vote ahead.

Javier stepped forward to emphasize the mechanics of what securing the land would mean for their cooperative. He detailed the plans for sustainable practices that could cultivate not only crops but also community resilience. "With this land, we create a foundation—not just for an economic model, but a legacy of ownership and pride," he said, his words resonating strongly with those present.

After further discussions and passionate testimonies from others in the cooperative—each reinforcing Isabella's vision—the time arrived for the vote. It felt heavier than any ballot they had cast before, symbolizing not just a choice but a commitment to their collective future.

As the results were tallied, everyone held their breath—the anticipation palpable in the air. Finally, the announcement came: the vote was unanimous. Cheers erupted in the room, a chorus of joy and relief cascading over one another. Isabella felt tears of happiness streaming down her face as the realization of their victory settled in. They had achieved what once seemed impossible.

The news of their triumph spread quickly throughout the community. Each conversation buzzed with excitement, igniting a sense of pride and hope among the women who had fought for this dream. Isabella's tireless efforts had resonated deeply, transforming skepticism into belief and empowering others to embrace the cooperative's vision.

Celebrations erupted as the community came together to honor their victory. A festive gathering was organized, filled with laughter, music, and shared stories. Women who had once been hesitant now stood proudly, showcasing produce they had grown, crafts they had created, and the bonds they had forged. Their joy was mirrored in the colorful decorations that adorned the celebration, symbolizing their unity and newfound purpose.

Isabella moved through the crowd, receiving hugs and smiles of gratitude. She thought of the journey—the late nights spent planning, the challenges they had faced, and the indomitable spirit that had fueled their fight. This victory was not solely hers; it belonged to every woman who had contributed to the cooperative, every voice that had risen in support, and every heart that believed in a brighter future.

At the center of the gathering, Isabella, alongside Javier, took a moment to address the crowd one last time that evening. "What we've achieved today is just the beginning," she said, her voice filled with pride. "Let this land be a testament to our strength and a promise of what we can accomplish together. We will cultivate not only food but also hope and empowerment for generations to come.

The crowd erupted again into cheers. Isabella felt an overwhelming sense of belonging and purpose—a connection to something greater than herself.

As the sun set on the horizon, casting a warm glow over the festivities, Isabella knew that despite the challenges ahead, they had forged a solid foundation for their future. The cooperative was more than just a place to work; it was a community built on resilience, solidarity, and love. They had transformed not only the landscape of their village but also their own destinies.

With renewed commitment, they looked toward the future, ready to embrace the transformative journey ahead—together.

With the land secured, Isabella felt a renewed energy pulsating through the cooperative. The realization of their collective dream was finally tangible, and it was time to put her vision into action. She gathered the women around, their faces bright with anticipation as they set to work planting their first crops together.

"Let's start this journey by cultivating not just our land, but also our values," Isabella encouraged, her enthusiasm infectious. "We will focus on organic farming techniques that protect our environment while nourishing our community. Together, we can create something truly impactful."

They dug into the soil, hands dirty and laughter echoing all around them. As the seeds were sown, so too were the stories of hope and ambition that would blossom in the months to come. The cooperative soon became a beacon of innovation and resilience, showcasing sustainable farming practices that highlighted their commitment to environmental stewardship and community welfare.

Isabella's leadership, grounded in her passion and dedication, quickly earned her respect not only among the women of the cooperative but also within the broader community. Word of their achievements spread, capturing the attention of local media. Articles and features began to surface, highlighting the cooperative's successes and innovations. Each story depicted the transformative journey of the women who had come to reclaim their power.

At community gatherings and farmer's markets, Isabella became a sought-after speaker. Her captivating presentations detailed the cooperative initiatives, touching on topics not only related to agriculture but also to education and self-empowerment. She spoke passionately about the importance of knowledge sharing and collaborating for the greater good.

"By empowering ourselves, we are empowering our entire community," she proclaimed at one such event, her voice resonating with conviction. "Every seed we plant embodies our dreams and our determination. We are not just growing crops; we are cultivating our future."

Her words resonated deeply, inspiring other women from neighboring villages who attended her talks. Many approached her after the events, eager to learn more about the cooperative model and how they could implement similar initiatives in their own communities. "Your story gives us hope," one woman said, tears glistening in her eyes.

"We want to create a supportive network like yours."

Recognizing her accomplishments, local and regional organizations began to reach out to Isabella for partnerships. They saw in her an emerging community leader, a powerful voice for women's empowerment and sustainable initiatives. Invitations to collaborate on projects flowed in, expanding the cooperative's reach and influence.

One afternoon, as Isabella met with representatives from a regional agricultural organization, she felt a swell of pride as they discussed potential training programs for aspiring female farmers in the area. "Your work is inspiring," one of the representatives stated. "We'd like to partner with you to facilitate workshops that will enable women from surrounding communities to learn sustainable practices."

Isabella's vision was gaining traction, and the cooperative stood at the forefront of a movement that embraced environmental responsibility and equity. She saw this not only as an opportunity for her community but as a chance to uplift women everywhere.

As the cooperative flourished, it became a model for others to follow. Isabella organized community forums where women could share their experiences and successes with agriculture, business, and education, fostering a spirit of collaboration and knowledge exchange.

The cooperative also launched educational initiatives targeting local schools, where children learned about sustainable farming practices, nutrition, and environmental stewardship. They organized workshops that encouraged the next generation to engage with the earth, instilling the values that had guided their journey.

"Imagine the difference we can make if we teach our kids these principles," Isabella said during a community meeting, excitement lighting up her eyes. "They'll carry these lessons forward, building on what we've created."

As these programs gained popularity, Isabella's reputation grew beyond the local sphere. She was invited to speak at regional conferences and festivals, sharing the cooperative's journey with broader audiences. Each presentation propelled her status as a community leader, while also emphasizing the need for support systems that uplift marginalized voices.

Isabella took every invitation seriously, recognizing the importance of being a representative for her community. "We are paving the way for future generations, and I want to ensure that our stories are heard," she emphasized at one conference, addressing a room full of eager listeners. "There are countless women like us who have the potential to lead and innovate, and we must create spaces for their voices."

As the months passed, the cooperative thrived. Their first harvest was bountiful, a tangible manifestation of their hard work and perseverance. They decided to celebrate this milestone with a Harvest Festival, inviting everyone from the surrounding regions to take part in the festivities. This event highlighted their journey and showcased their produce, crafts, and homemade goods—a true testament to their achievements.

The festival was a vibrant display of community spirit, complete with traditional music, dancing, and potluck-style meals featuring dishes made from their harvest. Families gathered, enjoying the culmination of their labor while sharing stories and laughter.

Isabella took the stage during the celebration, surrounded by her fellow cooperative members. With heartfelt gratitude, she addressed the crowd. "This is more than a harvest; it is a symbol of our resilience and unity. We have turned struggles into triumphs, and this land will continue to nourish us—body and spirit."

The community erupted into applause, tears of joy mingling with smiles. As Isabella looked at the faces of the women beside her, she felt the profound significance of their shared journey. They had not only secured land but had also transformed it into a sanctuary of empowerment, knowledge, and hope.

The Harvest Festival closed with a performance by local musicians, joyous melodies weaving through the air as Isabella danced with her friends, embracing the moment. She felt a sense of fulfillment, knowing that their efforts had not only reshaped their community but had also sparked a movement that would inspire countless others.

Together, they had blossomed into leaders, who were able to share their knowledge, strengths, and experiences. They were not just cultivating crops; they were cultivating a legacy—one rooted in respect, recognition, and unwavering resilience. The future was bright, and Isabella knew that they would continue to forge their path, united in purpose and spirit.

Emboldened by their recent successes and the unwavering support of the community, Isabella was determined to build upon the cooperative's achievements—not just in agriculture but in education as well. She envisioned a comprehensive educational program that would empower women with skills and knowledge extending far beyond the fields. Recognizing that nurturing the mind was just as crucial as nurturing the land, she set out to bring her vision to life.

Isabella reached out to local educators and organizations, forming strategic partnerships that would enhance the cooperative's impact. Together, they identified critical areas where women would benefit most: financial literacy, health education, and leadership training. "We need to equip our women with the tools to make informed decisions," Isabella emphasized during a planning meeting. "Empowerment is knowledge, and together we can cultivate a stronger community."

The workshops they designed included interactive sessions on budgeting, saving, and investing. Recognizing the importance

of financial independence, Isabella brought in knowledgeable speakers who could demystify economic concepts. "Understanding our resources is crucial," she stated at the first financial literacy workshop. "When we learn to manage our finances, we can secure our families' futures and contribute to our community's growth."

Health education workshops focused on nutrition, reproductive health, and disease prevention. Isabella believed that understanding health was foundational to empowerment. "If we are to thrive, we must take care of ourselves and each other," she told participants in one session. "Let's learn how to make informed choices for our health and well-being."

The leadership training workshops aimed to inspire women to take on active roles within their families and the community. Isabella invited successful women leaders as guest speakers, women who had faced adversities yet emerged as powerful advocates for change. The stories shared in these sessions resonated deeply, sparking discussions about aspirations and personal goals.

"Leadership is not just about holding a title; it's about taking initiative and being a voice for those around you," Isabella encouraged attendees. "Each of you has the potential to lead. Believe in yourselves and act."

As the educational programs took shape, the cooperative became more than just a source of agricultural produce—it evolved into a vibrant center for learning and growth. Women from neighboring villages began attending the workshops, eager to benefit from the knowledge being shared.

With each workshop, Isabella witnessed a transformation within the village's social fabric. As women gained skills and confidence, they began to foster a culture of learning and collaboration. They shared insights, support, and resources, building a network of empowered individuals committed to uplifting one another.

Participants in the workshops often became mentors, guiding others in their communities and reinforcing the spirit of collaboration. "We are stronger together," one young woman remarked during a discussion on networking. "When one of us rises, we all rise."

The cooperative thrived as a hub of knowledge, attracting attention from other regions interested in replicating the model. Isabella began receiving inquiries from neighboring villages wanting to implement similar programs. "Your work is inspiring," one leader from a nearby town said during a visit. "We want to create opportunities for our women too."

To celebrate the successes of the educational programs, Isabella organized an annual Education Fair. It provided women an opportunity to showcase what they had learned through projects, presentations, and displays. The fair buzzed with excitement as women shared stories of how the knowledge imparted had transformed their lives.

Isabella's heart swelled with pride as she walked through the event, observing the vibrant displays of crafts, financial plans, and health presentations. Each exhibit reflected not only newfound skills but the spirit of empowerment that radiated throughout the cooperative.

During the closing remarks at the Education Fair, Isabella addressed the gathered crowd. "This fair is a testament to the strength and determination of our women. Education is the seed we have planted in our community's heart, and as we nourish it, it will grow into a robust tree of prosperity and knowledge.

The crowd erupted in applause, sensing the palpable energy of achievement and promise in the air. Women hugged each other, rejoicing in their shared victories and newfound capabilities. Together, they were dismantling barriers and challenging societal norms that had once limited their potential.

As the cooperative continued to flourish as an educational center, Isabella's influence expanded beyond the village. She received invitations to local and regional conferences, where she shared the importance of integrating education into cooperative initiatives. She advocated for policies and support systems that recognized women's services as invaluable to community development.

"We must advocate for educational access for all women," she urged during a regional gathering. "Investing in women is an investment in the entire community. When women thrive, families thrive, and society flourishes."

The call for recognition of women's contributions and needs resonated with many attendees. Isabella's passionate advocacy inspired other communities to launch their own educational initiatives, creating a ripple effect that fostered empowerment across the region.

Through her tireless efforts, Isabella not only transformed her cooperative but also ignited a movement that championed education as a catalyst for change. The seeds of knowledge she and her fellow members had sown would continue to grow, creating opportunities for future generations to rise collectively and advance.

They had embarked on a journey of empowerment through education, forging a path that would lead to a brighter future for their village and beyond. Together, they began nurturing a new era where women's voices would echo with strength, wisdom, and resilience.

With the cooperative thriving and educational programs established, Isabella recognized the importance of strong support networks for the women involved. She wanted to create an environment where experiences, knowledge, and encouragement flowed freely, enabling each member to reach her full potential. "A united community is a powerful one," Isabella expressed in a meeting, her voice brimming with conviction. "We can amplify our strengths by sharing our stories and growing together."

Isabella introduced the concept of mentorship circles, where women from various backgrounds could come together to share their experiences, challenges, and successes. These circles became safe spaces for open dialogue, fostering a sense of belonging and camaraderie among the participants. Women of different ages and expertise gathered each bringing unique perspectives to the table.

During the inaugural session, Isabella welcomed participants with warmth. "Tonight, we are here not just to listen but to learn from each other," she said. "Every story matter; every voice is significant. Let us uplift one another as we share our journeys."

As the women exchanged stories, laughter and tears intertwined in the room. They discussed their aspirations, the hurdles they faced, and the victories they achieved, however small. An older farmer shared her knowledge of traditional planting methods, while a younger member spoke about modern techniques she had learned in the cooperative. This exchange of wisdom bridged generational gaps, creating a rich tapestry of shared knowledge.

The mentorship circles quickly grew into a vibrant community, offering both emotional support and practical advice. Women began forming deep connections, celebrating each other's successes, and providing encouragement during difficult times. "We are here for each other," one participant reminded her peers during a challenging discussion. "No one in this circle stands alone."

Isabella's initiative not only built relationships but also instilled a sense of accountability. Participants felt motivated to pursue their goals, knowing they had a network of women cheering them on. These sessions became biweekly gatherings filled with empowerment and collaboration, where women honed their skills, brainstormed solutions to common challenges, and celebrated milestones.

Throughout this transformation, Javier remained an integral ally to the cooperative. His commitment to the women's vision was unwavering, and he utilized his connections to facilitate workshops and training sessions. Recognizing the value of diversifying knowledge, he reached out to experts in various fields to provide specialized training in areas like business management, effective communication, and conflict resolution.

When Isabella approached Javier about securing additional funding to support their initiatives, he was eager to help. "Let's make sure your vision for the cooperative goes as far as it can," he said, determination evident in his voice. "We'll look for grants that focus on community-driven projects, and I'll help you craft compelling proposals."

With Javier's guidance, the cooperative successfully secured funding from local organizations and foundations that emphasized women's empowerment and community development. This influx of resources enhanced their programs and solidified their status as a model of success. The collaborations between the women of the cooperative and Javier highlighted a crucial point: men can and should be allies in the fight for women's empowerment.

Javier frequently emphasized this message in community meetings, advocating for more involvement from men in supporting women's initiatives. "Empowerment is not just a women's issue; it's a community issue," he explained. "When we rally together—men and women—we build a stronger society for everyone."

His voice echoed throughout the village, encouraging men to take active roles in supporting the cooperative's efforts. Many started attending events, learning about the challenges women faced and how they could contribute. These changes sparked conversations about gender roles within the community, promoting broader acceptance of collaboration between men and women.

To commemorate the flourishing support networks, Isabella organized a Community Unity Day, inviting both women and men to join in the celebration. This event would showcase the accomplishments of the mentorship circles and highlight the strong relationships that had formed.

The day began with heartfelt testimonials from participants, who spoke passionately about how the mentorship circles had impacted their lives. One woman shared, "I never felt like I could voice my dreams until I joined this circle. Now, I am pursuing my goals with confidence, knowing that I have support."

As the event progressed, the atmosphere buzzed with excitement. Traditional dances and songs filled the air, symbolizing unity, and shared purpose. Booths showcasing the women's crafts, produce, and knowledge from the workshops lined the area, bringing the community together to celebrate their collective achievements. It was a vivid display of empowerment through collaboration.

As the day concluded, Isabella stood in the center of the gathering, her heart swelling with pride. The cooperative had transformed into a vibrant ecosystem of support, anchored by strong relationships that celebrated knowledge sharing and collaboration. She beamed at the women around her, knowing they had laid the groundwork for a brighter future.

In her closing remarks, she addressed the crowd, emphasizing the importance of unity. "Together, we have created a powerful network of support that empowers us all," she declared. "Let us continue to nurture these relationships and extend our hands to help others discover their strength. The path to equality and empowerment is a journey we must embark on together."

As the sun set, casting a warm glow over the celebration, Isabella looked around at the faces of people, all proud participants in the movement they had forged. They had built not only a cooperative but also a community infused with resilience, respect, and hope. The future was bright, and Isabella knew that together, they could achieve even greater things in their fight for empowerment and equality.

As the cooperative flourished and the support networks deepened, the impact of these changes began to reverberate throughout the entire community. What started as a grassroots effort for individual empowerment quickly evolved into a movement that transformed the village into a vibrant hub of resilience and collaboration.

With the newfound confidence and skills gained from the cooperative and mentorship circles, women began actively participating in local governance and decision-making processes. Their voices, once overshadowed, emerged with clarity and purpose. Isabella encouraged this shift, holding workshops on civic engagement, explaining the importance of attending village meetings and advocating for community needs. "Your opinions matter, and together we can influence change," she urged the women.

During village council meetings, women who had once been silent now stood up to address concerns directly impacting their families and community. Their insights on issues such as education, healthcare, and infrastructure began to reshape local policies. "When women are included in the decision-making process," one woman argued during a meeting, "we bring perspectives that lead to more comprehensive solutions for our village."

This cultural shift was palpable; the village began to witness a diverse range of ideas and solutions emerging from discussions that included the voices of women. The leadership roles women began to assume were breaking down long-standing barriers, fostering an environment where collaboration led to progressive change.

The cooperative's success and the economic contributions of its members began to improve the overall standards of living in the village. As women became financially independent, families benefited from increased household incomes. They could afford better nutrition, healthcare, and educational opportunities for their children. It was not just individual families that thrived; the entire community felt the positive effects.

Local women proudly shared stories of their accomplishments—one woman had enrolled her children in a nearby school, and another had saved enough money to expand her home. "We are not just feeding our families; we are investing in their futures," another participant in the cooperative added. This collective rise in living standards fostered a sense of pride within the community.

Local markets began to thrive as the cooperative became a key supplier of fresh produce and made products. The women's handmade crafts and organic goods attracted buyers not only from the village but from neighboring towns as well. Farmers' markets buzzed with activity, showcasing a vibrant array of goods that reflected the hard work and creativity of the cooperative members.

"I've never seen the market so full!" a local merchant exclaimed during one bustling market day. "The quality of the produce is exceptional, and the crafts are unique. It draws customers from everywhere." The cooperative's presence not only alleviated food insecurity but also stimulated the local economy, creating ripple effects that benefited all local businesses.

Isabella, always a visionary, organized "Market Days," where the cooperative would host events featuring local artisans, musicians, and chefs demonstrating culinary skills, turning these gatherings into celebrations of community and collaboration. Families came together to enjoy the vibrant atmosphere, share meals, and support local entrepreneurs.

The cooperative's influence continued to grow as women recognized the power of collective investment in their community. They began to initiate projects aimed at enhancing local infrastructure, such as rebuilding parks, improving village roads, and restoring communal spaces. "We are not just building business; we are building our community," one member noted during an initiative planning session.

Together, they drafted proposals for community developments that emphasized sustainability, inclusivity, and growth. These initiatives garnered support from local government and NGOs who recognized the cooperative as a model of how grassroots movements drive positive social impact.

The cultural shift within the community was profound; women were now seen as vital contributors to society. Their voices not only echoed in governance but also in social gatherings, education forums, and community events. Families began to adopt new models of cooperation, where men actively supported women's endeavors, further reinforcing the bonds within the community.

The cooperative has also fostered the importance of education and skill-sharing, with members volunteering to teach local youth about agriculture, business, and leadership. This investment in the next generation heralded a new paradigm in the village, one characterized by a collaborative spirit that promised hope and resilience.

As the cooperative's impact continued to broaden, Isabella gathered with the women at the community center one evening to reflect on their achievements. "Look how far we have come together," she said, glancing around at the smiling faces. "We have revitalized not just our cooperative but our entire village. We have created a future where women's voices are valued, and our community thrives together.

In that moment, it was clear: they had become a beacon of hope and progress in a world that often marginalized their voices. Their journey showcased the transformative potential when communities invest in themselves, foster collaboration, and empower everyone.

Isabella felt a wave of gratitude wash over her. She understood that they were laying the groundwork for future generations,

ensuring that their daughters and granddaughters would inherit a community filled with opportunities and possibilities. The cooperative was not just changing lives; it was reshaping the very identity of their village—one built on cooperation, respect, and unwavering strength.

With this vision for the future, they looked ahead, ready to face new challenges and build upon their successes. The cooperative would continue to thrive as a model of empowerment, inspiring others to embark on their own journeys of growth and community revitalization. Together, they had not only planted seeds of economic prosperity but also sowed the foundations of unity—a legacy that would echo through the generations to come.

With the cooperative flourishing and the community increasingly united, Isabella envisioned a grand celebration to honor the women's hard work and the transformative impact of the cooperative. Thus, she organized the first annual Festival of Unity, a vibrant event designed to showcase their achievements, products, and the stories that had fostered newfound strength and resilience within the village.

Isabella rallied the members of the cooperative, discussing ideas for the festival during one of their regular meetings. The excitement was palpable as women shared their visions for the event. "This festival should celebrate everything we've accomplished," one member suggested.

"Let's invite everyone and show them the power of our work!"

Isabella agreed. "It is not just about the products we create; it is about our stories and journeys together. Let us make it a true representation of our community spirit."

Over the next few weeks, the women poured their energy into planning the festival. They coordinated logistics, arranged for booths to display their crafts, and produce, and organized demonstrations of traditional cooking and artisan skills. Music, dancing, and storytelling would fill the air, reflecting the rich culture and heritage of the village.

When the day of the festival finally arrived, the village was transformed into a lively hub of activity. Colorful banners fluttered, stalls adorned with vibrant crafts and fresh produce lined the pathways, and the air was filled with the enticing aroma of local cuisine. Children ran through the crowd, laughter echoing as families gathered to celebrate.

As the festival opened, Isabella stood on a makeshift stage, a warm smile on her face as she addressed the crowd. "Welcome to our Festival of Unity! Today, we came together to celebrate not only the fruits of our labor but the bonds we have formed as a community. This cooperative represents our strength, resilience, and shared dreams for a better future."

The cheers from the crowd reinforced the sense of pride that filled the air. Women displayed their crafts—handwoven baskets, intricate textiles, and beautiful jewelry—all crafted with care and creativity. Booths overflowed with fresh, organic fruits and vegetables, proudly labeled with the names of their growers.

Throughout the day, women took turns sharing their personal stories at the storytelling corner. They spoke of challenges they had faced, the lessons they had learned, and the empowerment they had found within the cooperative. Each narrative resonated deeply with the audience, illustrating the profound impact this journey had on their lives.

"I remember when I first joined the cooperative," one woman began, her voice steady yet emotional. "I was hesitant and unsure of my abilities. Today, I can proudly say that I not only support my family but also inspire others. We have built something beautiful together."

As the audience listened, heads nodded in recognition and support. These stories reinforced the community spirit, reminding everyone that they were not alone in their struggles or triumphs.

The festival caught the attention of neighboring villages and local media, drawing visitors who eagerly participated in the festivities. Reporters and bloggers wandered through the stalls, capturing the essence of the cooperative and its significance to the community. "This cooperative is a vibrant example of what can be achieved through collaboration and empowerment," one journalist noted in a live broadcast.

As discussions unfolded among attendees, new friendships and partnerships began to form. Local artisans exchanged ideas with cooperative members about potential collaborations; aspiring entrepreneurs learned from the women's experiences in starting their ventures.

As twilight descended on the village, the festival reached its peak with a grand unveiling of a mural painted by cooperative members, representing unity, strength, and the journey they had taken together. Isabella stepped forward to unveil it, her heart swelling with pride. "This mural symbolizes our collective spirit and resilience," she announced. "It will forever remind us of the progress we've made and the future we are building together."

The crowd erupted in applause as the mural came into view, depicting women working side by side, nurturing both the land and each other. It was a powerful representation of the transformation that had taken place within the village.

As the festival wound down, Isabella reflected on the day's successes. The Festival of Unity had become a pivotal event, solidifying the cooperative's role in the community and showcasing the strength of women united in their purpose. It was not just an acknowledgment of their achievements; it was a celebration of their identities and commitment to a brighter future.

"Let this festival be a reminder that our journey is far from over," Isabella spoke as the last attendees began to leave. "Together, we will continue to uplift one another, support our community, and pave the way for generations to come. This is just the beginning!"

With laughter, music, and the scent of delicious food lingering in the air, the village thrummed with a sense of unity, pride, and hope. The cooperative had not only transformed the lives of its members but had also revitalized the very heart of the community, showcasing what could be accomplished when women came together to empower one another. The Festival of Unity would become an annual celebration, a testament to their journey and a vibrant reminder of their strength and resilience in the fight for a better future.

As Isabella took time to reflect on her journey and new-found purpose within the cooperative, she often found her thoughts drifting back to a pivotal moment in her past—her 18th birthday spent in St. Kitts. That experience had shaped her in unexpected ways, marking the beginning of her transformation long before she recognized it.

On the morning of her milestone birthday, Isabella awoke to the gentle sound of waves lapping against the shore. Sunlight streamed through her uncle Gardia's quaint beachside cottage, illuminating the vibrant colors of the Caribbean. The air was filled with the scent of fresh fruits and the faint but fragrant aroma of island species. Excitement bubbled within her as she recalled her journey to this beautiful island to visit her mother's brother.

After a warm breakfast of ackee and saltfish, Gardia hugged Isabella tightly and said, "Happy birthday, my dear! Today, we will celebrate you!" He was a kind man with a heart as open as the sea and a zest for life that matched the rhythms of the island.

Gardia took Isabella on an adventure across St. Kitts, sharing stories about their family's history and the rich culture of the island. They visited local artisans who created intricate crafts and sampled delicious local dishes at bustling market stalls. Each experience enchanted Isabella, igniting her curiosity about the world beyond her own.

At one point during their exploration, Gardia led Isabella to the summit of Brimstone Hill Fortress. They stood together, gazing out at the breathtaking views of the island and the coastline stretching endlessly into the horizon. "This is where resilience lives," Gardia explained, gesturing to the fortress built by their ancestors. "It's a reminder of how we can overcome challenges and stand strong against adversity."

Isabella felt a spark inside her, resonating with Gardia's words. It was in moments like these that she began to grasp the weight of her family's legacy—struggles and triumphs intertwined, each forging the path she would walk.

As they wandered through the vibrant streets of Basseterre, Isabella marveled at the sense of community that enveloped her. People greeted each other with genuine warmth, embracing a spirit of togetherness that felt foreign yet inviting. This atmosphere contrasted sharply with her experiences back home, where societal expectations often kept individuals at bay.

That evening, as they returned to the cottage, Gardia surprised her with a small birthday celebration. He had invited a few family friends, creating an intimate gathering filled with laughter, music, and heartfelt wishes. As they gathered around the table laden with a feast of traditional dishes—flying fish, coconut rice, and fresh fruit cocktails—Isabella felt something shift within her. For the first time, she felt free to express herself, to dream without restraint.

"I want to do something meaningful," she said to Gardia and the others, her voice steady. "I want to help my community back home. I want to make a difference."

Gardia leaned closer, recognizing the determination in her eyes. "Then you must believe in yourself, Isabella. The world is filled with opportunities for those brave enough to seize them. Your voice matters."

As the sun set over the Caribbean, the sky painted in shades of orange and pink, Isabella felt an overwhelming sense of clarity. This birthday was more than just another year; it was a turning point, a gentle nudge toward her destiny. Surrounded by laughter and love, she realized that her aspirations were not just dreams; they were seeds waiting to be planted.

By the end of her visit, Isabella returned home not just as a young woman celebrating her birthday but as someone who had begun to understand her power and potential to create change. The memories of that day lingered with her, a guiding light through the challenges she faced ahead.

Back in her village, as Isabella embraced her role within the cooperative, she frequently recalled her uncle Gardia's words and the vibrant spirit of St. Kitts. Each time she faced doubt or difficulty, she conjured that image—a young girl stood at a fortress overlooking the sea, ready to embrace the world.

Now, as a mentor and leader, she drew upon the resilience she had witnessed during that pivotal visit. Isabella dedicated herself to uplifting the women around her, always reinforcing the belief that they, too, could discover their strengths and forge their destinies. In the unfolding story of her life, she was not merely a participant but a fierce architect, shaping her narrative and inspiring others to do the same.

And as she looked ahead to future challenges, Isabella knew that the essence of her journey—its roots grounded in family, culture, and love—would continue to fuel her unwavering commitment to empower others and uplift her community. The transformation she once began in St. Kitts was now blooming into something extraordinary, a beautiful testament to the power of dreams nurtured by unity and shared purpose.

As the cooperative blossomed and the village dynamic shifted towards unity and collaboration, Isabella's personal journey embodied the very essence of transformation. Once hesitant and weighed down by societal expectations, she emerged as a force of strength, inspiring the community around her and redefining her role as both a leader and a mentor.

Reflecting on the early days of the cooperative, Isabella recognized how far she had come. The shy woman who once stood in the shadows, reluctant to voice her opinions and dreams, now radiated confidence. Through her commitment to the cooperative and the empowerment of her peers, she had cultivated a leadership style grounded in empathy and encouragement.

Isabella began actively encouraging other women to step into leadership roles, both within the cooperative and in the broader community. During meetings, she would often say, "Leadership isn't about being in front; it's about lifting others up and fostering their strengths." This mantra became an integral part of the cooperative's culture, encouraging women to embrace their potential.

As Isabella's stature as a leader grew, so did her role as a mentor. Women sought her guidance, eager to learn from her experiences and insights. She readily shared her journey, including the challenges she faced and how she overcame them. "It's vital to acknowledge the obstacles we encounter," she advised during one of her mentorship sessions. "Each challenge is an opportunity to grow stronger and more resilient."

Isabella organized leadership workshops, inviting women to explore their potential and develop skills in public speaking, negotiation, and community organizing. "Let's practice together," she would say, encouraging participants to present their ideas in front of the group. This environment of support fostered a sense of camaraderie, as women cheered for one another's successes and growth.

In quiet moments of reflection, often accompanied by the golden hues of sunset over the fields, Isabella contemplated her transformation. She understood that her success was not solely an individual triumph. It was a tribute to every woman who had stood by her side, fighting for a collective vision, and dedicating themselves to building a brighter future.

"Every story shared, every challenge faced together, has fortified us," she mused one evening as she conversed with a group of women after a workshop. "We are quilting together a tapestry of our experiences and aspirations, and this beautiful creation is our legacy."

This realization deepened her commitment to nurturing the bonds formed within the cooperative. She initiated "community circles," where members could come together to share not just their triumphs but also their fears and vulnerabilities. "It's important to stay connected," Isabella reminded the women. "Our strength lies in our unity and the support we provide one another."

Isabella also began advocating for initiatives that fostered broader community engagement, recognizing that the cooperative could serve as a model for other villages. She reached out to neighboring communities, organizing cross-community workshops, and sharing best practices in cooperative building and women's empowerment.

As these connections grew, Isabella spoke passionately about the power of solidarity. "When we uplift one another, we create an unstoppable force for change," she would express during gatherings. The community responded positively to her messages, rallying around the idea of collective progress and support.

As Isabella's influence expanded, she began to receive invitations to speak at local events, sharing her story of transformation and the cooperative's impact. Each time she addressed a crowd, she emphasized the importance of community and female empowerment, inspiring other women to follow her. "Your voice is powerful; never underestimate its ability to effect change," she encouraged her audience.

These speaking engagements allowed Isabella to amplify their collective message and inspire a larger movement. Women from various backgrounds approached her, sharing their struggles and seeking guidance on building their own initiatives. Isabella welcomed these conversations enthusiastically, eager to help others embark on their journeys.

As the seasons changed and the cooperative continued to thrive, Isabella's transformation served as a beacon of hope within the community. No longer just a member of the cooperative, she had become its guiding light, a symbol of empowerment and resilience.

In moments of solitude, she would often look around at the bustling village, filled with laughter, creativity, and collaboration, and feel immense gratitude. She had come to understand that her journey was part of a larger narrative woven by the efforts and dreams of many women before her. Their struggles, sacrifices, and victories played a crucial role in shaping not only her path but also the path of future generations.

Emboldened by this understanding, Isabella stepped into each new day ready to face challenges and embrace opportunities, knowing that together with her sisters in the cooperative, they were not only changing lives but also building a legacy of strength, unity, and hope. The future shimmered with promise as Isabella embraced the role of mentor, leader, and visionary, celebrating the remarkable journey of transformation that had brought them all this far.

As the sun rises over the vibrant setting of the cooperative's newly constructed main building, a feeling of anticipation fills the air. The community gathers to celebrate the grand opening ceremony, a moment that symbolizes not only Isabella's dreams realized but the collective aspirations of the women who have stood by her side. Colorful banners flutter in the gentle breeze, and laughter mingles with the sounds of music and conversation, creating an atmosphere charged with joy and hope.

Isabella stands at the front of the gathering, her heart swelling with pride as she looks around at the sea of familiar faces—women of all ages whose lives have been transformed through the cooperative. They are mothers, daughters, and sisters, united not only by their past struggles but by a shared vision for a brighter future. Each one has contributed to this moment in their own unique way, whether through their labor in the fields, their creative talents, or their unwavering support for one another.

Taking a deep breath, Isabella steps forward to address her community. Her voice, once hesitant and unsure, now carries a resonance that commands respect and attention. She reflects on the challenging journey that brought them to this day, recalling the moments of doubt, the betrayals, and the triumphs. She shares her personal struggles, illustrating the growth she has experienced alongside her fellow women.

"Valor," she begins, "is not just about achieving dreams for ourselves; it's about lifting each other up, fighting for one another, and building a future where we can all thrive." Her words echo through the crowd, striking a chord that resonates deep within each listener. Isabella emphasizes that their strength lies in unity and collective empowerment, an enduring bond that has been forged through adversity and perseverance.

As she speaks, Isabella's gaze sweeps the crowd, meeting the eyes of women who once felt powerless, who now stand tall and confident, fully embracing their roles as leaders and changemakers. She recognizes the profound transformations within them, their laughter, their determination, and their newfound agency. This cooperative is not just a business; it is a movement, a testament to their resilience and shared vision for transformation.

With tears of joy in her eyes, Isabella concludes her speech by inviting the women forward to officially inaugurate the cooperative together. They each take turns cutting the ceremonial ribbon, symbolizing a new chapter that embraces collaboration, opportunity, and empowerment. The crowd erupts into cheers, celebrating what they have achieved as one unified voice.

As the festivities continue, Isabella takes a moment of quiet reflection, stepping aside to absorb the vibrancy and energy around her. She feels a profound sense of gratitude, washing over her as she acknowledges the immense journey they have undertaken. In these serene moments, she understands that her story is intricately woven with those of all the women present. Each has played a role, contributing to a collective identity that is more powerful than any singular effort.

Looking towards the horizon, Isabella envisions a future overflowing with possibilities—further educational initiatives, expanded agricultural practices, and even broader networks that connect them to other women's cooperatives beyond their village. She dreams of a time when their successes inspire others across the region, transcending boundaries and proving that empowered women can transform entire communities.

With hope in her heart, Isabella knows that the journey does not end here. This opening is merely the beginning of a much larger narrative—one filled with the promise of growth, collaboration, and an unwavering commitment to uplift every woman. As she merges back into the celebration, surrounded by those she loves and has fought for, she carries forward the knowledge that together they can redefine their destinies and create a legacy of valor, resilience, and hope.

The novel closes on this note of optimism, where the cooperative stands as a living testament to what can be achieved when dreams are pursued boldly, and when women choose to stand alongside one another, ready to forge their future together, hand in hand.

EPILOGUE
A NEW DAWN

Years had passed since Isabella and the women of the cooperative faced their greatest challenges, and a palpable sense of empowerment now radiated through the community. The sugar cane plantation had transformed into a thriving enterprise, proving that their collective efforts could reshape not just their lives but the very fabric of society.

Isabella stood on the balcony of the newly established community center, overlooking the lush fields where rows of sugar cane swayed gently in the breeze. She had often dreamt of this moment when their hard work and perseverance would bear fruit, both literally and metaphorically. Today, the cooperative was a model for women's empowerment, attracting visitors and collaborators from neighboring regions who sought to learn from their success.

The spirit of camaraderie among the women had only deepened over the years. Together, they had navigated the complexities of running a business, empowering one another to take on leadership roles, and challenging the societal norms that once confined them. Many of the women who had initially doubted Isabella's vision were now proud advocates, sharing their stories at workshops and community events, inspiring younger generations to dream bigger.

As the sun began to set, casting a golden hue across the landscape, Isabella reflected on her journey. The whispers of skepticism that had once clouded her dreams had long been silenced. Instead, her heart swelled with gratitude for the unwavering support of her community, a community that had learned to rise together against adversity.

Clara, who had once voiced her fears so long ago, joined her on the balcony, a smile lighting up her face. "Look at what we've accomplished," she said, her voice filled with awe. "I never imagined we would reach this point."

Isabella nodded, filled with pride. "We did this together. Each of us played a part in this transformation."

Just then, a small group of young girls approached, their eyes wide with curiosity. They had come to the center for a community event, excited to learn more about agriculture and entrepreneurship. Isabella knelt to their level, smiling brightly. "Do you all want to learn how to plant your own gardens?"

The girls erupted in cheers, and Isabella felt a warmth spread through her. She understood that they were not just cultivating crops but also sowing the seeds of ambition and strength in the next generation of women. The cycle of empowerment would continue, each young girl inspired by the stories of those who had come before them.

As evening fell, the community center filled with laughter and chatter, a celebration of their achievements and a beacon of hope for the future. Isabella knew that while the journey had been fraught with challenges and betrayals, it had also been a testament to the resilience and spirit of women who dared to dream.

Standing hand in hand with Clara and the other women of the cooperative, Isabella looked out at the vibrant community they had built. It was more than a cooperative; it was a movement—a movement of valor, unity, and hope. Together, they had proven that with courage and collaboration, they could change their destinies and inspire others to follow in their footsteps.

In this new dawn, Isabella felt a renewed sense of purpose. The journey continued, and she was ready to lead the way, heart full of dreams and determination. Together, they would write the next chapter of their story, one filled with endless possibilities.

THE END

ABOUT THE AUTHOR

Kurell Vidal is a passionate storyteller and advocate for women's empowerment, drawing inspiration from her own experiences and the rich tapestry of culture in her community. With a background in sociology and community development, Kurell has dedicated her career to uplifting voices often overlooked in society, inspiring and motivating others to embrace their strength and potential.

Born in the village of Colihaut and raised in Salisbury, Kurell proudly identifies as a West Coast lady and a descendant of the Philogene clan. She brings a unique perspective to her writing, skillfully weaving together themes of resilience, unity, and transformation. Her debut novel, "Woman of Valor," draws inspiration from the stories of her ancestors and the remarkable women who have faced adversity and emerged empowered, highlighting their journeys and the legacies they leave behind.

When she is not writing, Kurell enjoys traveling, hiking, mentoring young women, and engaging in community projects that foster growth and change. Currently residing in the USA with her family, she continues to advocate for social justice and inspire others through her words and actions, striving to create a world where every voice is heard and valued.